Sorrow Street
By Jerilyn Watson

*Joy-Dee
Dedicado
hacia Ti
Jeri Watson*

Text copyright © Jerilyn Watson

All Rights Reserved

This is a work of fiction. Except where actual historical events, situations and characters are described for the storyline of this novel, any resemblance to persons living or dead is purely coincidental.

For C.J.W. and M.G.W.

So we beat on, boats against the current, borne ceaselessly into the past.

-- F. Scott Fitzgerald

ONE

Small hands reached at Sandra, pulled on her skirt hem. "Please, oh, please, miss, por favor, please. Please, lady, please."

The English was heavily accented, but Sandra couldn't misunderstand the message. She tried not to look down as she hurried from her car to the gate of the building where she worked. Several children surrounded her, then darted away, just blurs before her eyes. But one little girl, maybe five or six years old, grabbed Sandra's sleeve and hung on. The child wore a ripped T-shirt that might once have been white. Her bare feet were bleeding, and she was so thin that her sandy-colored hand on Sandra's arm looked like a bird's claw.

Sandra stopped. She reached into her white raffia bag to get some money. But the child took off.

Sandra did not react for several seconds. Slowly, she realized the little girl had stolen all the reais in her purse. Sandra started after her, but stopped abruptly as her right ankle turned in her high-heeled sandals.

The blonde American woman stood as though cemented into the pavement. Her pale complexion faded even whiter than usual.

Another child, a boy wearing only torn gray shorts, ran between Sandra and the thief. Sandra watched his short legs accelerate. He overtook the girl.

Dust billowed from the sidewalk; it hadn't rained in Rio de Janeiro for several days. Then Sandra spotted the girl running into the distance. The boy turned to Sandra.

His fist was tightly balled, and he unclenched it to reveal the money. "Aqui, Tia. Here, Auntie," he said, out of breath. He extended his hand. Sandra accepted the roll of pastel-colored bills and blurted some sentences in English.

"I'm very grateful. I was going to the Rio Sul to buy groceries with that money." She studied the child. Maybe he was ten or eleven years old—wild, spiky brown hair, deep brown eyes, peach-pit skin, very prominent buck teeth and ears that stick out from his head. "What's your name?" she asked, switching to Portuguese.

"Pedro."

"Pedro what? What's your last name?"

"Just Pedro. That's all."

He stared at the roll of bills now in Sandra's hand. She pulled off several of the pretty notes and handed them to him. "Thank you for helping me."

The child looked back at her as he turned away, but didn't smile. She got another fleeting look at him. She thought he said "OK" in English, but maybe it was another word. He didn't exactly run, yet within an instant he seemed to have dematerialized in the haze. She wished she'd had a better look.

Sandra wondered about the boy as she gazed into the vacant space where he'd stood. A blue van passed her as she turned away from the spot, but she was thinking hard and failed to notice that a figure in the driver's seat was holding a gun.

Sandra started walking up Siqueira Campos Street, her legs taking long strides despite her high heels. But then she realized her trusted shoes were beginning to betray her. A blister was forming under the instep strap of her white sandal, and she stopped to try to slide the strap off the sore spot.

"Darn you," she scolded the shoe. But she quickly resumed walking. Before long, the sun would break through, and the unconscionably lush sprawl that is Rio would stew and boil in the full, cruel heat of summer. It would feel good to get inside.

A few minutes later, she got out of the elevator on the fourth floor of the building where many foreign media have headquarters in Rio. The venerable dust-colored building wasn't very far from the famous Copacabana ocean front, but it lacked the glamour of the hotels and businesses near the water.

Sandra made her way down the hall, told her story about the theft and rescue to Tomás Mello, her boss and Rio bureau editor of the Worldwide Broadcasting Network.

Tomás laughed. The action shook his distinctly red beard. How young he looked, Sandra thought, and how mockingly flirtatious. His dark eyes lightened as she talked. Tomás was not very tall, maybe five feet nine at most. The thick hair on his head was black, yet his eyebrows were quite red, like his unfashionably long beard. His brows slanted distinctly upward, giving him a sardonic appearance. No lines or wrinkles creased his forehead, which seemed high. She hadn't decided if his face was handsome or just average, or maybe even unattractive.

But then, they say Don Juan was ugly.

Tomás looked her up and down in a way that made her uncomfortable; then his expression changed.

"Sandra, that girl was probably his sister or some other accomplice. Kids play games like that in hopes of getting rewards from tourists." He absently picked up a stack of shining white printer paper. "Sometimes whole families of little thieves operate together. Clever little bastards. These kids that run the streets have almost no education, or none at all, but they're very good at thinking up tricks and appealing to the guilt complexes of tourists. Oh, they know how to get money, these brats, even the very young ones."

"But why would this kid return my money? How would he know I'd give him a reward?"

"If you're starving, you're willing to take a chance." Tomás snorted. "The kids' tricks often work. You might have caught the girl as she was running away. If you'd succeeded, her little gang would've had nothing. You might even have had a policeman after them." He tugged at the beard, which badly needed trimming.

Doesn't he know that the today's fashionable beards looked more like a five-o'clock shadow than the bird's nest he was wearing?

"This way, the boy distracted you from trying to catch the girl. It was worth a try. For the youngest kids, the ones who aren't strong yet, it's less chancy than hitting you and grabbing your purse or wallet. Besides, you have a kind face."

But Sandra heard, *"Because you look like a sucker."*

"Listen to me, Beautiful One. Don't waste your sympathy on little criminals."

"But why aren't these kids in school? Every child has a right to go to school in Brazil."

"Who says rights are means? Those brats probably have no one to send them. The parents likely are thieves as well. They're in jail or drugged out somewhere. If you're smart, you'll avoid street kids.
They can be dangerous."

She decided not to reply. This wasn't the first time Tomás has struck her as hard and uncaring.

How could being interested in kids like Pedro be dangerous?

###

That evening, a good distance from Sandra's office, Sandra's skinny rescuer pumped the small, chubby hands of his sister.

"Look at all this money! We'll eat good tonight!" He spoke loudly in the Portuguese of the Cariocas, the people of Rio.

Pedro quickly wrapped the money in a rag so nobody would see it. Dusk had enveloped the long, rusting industrial awning near the favela—the shantytown —where he and his sister camped. A blue van passed close to the makeshift homeless village, and other kids looked up as the driver slowed and peered out the window at them. But Pedro was too busy fondling the money to notice.

###

The next morning, Sandra parked her lemon-colored Volkswagen as close as she could to her office building and steeled herself against beggars. In the present downturn of the Brazilian economy, she often encountered people pleading for money or trying to sell her trinkets or food she didn't want. And she couldn't begin to help everyone who asked for help or peddled little flags or necklaces.

The desperation of some Cariocas increased her depression about being sent here. She longed for a transfer to another reporting assignment, or maybe a job with a different network.

But today, thankfully, no kids were in sight. She was fumbling for her key to the black iron courtyard gate when she caught sight of someone scooting around the corner.

There stood the boy who called himself Pedro, looking up at her. His front teeth seemed even more prominent than before. But they were straight, and they shone brightly white.

"Want a shoeshine?" The kid held a crude wooden footrest in one hand, a dingy gray rag in the other. She shook her head, darted inside the gate, slammed it. It had gargoyle-like animals of some sort—lions, maybe?—tucked between the wrought-iron points. They weren't a friendly sight, she thought, but surely that was on purpose.

Sandra took a few steps, then turned back. She keyed open the gate, only to see the child retreating, head down, his bare feet moving slowly on the hot pavement.

"Pedro!" she called.

In a few bounds, he stood next to her again, next to the American woman and the deep purple bougainvillea and white hibiscus on the fence. Somewhere close by, tiny beija flor birds chirped in the relative cool of the morning.

"Was that your sister yesterday or some friend of yours who took my money? Did you fool me into thinking you'd saved my money?"

Pedro's eyes darkened, and he paled. His skin faded so light that his freckles stood out like drops of blood. He shook the footrest.

"No! I don't fool people. I work." He grabbed at Sandra's sleeve. "My sister is no thief. Come see my sister. She's just over there." He pulled.

Sandra thought, what a nervy little guy. But she went with him.

"Just over there" proved accurate. Their steps led just around the corner. Here, the neighborhood became residential and took a turn for the worse. Big buildings gave way to some of the city's few detached houses. They were large and once grand, but now needed fresh paint over their faded, chipped coats of pink, yellow, and burnt sienna. Some of the houses had overflowing garbage cans in front, and Sandra smelled rotting fish amid the scented orange and magenta bougainvillea and frangipani.

The smell seemed symbolic of Brazil, impossibly beautiful yet tinged with corruption.

The boy gestured to a battered cane chair on the grass near the corner. He'd picked a spot beneath a jaca tree, hidden from passersby but close to his impromptu shoeshine stand. A stack of rags lay piled next to the chair.

On a tattered blue blanket sat a little girl, playing with a torn black backpack. She wore only dingy-white underpants.

"Zaida," said Pedro.

Sandra stared at the child. "What?"

"Zaida, my sister."

"She's hardly older than a baby."

The reporter looked to the left and right, then down the street. The traffic was thick and noisy, but she saw few people on the sidewalk. The only pedestrians seemed to be teenage males. Spotting nobody who looked like a parent or sibling nearby, she rocked back on her high heels.

"Where's your mother?"

"Zaida's a pretty girl, isn't she, Tia?"

"Yes."

The little girl was so dirty that it was really hard to see what she looked like. But two sparkly green eyes peered out at Sandra from under curly, snarled bangs of indeterminate color. Was the hair auburn, perhaps?

"Wanna cookie. Wanna Guayana. Wanna Ho-wood."

Coming from such a small body, her chirping sounded loud.

"What's a Ho-wood?"

"Zaida is two. I think she'll be three soon. I'm ten, almost eleven."

"What's a Ho-wood?" Sandra asked again.

Pedro looked away. "A Hollywood, a cigarette. Someone once gave her a cigarette to chew on. I took it away from her right away, but she remembers it."

"Where's your mother, Pedro?" Sandra raised her voice. "Is your father around? Do you have a big brother or sister? Surely you don't take care of this little girl alone."

"I take very good care of her. And I keep her away from bad people and the police. Georges and the other big kids told me if the police catch me, they might take her away from me. And they might make me go to school."

His expression clouded; fear shone from his eyes.

"Say, Tia, don't you want me to polish your shoes?" He gestured toward the rickety folding chair. "I bought this chair with the money you gave me."

Sandra didn't quite believe what she was doing, but she plunked herself down. She wondered if smirches or dirt would stain the seat of her white cotton shift, so she was careful not to sit back. Instead, she leaned forward and studied the boy.

His complexion looked somehow darker today, and his brow knitted and contracted as he concentrated on his work. The expression made him look years older than ten or eleven. She thought it wouldn't be too many years before the furrow between his eyebrows became permanent.

He looked thin in his torn denim shorts and a filthy grayish T-shirt. His knees and shoulder bones poked forward, alarmingly so. But the muscles in his arms and legs looked well developed.

"Pedro, you're a tough interview." She smiled. "You're not going to give me any information, are you? Come on, tell me about your family. Where are they?"

"Hey, Tia, do you want some polish?" Pedro reached under a corner of the tattered blue blanket where Zaida sat and produced a bottle. "I'll do a very good job."

TWO

Efrain de Carvalho took the sharp curves of the winding road without looking at the lane markers. Instead of the road, Efrain gazed at the ultra-luxurious Sheraton Grand Rio Hotel and Resort, set on the ocean under the very steep hill of the Rocinha favela. He turned to the fat man in the passenger seat. "That's damn funny, isn't it, Rodrigo? A palace like that in sight of a slum?"

"Watch the curves, will ya?" his boss replied. "You'll smash up this gorgeous bitch of a car. You're damn lucky I let you drive my BMW."

Efrain paid no attention. He was thinking of another favela, Misericordia, where Rodrigo Suares commanded an impressive empire. In the teeming neighborhood's narrow climbing streets, young kids in the Suares milicia, his gang, helped operate his drug empire. Some of them were no older than fifteen or sixteen, but most were good at daily operations.

The drugs had been going well, especially cocaine and what Rodrigo called "old fashioned marijuana," which wasn't. Everything was running smoothly—too smoothly for Efrain's liking.

Rodrigo's cellphone rang, its loud, harsh jangle resounding over the samba tune playing on the radio. He listened to the caller for a full minute. His expression darkened. A second later, he yanked off the safari hat that had nearly covered his brown eyes and pockmarked face. He pitched the hat into the windshield.

"Murilo says some of the kids, the runners, have been holdin' out on me. They haven't turned in all the money."

"Terrible!" Efrain hesitated a nanosecond. "Rodrigo, how 'bout if I punish those kids, teach them a lesson? Word'll spread fast, and nobody else will try cheating—ever."

Rodrigo stroked his balding, perspiring head. "Murilo can do it."

Efrain winced. "Why always Murilo when there's something to be done? What about me?"

"Nope."

"I'd like a chance."

"I said no."

"Why not?"

"You're a foreigner."

"You promote other foreigners in the organization. There's Lopez and Charlton and Vargas and El Flaco…I've done good work for you for a long time. You're holding it against me that I came from one country down on the map?"

Rodrigo pulled out a cigar, snipped the end, lit it.

"I just don't trust you enough to work those kids over without a hassle."

"You trust me with the sales for my district. You trust me to drive you around in your BMW and keep it other times. Why wouldn't you trust me to do this job?"

"I dunno."

"Come on, boss."

"I told you. You're a foreigner."

But Efrain noticed that Rodrigo Suares was starting to look bored. Maybe he'd worn him down.

"I'll do fine. Nobody will ever dare cross you again."

"OK. But don't screw it up."

Efrain increased his pressure on the accelerator, anxious to dump Rodrigo at his office in the favela and do the job that would advance him in the organization

Foreigner, am I? Well, I'm going to be something far more than the drug salesman for district nine and a chauffeur for this fat pig. And as soon as that's done, I'm going to launch my new business, benefitting only Efrain de Carvalho.

###

Efrain drove up to his large pink house in Misericordia. Like so many others in the favela, it was perched on a steep incline. But neighboring buildings were narrow, multileveled. His home was wide, not to say sprawling, and many asparagus ferns and palms blocked it from the street. If passersby could have seen it better, they would have noticed that the brick wall was crumbling in several places. Part of the porch was missing, too, collapsed into a slice of exhausted, broken cement.

Much as he would have liked to fix up the place, he didn't want to communicate the fact that he lived there. The exterior looked run down because that's the way he wanted it. The yard in back existed because he'd ordered the space hacked out of the hill. It contained his blue van and a motorcycle and, most days, Rodrigo's BMW. Two large Rhodesian dogs guarded the property. They barked fiercely as he got out of the car.

"For God's sake, shut up, hounds. I'm your master, not a burglar."

Indoors, his lair looked far different from its exterior. Efrain's home contained the best of everything he could steal. He was about to enter the house when he changed his mind.

"I don't wanna pretend we're a happy family," he said aloud. "Sometimes Isobel gives me a pain that starts over my heart and radiates down into my gut and then starts all over again. She doesn't satisfy me anymore. Nobody satisfies me anymore."

He knew if he went in, the night would be long, the sex less than mediocre. He would sleep only in short naps punctuated by latenight television programs, smokes, booze, and maybe, if he got too bored, a snort of coke. He liked cocaine; he seemed to be one of those rare people who could do a line now and then without ever getting to need it. He thought of himself as different from others working in drug gangs in Rio.

Efrain turned around, got back in the BMW and drove away. He steered lightly, carelessly, with the index finger of his left hand. He pulled down the vanity mirror on the visor with the other hand and took a long look at his face. The action caused him to swerve sharply and cross the median line of the road.

He narrowly missed a white truck approaching from the opposite direction. The man in the big, pregnant-looking vehicle waved his fist. Efrain studied the mirror intensely, too busy to respond.

His skin looked very white, his eyes, quite startlingly blue. His hair had grayed a little at the temples, and white map lines had formed around his eyes. Tiny cracks shadowed his down-turned lips.

"OK, these aging signs, they're kind of distinguished. It's the fucking scar that bugs me." He ran his hand over the mark. It arrowed from beneath his left eyebrow down to his collarbone. Sometimes it still hurt.

Efrain remembered how it got there. He closed his eyes for a few seconds, nearly caroming off the road.

Sandra Shelton trekked up the carpeted stairs to her thirdfloor apartment in Rio's Leme district. Opening the door, she found the big orange cat that had adopted her during her first weeks in Rio. One of her neighbors, an old lady with hair as brightly orange as the cat's fur, had told her that the animal was a Maine coon cat.

"How can you be a Maine coon when you live in South America?" Sandra inquired as she petted the animal. But he just purred and failed to answer the question. She wondered if Marmalade would be her only dinner companion, as usual. "I'm fond of you, all right, but you're not such a great conversationalist."

The cat had appeared one day when Sandra took a walk. It looked skinny and kept following her. Each day for a week, it had met her when she arrived from work, each day looking hungrier.

"Hey, you surely know how to work a person. And here you are, enjoying two big meals a day in my kitchen and snoozing on the foot of my quilt at night." In Sandra's sometime vagabond days as a correspondent on temporary assignment here and there, she'd always kept the red and white comforter made by her great grandmother in the 1920s.

"Listen, Marmalade," she said into the animal's ear. "You're lucky you're a cat. You're easy to take in."

Sandra shucked her shoes on the carpet, which seemed to be neither beige nor gray, but a dull combination that reminded her of ski wax. She flopped on the sofa, picked up a book of crossword puzzles, chose one. For a few minutes, she readily filled in the squares, but couldn't think of a five-letter word meaning "recession" that fit. She tossed the book aside and let gloomy thoughts take over.

Those thoughts started with Pedro and Zaida. They surely needed help, and how could they possibly get it? She was a neophyte in a strange country, after all, and had no idea where to start.

Hey, wait a minute, who says I'm going to get involved?

Besides the children, her new surroundings also added to her blue mood. Affordable housing was scarce in Rio, and when she'd heard that the New York Times correspondent was moving back home and relinquishing this place, she'd rented it in a hurry. But she thought the apartment's decor, with its contorted modern metal furniture and dark drapes, was obviously designed by someone with a migraine or a hangover.

The one attractive feature of the building was a swimming pool lined with graceful palms and pots of dazzling camellias. She'd tried it only once; the cloudy, heavily chlorinated water was warmer than her usual shower. And jogging, her favorite exercise since high school, seemed out of the question here. Young men, mostly teenagers, had followed and harassed her every time she'd tried to go for a run on the streets. Tomás had invited her to his sports club, but she thought there was danger there.

Soon she felt the cat rubbing at her bare toes, and the purr she heard sounded demanding instead of content.

"Oh, OK, Marmalade, I'm so out of it that I forgot to feed you." She pulled her long body off the sofa, but didn't go directly to the kitchen. Instead, she flicked on the television set.

A scene flashed on showing a palatial, distinctly Old World room. People surrounded a tall, mustachioed official of some sort. He was holding forth in French; subtitles translated his words into Portuguese. It seemed that CNN International was interviewing a representative of the European Commission. And amid the throng of reporters loomed a familiar face. For a second, Sandra stood anchored onto the carpet.

The man looked a little disheveled. His tie was loosened and pulled to one side. He looked heavier, but definitely recognizable.

"Charles!"

A physical pain coursed through her, like the grating flash that always assaulted her innards when she saw something grisly. Rage and grief welled up within her in bitter competition.

How could she have chosen this instant to turn on the television? She took a few quick steps and silenced the set. The image flickered, then faded. Sandra squeezed her eyelids tightly together, trying to block the memory of the man she'd just seen.

"I've got to forget!" she yelled at the silenced TV.

Marmalade stared at her. Sandra hadn't turned on any lights in the apartment, and in the gloomy twilight, she thought the cat's wild and yellow eyes looked disbelieving.

It took an hour for her to settle herself enough to put her frozen dinner in the microwave. But the meal was as desolate as she'd expected. The main course, chicken with lemon sauce, tasted bitter.

"As well it should," she told the cat. Then she dug her cellphone from her oversized, stuffed purse. Before thinking, she pushed a string of numbers, steps on the yellow brick road to Rome. Her father had served many years in the U.S. State Department. After the death of Sandra's mother and his retirement, he'd moved to Italy, his favorite posting.

"Just thought I'd say hello," she said to Howard Shelton, who lived in an apartment with a view of the Coliseum. "How're you?"

There was a tiny hesitation before he replied. Sandra instantly pictured someone else in the room with him.

"Honey, how good to hear from you. How's the job? Are you enjoying Rio? We had such great visits there when I was working in Buenos Aires and you were in high school." His voice was deep, perhaps deeper even than when he was younger. "One of my great regrets is that they never sent me to Rio. There's poverty, but such good times, too. Endless entertainment in Rio to lighten your workload."

"Well, I'm getting kind of a slow start on the job." She thought that was the understatement of the three months she'd been in the city. "It's such a far cry from covering the White House."

"I know it was a disappointing assignment for you, after all your hard work." He hesitated, and Sandra heard a woman's voice in the background.

"Gee, I'm sorry, Sandy, but Elizabetta and I have to get to the airport. Security's taking forever these days. We're having a little break in Sicily, actually. Checking out some archeological sites…" Sandra had a sour thought: In a way, her father had unwittingly dealt her another rejection, just when she'd called him to hear a welcoming voice. She shook her gold mane, now loose from her long braid, pushed aside that thought, and mentally chewed on his reflections about Rio.

You needed to look beyond both the excesses of the rich and the starkness of the poverty, like those sad children she'd just met. The city itself offered indecently beautiful sights, and the people were among the most gracious and welcoming she'd ever encountered. Not to mention the endless merriment that seemed the order of the day for many a Carioca. But the friendliness of strangers and their often warm generosity only seemed to emphasize her losses.

She picked up Marmalade and whispered a question into one furry ear. "What kind of a spineless whiner am I?"

Sandra swallowed hard and determined to try to divert herself. But she couldn't think of anything she wanted to do. Maybe she'd just go to bed early tonight. She took a shower, brushed her teeth, and climbed in bed with a novel by Doris Lessing, the Nobel Prize-winning British writer. She'd chosen the book because one main character was an old lady, and, if there was a love scene in the book's many pages, she hadn't found it.

She thought she'd read herself to sleep. Instead, her last thought before dozing off was of the boy on the street who'd saved her money. Pedro. Just Pedro, he'd said, refusing to give a last name. Somehow, she was sure Tomás was wrong. The kid, caring for his small sister, didn't seem like a thief.

She fell into a dream about having dinner in a posh restaurant in Washington. She was eating something expensive—

what kind of food wasn't clear—and laughing and talking. But then a skinny child with hollow eyes came to the table, begging.

Behind him toddled a smaller child. Their faces were indistinct, but she understood that they were crying with hunger. And she heard herself say, "Run along!"

Then the dream took an even more disturbing turn. The scene switched to a blackened street, where a dark van drove straight into the blurry dream-children.

Sandra sat up, shaking.

THREE

In an isolated rural patch of scrubby land miles from Sandra's apartment, a bad dream about children also awakened Father Peter Mulroy. Momentarily chilled, the parish priest put on a grayed cotton robe over his seersucker pajamas and went into the rectory kitchen. It took him only a few steps to feel too hot again, the cold of the nightmare gone. He paced the slightly sloping linoleum tile floor.

The priest couldn't sleep very well in the heat, and it seemed to him that his small piece of Brazil was unrelentingly hot. The air conditioning in his living quarters chugged feebly, as usual. Sometimes he thought his diocese had forgotten its priests out here.

The images of his dream followed his footsteps. They'd focused on a family in his parish that had bad luck. Indeed, most of the families in his parish were unlucky, one way or another. But this particular family seemed singled out for the very worst.

The father had lost his job on the railroad; the last of their many babies was born with a badly formed heart valve. The tiny boy lived through several surgeries that emotionally and financially bankrupted the family before he died.

The priest thought he hadn't done all he could for them. But he wondered how he could have done more. So many people in his parish had desperate needs, needs of all kinds. His black sandals thumped on the uneven blue and white linoleum as he paced.

Sometime in the past, the floor must have been intended to copy the Delft tiles of The Netherlands.

    The telephone rang, but when he picked it up, it was a wrong number. The caller swore repeatedly and sounded like he was crying. "Drunk!" The priest ended the call. But he willed his disgust to mellow. The people here led hard lives, and it wasn't right to be too judgmental. Judgment wasn't the job of humans, after all. Long ago, when he was young, he'd thought life in Enniskillen was hard—not much employment. What existed seemed reserved for Protestants. And it seemed to him that everyone was Protestant.

    Mulroy decided to check if the parish dog was in the small shanty in the garden back of the kitchen. He thought, how pathetic, looking for a dog for company. In other, bigger parishes he'd served, there'd been a clergy residence, a place where another insomniac priest might be up watching a movie on television in the parlor. They could have a word about local politics if the other cleric were at least passably interesting, maybe a glass of wine, a game of chess. Here it was just him.

    Mulroy had named the dog James Joyce. Joyce may have been a Prod, but he was also the priest's favorite writer. The James Joyce of the canine variety was a mix between a collie and who knew what, and he began scuffling around excitedly when he heard his master's sandals swishing through some weeds. James Joyce barked a single, throaty welcome, accepted an ear rub, and trotted behind Father Mulroy as his human started through the kitchen garden for the house.

    "Don't root in the tomatoes," he cautioned the animal, and it obeyed. The priest opened the back door for the dog, who configured himself on a patch of especially saggy tiles.

    Despite the heat, Mulroy decided to make himself some hot coffee. He couldn't seem to erase the dream-children from his mind. And the dream made an easy transition to thoughts of the young dying woman when he'd administered the anointing of the sick.

    "Promise me you'll watch over the children, see my cousin is good to them," she'd whispered. "So little to be left alone…" Her voice had failed then. Although she tried to say more, he couldn't understand her.

    And he'd promised.

The next morning, Sandra Shelton found her editor, Tomás, bent over his computer, smoking a cigar. She coughed a little.

"OK, be like that, Ms. Fussy." He flicked the ashes of the stinking thing into a glass tray. Sandra tried to recall the last time she'd seen an ashtray in an office back home in Washington, D.C. She couldn't.

Through the haze, she stared at Tomás. He was a compact sort who might not have been noticeable in a crowd except for his red beard, which contrasted so startlingly with his head of raven hair. Sandra assumed he wore the beard to make himself look older. She thought that he must be the youngest Rio bureau chief their network ever had, at least ten years her junior.

So far, though, the age difference—and his status as husband and father—hadn't stopped his stares when he thought she wasn't looking, and sometimes even when he knew she saw him ogling her. Not much, she'd noticed, seemed to affect the assertive flirtation game played by some young males in Rio.

"I saw those kids again." Tomás rolled his eyes, which seemed blue when he wore blue and green when he wore green. Today, though, they seemed as yellow as a wolf's.

"For God's sake, worry about the news, not the street kids. Their mother probably puts the kids out every day to make money for her drug habit."

Sandra tugged at the single blonde braid she wore over one shoulder. The braid was clasped with an elastic fastener that matched her outfit. Sometimes she thought this style was too youthful for her thirty-six years, but she'd worn her hair this way for a long time and never quite got around to changing it. The same was true of her bangs, which often seemed to creep down into her eyes.

"If the kids' mother's got a drug habit, they should be in foster care. Pedro's obviously not going to school."

But Tomás had opened a copy of *The Economist* in English; his face was no longer visible. His voice sounded far away as it came out from behind the paper. "Aren't you going to start on that nun's situation in Pará?"

Sandra followed his cue. Between telephone interviews, she reflected again on the irony of reporting about a do-gooder nun in a tropical rainforest area of Brazil. It seemed such an old story, anyway, a tragedy that could repeat itself.

Instead of starting to write, though, she decided to share a thought with Tomás. "How come hundreds of poor people have died trying to stand up against the men who burned the forests, but it took a foreign nun to get public attention?"

Sandra couldn't understand sending religious workers to the Brazilian rainforests—or anywhere dangerous, for that matter. They risked their lives, and sometimes lost them, for hopeless causes. What was the point?

"What, you don't admire their courage?" But his tone was wry.

"Well...." Sandra's memory of the nuns who had taught her during childhood stuck in her mind, an unwelcome implant. Sometimes she thought she could still feel the sting of the ruler wielded by her piano teacher, Sister Mary Augustine, when Sandra missed a beat of the metronome. And then, there was also the way the nuns had silenced her concerns after that awful day long ago in Buenos Aires.

Tomás' voice got louder, breaking her reverie. "Sandra! You're delaying. You don't have much time before you're due in the studio, and I still have to edit your broadcast. Are you almost done?"

Well, what d'you know, Sandra thought. For once Tomás sounded more like an impatient boss than a leering would-be lover. The radio and web division of Worldwide's tiny, unimpressive Rio bureau had a recording studio of its own. But it had to share a live broadcast studio with two other news agencies, and if she weren't ready by the appointed hour, Sandra knew she would lose the studio time. Each time she thought of the luxurious separate quarters and elegant equipment provided for the network's television sports staff, her skin prickled with resentment. It seemed to her that nobody cared about news except for the Olympics.

"I'm hurrying," she mumbled. She hoped she could make the deadline. She hated everything about this story—the research, the writing, voicing it on the air. But she disliked that story less than the continuing crime saga she'd had to broadcast several times. The gory events of drug wars in the favelas always struck her as another public favorite.

It seemed when foreigners thought of Brazil, all they cared about were soccer games—futebol matches—and the upcoming Olympics. Oh yes, and do-gooder nuns, gang violence, the samba, and Carnival, the tuneful and colorful pre-Lenten festivals that sometimes turned wild, even violent.

"Why are you stalling?" Tomás said. "You're cutting the time too close."

"No, I'm OK." She had the notes from on the scene, the material filed by the often-absent Brazilian reporter, Nilda. But what had she named the file? Lord, she couldn't have forgotten. Why wasn't she applying the same effort she'd always brought to her work? Thankfully, she recalled the name, scanned the information, and banged frantically on the keyboard.

Words formed on her computer screen:

"Tension is high in Pará as police continue to search for people who threaten the life of Sister Jean Hightower. For months now, the American nun has angered local lumbermen and cattle ranchers with her activism for preservation of the rainforest and legally owned farmland."

Somehow, other sentences flowed until she'd filled the required lines for her five-minute broadcast.

Sandra named and saved the story and hastily dragged the template to the editing file. "It's in the drawer," she called, then stared as she watched Tomás do a hasty bit of chopping at his keyboard. She saw him recheck the clock.

"Run!"

Sandra raced to the printer for the hard copy of her story and dashed out the bureau door and down a long hall. She flung open the studio door and threw herself into a chair in front of the microphones. The engineer in the control booth muttered something she couldn't hear. There was no time for him to test the level of her voice. What was his name again? He glared at her through the glass partition as he slid control switches around.

"Hey, you could come in here a little later if you worked on it." It sounded like more of a growl than a statement. He started the music and waved his hand to cue her. Then he opened the microphone that would send Sandra's words into the atmosphere.

She could feel the man's stare as she read. Sandra knew she had no excuse to be late. But somehow she managed not to sound winded and remarkably didn't bumble her lines. The engineer had just turned off her microphone and brought up Worldwide's theme music when, to Sandra's amazement, the long-absent Worldwide reporter, Nilda Oliveira, burst into the control booth.

Sandra scooted out of the studio and opened the booth door. But before she could phrase a question, Nilda yelled at her.

"Come on, Sandra, get your stuff and hurry up. There're murders in the Misericordia favela. Drug crimes, I 'spose."

"But I haven't covered a murder since grad school."

Nilda grabbed her arm. "Move it!"

"Hey, they'll still be dead five minutes from now."

Nilda was a tiny woman in her late fifties, and although she toddled around in impossibly high heels, her speed surprised the much taller, much younger Sandra as they ran down the hall.

The American trailed Nilda back into the Worldwide office and helped her gather the most efficient tape recorder the bureau owned. It had several twisted cords and microphones and seemed to Sandra to weigh about a hundred pounds. Where was the compact digital device she'd used back in Washington?

Indeed, where was a soundman like the one who'd accompanied her on big stories in D.C. and in several hotspots around the world? Here in Brazil, members of the sports bureau of her network were treated like kings and queens. But other than those TV reporters and producers, Worldwide neglected the Rio bureau.

The editors demanded wide coverage of demonstrators and rioters enraged by the government's clearance of housing near Olympic sports venues—and the cost of repairing and building the venues themselves. But like firecrackers, these stories burst forth and faded. So did accounts of Rio's lawlessness and the germs said to occupy swimming and rowing waters for the 2016 competitions. Brazil's faltering economy and its effect on the world got little indepth treatment.

So far, Sandra's requests to deepen this coverage had little impact. Now, an unfamiliar and unwelcome assignment faced her.

She moved slowly, urged on by Nilda, the awkward recorder case biting into her shoulder.

###

Tomás' smile looked amused, sardonic as he posted the story she'd just read on the air on Worldwide's streaming website.

"Ladies, I'd go cover this murder story myself if I had time. But I have an opinion piece for the six p.m. 'cast. Just don't get too bloody."

Nilda steered Sandra to her own Volkswagen, a blue one, and launched into a lecture.

"You know, part of the problem of these drug killings is the United States' fault." Nilda whisked the little car around a big truck as she talked, looking more at Sandra than the road.

"Oh, right, everything is the United States' fault."

Nilda swerved sharply back into the right lane. But her colleague's sarcasm didn't deter her.

"The United States adopted the drug policies of President Reagan in the 1980s. They forced a lot of the drug trade down here and into the rest of South America."

Sandra shifted inside her seat belt, which constricted her as Nilda again abruptly changed lanes. Why was it that many Cariocas seemed to look upon driving as a blood sport?

Impervious to the traffic, Nilda plunged on with her sermon. "The Policia Federal, our federal police, couldn't handle it."

"Nilda, please be more careful!"

The car jerked repeatedly. But the woman in the driver's seat took no notice. Brazilian law enforcement, she said, couldn't deal with the flow of heavy armaments from around the world into their country. As a result, gangs of young people in Rio's uncounted favelas had gotten artillery, Russian AK47s, Belgian-made automatic rifles, AR-15s, G-3s.

"Even landmines and shoulder-launched missiles ended up in the Favela da Coréia, which has a lot of our city's poor." She grinned, paused for a reaction from Sandra, who denied her one, and started again. "Remember the time the bad guys shot down the police helicopter in Coréia? There's no way our official rule of law could stop traffickers from controlling these neighborhoods."

"Well, you're stopping at least some of them now. People say the government raids and occupation of Coréia and some other favelas defeated the drug lords. Brazil is taking Rio back from criminals. The pacification squads are doing their work. Look what's happened in Rocinha—violent deaths are down by at least eighty percent, maybe much, much more."

"Don't believe it! There's improvement, all right, in that favela and some others. But if the troops ease up or leave, things will go right back to the way they've been. That'll probably happen after all the Olympic stuff is over and the tourists go home. Besides, it's places like Coréia and Rocinha and maybe Vidigal that are supposedly under anything like good control." Nilda stressed her last words. "There're other favelas like Misericordia, where we're going. It may be smaller, but it still has huge numbers of people."

Sandra shrugged. "You can't blame all the crime on the United States." She felt pretty sure that Nilda was telling the situation accurately. Still, she didn't want to give her the satisfaction of agreeing with her. Anyway, drug crime was as far from Sandra's expertise as she was physically far from Washington.

She remembered her shock and disappointment a few months before, when Worldwide's managing editor had called her to his office. She'd thought he was going to tell her the news she'd expected: that she'd be assigned to cover the White House.

But today, here she was, between now and someday, laboring on a continent few people back home seemed to care much except for its sports extravaganzas and its Carnival. Anti-government riots, drugs, and the economy held some interest. Still, as world news went, Brazil didn't rival covering the American presidency—at least not for her.

The little car swerved wildly again, throwing Sandra forward and then back, halting her reverie.

"Nilda, please. We can't get a story if we're dead!"

FOUR

Sandra struggled to grasp the reality of her situation. Why was she speeding down a Brazilian highway to cover murders? If she wasn't to write about the White House, why hadn't she been sent to Kabul or Cairo or Aleppo or just about anywhere around the Gulf of Aden?

She'd left her last job in a television news bureau because her on-camera appearances were almost always restricted to four sentences per story, seemingly no matter how important the news. She'd thought if she worked for Worldwide in radio and on the web, she'd get to cover national politics in Washington in depth. She'd been so sure—yet here she was.

At last the car slowed, and Sandra began to breathe normally. But not for long. They pulled into the end of a street that seemed to have suddenly gone from a wide highway to cinders.

"Welcome to one of the meanest favelas in Rio!" chirped Nilda. She whirled the car next to a barricade maybe twelve-feet high, formed of gleaming white stone and what looked like bleached, baked mud. Huge jaca trees and palms drooped over the stones in the intense heat. Parked all along this unlikely "wall" were two cars of the Rio State police.

The women jumped out of their car, Nilda with grace. But Sandra, loaded down with most of the sound equipment, moved more slowly. Outside the car, she felt like the sun was frying the top of her head. She removed a stray metal clip on her braid that burned her scalp and stood still for a moment, wondering what to do next.

"There's the cop we need, Osvaldo Carneira, the police chief for this part of Misericordia. He speaks English."

She pointed at a lone man in civilian clothing who stood beside a narrow passage through the wall. As the women approached, the figure shielded his eyes. Nilda didn't wait until they got close to the police officer to start questioning him. "Delegado Carneira, what's going on here? Where are all your people?"

"They're where you two are definitely not going." His thin, darkly tattooed bare left arm, revealed by a short-sleeve multicolored shirt, gestured to the hole in the wall. He moved quickly to cover the space. "There's two stiffs just inside. They're removing the bodies." Nilda made a strategic move toward the opening, but Carneira blocked her. The women were so close to the "door" that they could hear men shouting on the other side.

"Delegado, isn't this unusual? Isn't this favela usually the territory of Rodrigo Suares? Doesn't he keep tight control on the gangs here?" Nilda poured out the questions staccato voce. "How are we going to get the story if you won't let us see what happened in there?"

Sandra stared at the cop. His face was so long that it looked like it belonged in an exaggerated political cartoon. His chin resembled a shovel. His very deep-set dark eyes darkened further as Nilda spoke.

"Officer," Sandra said in English. "We're broadcasting internationally." She unwound the cord and placed the microphone close to him. "Please at least tell us what happened."

He grunted something Sandra didn't understand, then apparently decided to answer her question.

"Usual thing." His voice sounded rather high for a man, his words running together. "Don't know any details yet. No identification, no idea of the identity of the shooters. The kids were gunned down execution style." He cleared his throat. "Maybe gangs fighting over who would keep money from the drug boss. They deliver the stuff and do what they're told. But they're competitive. The bosses enjoy the competition, too. Pleases 'em to keep things stirred up, to keep the kids vying for favor and a chance to move up in the structure."

Good, thought Sandra, he's going to cooperate; he's going to fill in the story. But the policeman stopped talking and turned away toward the hole in the wall. Before Sandra could phrase another question, Nilda tried a commanding tone.

"Come on, let us through. You know that if you don't, we'll just find another way."

"OK, if this is how you want to spend your day, be my guests."

A few seconds passed before the women decided to ignore him.

"Alice through the looking glass," Sandra quipped, and they ducked through the narrow opening. On the other side was a gravel road that ran horizontally in front of thick jungle growth.

"God!" She sucked in her breath in a gasp. What lay before her looked like a scene from a battlefield. Two young boys, not even in their late teens by the look of them, lay neatly arranged on their backs on the road in a line. Blood poured freely into the sheet partly covering the one on the left end, dripping onto the formerly pristine white gravel beneath.

The wound must have been at the back of the boy's head, for she couldn't see it. One arm lay at his side, but the other was extended, the hand seemingly reaching for something.

The two stared at the sky, not a mark visible on them. Had it not been for the red streams trailing from their heads, they would have looked like children playing the victims in a game of cops and robbers. Their faces seemed very alike: broad noses, full lips caught in the smile-like rictus of death. Were they biological brothers, maybe even twins? Would their mother soon learn that she had lost two sons, perhaps her only sons?

Policemen appeared. Or maybe they were special militiamen. They moved like streaks, so fast Sandra couldn't count them. Their khaki pants and navy flak jackets blended as they ran. One's jacket read "S.W.A.T."—at least she thought so in the blur of their activity. Body bags in hand, they were now placing the dead boys on stretchers.

Sandra's stomach turned and her legs seemed heavy. "God." She felt Nilda clasp her elbow.

Sandra was unwilling for the older reporter to see her losing control; she drew herself almost to her full height, just a few inches under six feet. She could hear her heart pounding in her ears. Her head felt light, and she instinctively backed up to a spot in front of the "door" in the wall. Through that opening she spotted a blue van pulling away. She had a fleeting, bizarre thought: The driver had regular features, but he also had a narrow stripe down his face and neck—a scar? He guided the van slowly, sedately out of sight.

Just then, a soldier in fatigues tending to the dead noticed the women and swung a big, meaty fist into the air.

"Move out!" he yelled at the women. Two others also looked their way, and one pulled out a pistol and waved it around. "What are you doing here? Get the hell out!"

"We're journalists. We have Delegado Carneiro's permission..." began Sandra, but Nilda grabbed her arm and pushed. Nilda found the "door" in the wall and shoved Sandra out first, then followed.

"Those cops looked pretty serious. Move it!"

They looked in vain for Carneira as they scrambled for the Volkswagen. But the officer was nowhere to be seen, and other police vehicles were beginning to move in.

"Nilda, what're we going to do?" Sandra sounded out of breath as she jumped into the little car.

"Nothing!" The other woman gunned the engine and spun the car around.

"But we have no story. I have about twenty seconds of the lieutenant generalizing. That's all. We've run away like terrified rabbits. What's Tomás going to say? Aren't we going to wait and try again?"

Nilda grinned and put her small right foot down hard on the gas pedal, shaking Sandra as she tried to fasten her seat belt.

"We're going back to the office, sweetie. We don't want to be around here." She stretched out her short fingers on the wheel, as though they were stiff. "Tomás doesn't really care about stories like these. He just has to show the editors in New York that he tried. Somebody from the local wire services will eventually get the information, and it'll get some lines on the evening news in Buenos Aires."

Nilda looked directly at Sandra and let go of the wheel to gesticulate with her right hand. "Then Tomás will put fifteen seconds of that into your 'Evening Round-up from South America.' He'll probably throw in a line or two about how his brave reporters were menaced trying to get the story."

"But, for God's sake…"

"Cool down! Your face is white as dough, and your hair's curled up all over your head. You look like an over-age Shirley Temple." Sandra just nodded, both disgust and relief flowing through her as Nilda piloted the VW into a line of highway traffic.

A moment ago they'd been witnessing dead bodies, corpses of young men who in death looked like children. Now they were entering an everyday big-city Rio traffic slowdown. They were again in the company of people going to work and school, people living normal lives. And at last, Nilda began to drive responsibly. Sandra was left to her reveries.

Guns, she thought, guns. She hadn't heard the gunfire that killed the young men. But she'd seen the result. Like so many other things, the violence reminded her of incidents with Charles. Both were serving as foreign correspondents at the time. They'd been near the border between Serbia and Kosovo, long after Kosovo had separated from Serbia.

The reporters had been investigating a rumor of gunplay. Their separate employers had called them to the scene, and theoretically they'd been competing for news coverage on their respective networks. But survival, not news, had become their goal as shots rang out. Sandra pictured the bright sunny afternoon in the clearing of a leafy area, the scene more suitable for a picnic than gunfire.

The shooting had quickly forced them to their knees.

"Who's firing?" they said, almost in unison. But they couldn't tell—Serbians, Kosovars, an ethnic skirmish, or maybe just enraged people going bonkers over an adulterous wife or husband, a stolen car or horse.

Over the heads of several other journalists crouched in front of them, they saw a little girl in a green jacket lying injured in the middle of the clearing, one arm stretched above her head. The two Americans could make out the small arm moving. Every few minutes, she would cry, "Mamá!" But no one had dared move for fear of becoming the next victim—no one except Charles.

"What're you doing?" Sandra screamed. The answer soon became apparent. "Come back!" But Charles had already run a good distance. The shots rang out thicker and faster.

Three unforgettable minutes later, he returned with the child in his arms. The little girl cried harder, but she had what appeared to be only a flesh wound in her arm. When the barrage of firing let up, Charles caught sight of his network's equipment truck as it pulled up.

"Deus Ex Machina!" he yelled as he ran. Sandra would always remember how Charles looked as he carried the little girl to a television truck that would take her to a hospital.

But what Sandra had to do now, light years from that day, was try to forget. She needed to erase the scene.

She had to think about this current assignment, and how she'd just failed. Tomás was not the boss she wanted, and this posting to Rio felt like purgatory. Her childhood years in Argentina as a diplomatic brat had provided her with all she really cared to know about South America. And she knew her attitude must be showing.

Tomás hadn't said anything negative about her work, but he hadn't said anything positive, either. Unfortunately, the only real attention he'd paid her so far had little to do with journalism.

As they neared the office, she gave Tomás more thought. He was attractive in a youthful way, a good reporter with a strong voice and a strong viewpoint that had undoubtedly helped him snare his job. But he seemed oddly cold to the plight of some of his own people. His attitude toward her interest in Pedro and Zaida was a good example—and he himself was a father.

Well, she was a foreigner, so why should she care about the street kids, either? But she knew herself well enough to know the answer.

Now, for no reason that Sandra could see, Nilda sped up drastically.

"Nilda! if Tomás doesn't care about this story, won't you please, please slow down?"

"No, I can't get us far enough from Misericordia."

FIVE

Dr. Olivia Kattah was driving to a shift at Wilson Azevedo Hospital, Rio's hospital for its most financially comfortable citizens. She'd recently finished her last year of the institution's training in pediatrics and had become associated with the permanent house staff there.

Her neighbor and passenger, her supervisor Dr. Lucas Gomes, related the story of the attacks in Misericordia.

"And just as you were picking me up, Olivia, I saw a bulletin on TV that there are at least two dead in Misericordia. Drug thing. Just kids. How awful."

Olivia pushed a lock of black hair from her eyes.

"That's different than usual?"

"Olivia, I said they're just kids. Mostly grown kids, maybe, but kids. Aren't you interested?"

"Sure, it's terrible. But don't we keep busy enough caring for the children of the comfortable to worry about favela kids?"

###

Olivia's passenger was not the only person who heard about the shootings in Misericordia that morning. The favela's drug boss, Rodrigo Suares, got the news on a widescreen television at a posh café near the Praia Vermelha beachfront. He choked on his cappuccino and brandy drink, and the burning in his throat brought tears to his eyes. A couple of minutes passed before he recovered his voice enough to pick up his insistent cellphone.

He heard the voice on the other end of the line and asked the person to repeat what he'd just said. Then Suares shouted a stream of invectives and threw the phone onto the floor. The face cracked, tiny pieces of plastic spattering in several directions.

Rodrigo reached into the Venetian leather briefcase next to his chair and pulled out another cellphone. He punched in a telephone number, listened, and listened some more.

Efrain de Carvalho's telephone line finally yielded up a robotic voice. It said he was unavailable right now and urged callers to leave a message. Rodrigo, calmer now, cleared his throat and enunciated carefully.

"I didn't ask you to commit a slaughter, and that's just what you did. You've involved the cops. What if you've drawn their attention to me? You're through in Misericordia, you stupid foreigner! You bastard, you better watch out. I've killed people for less."

When Sandra and Nilda finally defeated the traffic and returned to the office from Misericordia, Tomás greeted them with a sardonic smile. Nilda disappeared quickly, leaving Sandra to face her boss.

"How'd you like the bloodbath?" Tomás watched her carefully. He lifted one reddish eyebrow and laughed.

"You think it's funny that those young people are dead? For what? They're not even twenty years old."

"Oh, I see. You don't have drug killings like this in the United States, is that it? Young American men never lose their lives because they've been foolish?"

Sandra felt a blush firing her cheeks.

"Of course they do. You know that. But it's a terrible waste anywhere." She heard her voice rise. "And Nilda hinted that you won't make much of this in your broadcast, or have me follow up on it, either. Was she right? Did you send us just for a token presence, knowing we'd get next to nothing for the air? Did you send us for entertainment?"

Tomás' eyes narrowed.

"Listen to how you're speaking to me! I know you usually cover politics and general-interest stories. But you work here now!" Then he paused, cleared his throat, changed his tack.

"Still, you look like you need a drink. How about having a cocktail with me at Angela's Cafe? It's only a few blocks, and then you can work on the Pará story. Just let the murders go. You didn't get enough, anyway. We'll use the wire services."

She hesitated, realizing how far out of line she'd been.

Nilda, having miraculously reappeared, gave her a knowing look when the two left the office, a warning look, Sandra thought. But she trotted out the door after Tomás like a faithful soldier following the commanding officer's orders.

Angela's proved to be cool and quiet, a place of potted palms and a deserted bar. And instead of leering at her, as he so often did, Tomás launched into a lecture that was almost brotherly.

"Sandra, I'd like you to enjoy working in Brazil." He played with the swizzle stick in his drink. "I've asked you to eat lunch with me, come to my sports club. But if you won't do that, why don't you go to some parties at your consulate? Don't you want to increase your connections, meet and greet? Hell, it's part of your responsibility as a reporter."

Sandra almost blurted that she'd been too busy at work, but stopped herself in time. He of all people knew that wasn't true. "I wanted to get used to Rio first, I guess."

His face lit with that sardonic grin.

"There's the American Society of Rio de Janeiro—for homesick people, I think. Or how 'bout a church? They have social events." Seeing her expression, he paused for a second or two. "OK, but religion has some advantages, like getting to know people you ought to know."

"I'd rather sign up for Voodoo."

Tomás smiled.

"I'm with you there. Well, sort of. Religion is okay for women. My wife Margaretta goes to mass once in a while, and she insisted on having Sybila and Laura christened to please our families.

But I don't care for it."

Sandra thought the comment was interesting. In her time in the Rio bureau, she'd never before heard Tomás mention his wife. He'd made a number of references to his personal life, but they seemed mostly about handball, his favorite sport at his club. Sandra had wondered if their twins had sprung fresh from a vegetable garden.

"I guess you could say I'm disaffected, verging on bitter. I've got some unpleasant memories of high school in Buenos Aires."

"I know where you're coming from." Tomás spoke fluent English without an accent and liked to use popular idioms whenever he could.

One of his hands started to reach for one of hers on the table. "I'm glad to see you have enough confidence in me to chat a little. We should do this more often."

Sandra pulled her hand back. *No, we shouldn't.* But she smiled and said, "I'll pay my part of the bill."

"Are you kidding?" Frown lines she hadn't noticed before appeared on his forehead. "I'm just trying to show you some of our Carioca hospitality."

He's right about Brazilian hospitality being special. But I don't want to be indebted to Tomás, even if it's only for a few reais.

"I should pay my share, Tomás."

"You're serious?"

"Yes."

He combed his red beard with one freckled hand. "Is that American women's liberation speaking? I just want us to be friends as well as colleagues."

She didn't answer. *It's damn sure he wants a lot more than that.*

The corners of his mouth turned downward, moving his mustache and knitting his thick eyebrows closer together. "Let's pay, then, and we'll get back to work."

Inside the big pink house of Efrain de Carvalho, traffic sales director for the ninth district of Misericordia's drug operation, Isobel

Kwenten lifted her aching head. She hadn't meant to go to sleep before Efrain arrived. It was early yet, but she'd changed into a flimsy silk nightgown to wait for him.

To pass the time, she'd gotten into bed to watch their mammoth television screen, which took up most of one wall in the sprawling bedroom. Of course she'd fallen asleep.

Scolding herself, she unwound her body from the light orange comforter and stepped onto the floor from their four-poster bed. She wriggled her feet into puffy mauve silk slippers and padded just past the hall clock, a big Rococo affair. It read three a.m.

The realization hit her like a physical pain. Efrain wasn't here. He hadn't come home. Again. She felt cold, though the air conditioner in the big house wasn't set too cool. The same phrases played over and over in her brain: *I'm losing him. He's not interested in me anymore.*

Isobel opened the door of the mirrored bathroom, looked at the shining plumbing and the elaborate china hot tub. She turned on the gold tap and splashed her face with warm water. Bleary as she felt, she caught a glimpse of her oval face, dominated by huge green eyes, the lids a little droopy from sleep. Still, a beautiful woman looked back at her.

She extracted a bottle of anti-depressants from the carved rosewood medicine chest, hoping she would soon feel more cheerful. She kicked off the slippers and walked barefooted down the heavily carpeted long hall to Ana's room. Opening the door as quietly as she could, she peered in at her young daughter.

Ana had kicked off the bedspread. She lay on the short bed covered by a sheet decorated with pictures of toucans and monkeys. One chubby arm clutched a stuffed tiger. The other arm was at her side, the small fist opening and closing. Her lips opened slightly; she began breathing noisily through her mouth; her allergies were bothering her. To her mother, Ana looked vulnerable, very vulnerable. Asthma was always a threat.

Ana coughed and woke up with a little cry. She sat up in the bed, then started to stand, the skirt of her ruffled purple nightgown falling down in layers. It first covered her plump thighs, then her dimpled knees, finally resting at her ankles.

"It's all right, baby." Isobel spoke softly. "I'll get the vaporizer. We'll make the room moister. That will help."

Ana coughed harder, but subsided when her mother picked her up. Isobel filled the vaporizer in the gilded bathroom, then plugged it in an outlet in the nursery, near Ana's junior bed. After a few minutes, the moist air did the trick. Isobel leaned over the guard rail and eased her daughter back into the bed. Ana lay quietly now on those sheets covered with laughing monkeys and toucans.

Isobel began to whisper to her child.

"What would happen if Efrain doesn't care for me anymore? I have no skills. No woman lasts very long on the game, and that's all I know how to do—all I've done since I was sixteen, all I did 'til Efrain brought me here.

"What would I do if Efrain really tires of me?" Isobel bent over the now calmed little girl. "I can't go home again; there's no home to go to."

Sometimes she could hardly remember the farm where she'd grown up among a throng of sisters and brothers.

"You have aunts and uncles, Ana. I wonder if they'd even recognize me now. I'll bet I've been much luckier than they have. My mother—your grandma, darling—had a new baby every year. She must not have been much over thirty-five when that terrible fever killed her."

Her mother had provided the only tenderness Isobel had ever known. Isobel remembered her father as severe, made leathered and bent by years of trying to tease cassava from his piece of unforgiving dry land, that tiny piece of land in Mato Grosso. He allowed his sons to attend school only until they were about twelve. The girls were in the fields even sooner, as soon as they were strong enough to help bale hay.

As Isobel worked in the fields those many mornings just before dawn, she'd wondered if grubbing in the earth like this, if competing with her siblings for food, was all there was for her. Would she die young like her mother? Was this to be her future?

Now, light years later, Isobel pushed back a lock of amber hair that was teasing her right eye. At the same time, she patted Ana lightly on her small shoulder. "I escaped from the game in Rio. And one day about three years ago, I met Efrain and he saved me from prison and losing you."

She'd escaped because of Efrain.

Isobel spoke into the air of the silent house she and her child shared with him. "Efrain, please come home."

His Rhodesian dogs barked in the walled-in backyard. Isobel's heartbeat slowed. But then it was quiet again. Whatever had stirred the dogs, it wasn't her man.

The house was quiet.

SIX

When Sandra and Nilda had rushed out of the Misericordia favela that morning, they'd left behind two dead young men. Now darkness lowered in the uneven stacks of rock that crept up the hillsides of the favela. A few candles began to burn among little knots of people in the narrow streets, but soon the mourning spread to the meandering, wider Rua Orinoco. It was one of the few streets in the favela that had a street sign with an official name.

High above a main tourist area of Rio, the mother of one of the dead drug couriers stood on Misericordia's uneven bricks. Two of her children were so small that their older sisters were holding them in their arms. The mother's voice echoed shrill with grief in the darkness.

Every so often she would cry, "Justice! Justice for my sons!" Other people descended from the crumbling steps of their homes, and the group swelled to a throng. "No more of this, no more!"

Newcomers kept melting out of the dwellings carved into the side of the rocky hills. They descended the uneven stone steps from their houses. The throng continued enlarging. From above, the crowd looked like a sea creature that puffs itself large.

An old man, his white hair glowing silver in the candlelight, motioned for silence; the word passed through the crowd. The people must have thought he was someone important, or perhaps the mourners granted him a voice to honor his age. On the lane of crumbling cobblestone, they quieted as he began to speak.

"Friends!" Candles flickered in the moonlight as he shouted. "Our youth is being destroyed; evil men's greed is swallowing them. We must stop our kids from selling drugs and carrying messages and money to the drug lords. Otherwise, the kids die, destroyed like so many insects."

His voice broke. "The drug leaders must go." A roar went up from the mass of humanity, bouncing shrilly off the rocky hills.

Delegado Osvaldo Carneira received word of a demonstration in the Misericordia favela almost immediately. His delegacia, his police station, was just a mile or two inside the shantytown.

After the clean-up of several favelas that began in 2008, the Police Pacifying Units, the UPP, had invaded and occupied many dangerous areas, but not yet Misericordia. That was true so far, anyway. Carneira and his few Policia Civil subordinates were responsible for a large patch of the area without aid. If it weren't so ridiculous, he thought, it'd be funny.

The delegado was working late tonight; the paperwork for a double murder was unimaginable.

He squinted at his computer screen as he wrote the names of the dead. The monitor was old and didn't illuminate very well anymore. He sighed, sad for the lives that he suspected had ended at the hands of the favela's drug bosses. He turned to Saenz, a very newly minted detective who was the only other officer in the room.

Carneira put aside the cold pipe he was sucking on and looked at Saenz. The boy seemed slow, he thought, a kid who wanted to be a cop so he could play with guns. There didn't seem much use attempting to tell him anything, but he decided to try his familiar sermon.

"You know, Saenz, that we'll never be able to get proof against these killers. Rodrigo Suares runs this favela. He's as vicious as he is fat, but we never get anything much on him and his people. And this execution-style mess seems pretty crude for his operation.

Usually it's smooth." He glanced over to see if Saenz was listening and was pleased to see that the boy looked alert.

"The people in the favela may be singing and praying right now. They make a lot of noise, but some of them will blame the killings on us. Mark my words.

"That's the way it will be, because that's always the way it is. The drug guys in Misericordia are isolated and insulated." He tapped the pipe with a rhythmic touch.

"Even if we get them into court, they'll never be convicted. Nobody who wants to live very long will be a witness against them."

Delegado Carneira abruptly stopped talking and returned to his mortality list. He wanted to go home and sleep; he'd worked many hours now without a break. His eyes burned and his mouth felt dry. But curiosity overcame him. He was wearing plainclothes, and so was the young cop. He decided they should check out the impromptu demonstration in person.

Carneira stood stiffly. One hip twinged angrily, and his first steps favored that leg. I'm getting old, he thought as he walked gingerly to the door. "Come on, Saenz. You ought to see this."

Carneira put on his jacket, shouted to Danilo to cover the front desk, and headed out the door. He was careful to hide his limp as they made their way up onto the favela streets with no signs. The young cop, yawning, followed three feet behind.

"No point in trying to get a car through those narrow streets with a crowd around. We don't want to call attention to ourselves." Carneira chuckled, his tone sounding metallic. As they approached the fringe of humanity, people in a tiny square were singing. He didn't recognize the tune, though he thought it sounded vaguely religious.

The people's intent seemed real—for the moment. But in thirty years on the police force, Carneira had seen many mourners who'd sworn that the violence in the favela would end, and nothing much had ever come of it. The sentiment, the will to do something, would fade with the night and the candles and the singing. Fear—justifiable fear—of the consequences of opposition held many back. Poverty with little hope of improvement left others lethargic and passive.

Carneira turned to make sure Saenz was still trailing as they pushed their way into the crowd. He began talking to the young cop in a didactic monotone. "There isn't much work around for young men, and what there is doesn't pay well enough to live a decent life. "The boys see that the people who succeed here are drug dealers, and they follow the model. They go from avioezinos, little messengers for the dealers, to fogueteiros, lookouts. From there it's not too far to top jobs."

Carneira stopped to check that Saenz was taking in his lecture.

"They carry the stuff, sell it and use it sometimes—no, often." Despite the discomfort in his hip, he moved with practiced skill through a mounting crowd. "That means they die more slowly than these boys that were shot today."

"Uh, yes."

"Think this demonstration will make any difference?" Carneira asked an old man who was shoved next to him by the crowd. The man wore an undershirt and shabby beige slacks; his feet were bare. Up so close, Carneira decided that the guy wasn't as old as he'd thought, but he leaned on a crude wooden crutch. The policeman guessed that he'd mourned many fallen young people by now.

"Do you think things can change?" the policeman asked.

"Nah, this is Misericordia. There's no way out."

Efrain de Carvalho sat silently in his habitual bar in Misericordia, drinking beer. He'd consumed a half-bottle of whiskey and now worked on chasers. He'd drunk the beer by the chopp, a small cup. But he hadn't counted the chopps and dimly wondered if he should stop.

"Hey, what's-your-name!" he called to the bartender.

"Yeah?"

"How many of these have I had?"

"A lot."

"What's a lot?"

"As long as you keep paying me for every order, buster, I don't keep track."

"Don't get smart with me."

"OK, don't take offense. You're in here often, and you usually don't drink so much."

"Got problems."

The barkeep sighed. "Who doesn't?"

Efrain spilled beer on the counter, wiped his mouth with his forearm, and began his confession.

"I screwed up badly at my job. My boss is threatening me with firing—or worse. And I can't stand my woman anymore."

"Maybe you need to get out of Misericordia for a while. Let your boss cool off. Lose the work worries and hunt for broads someplace else. Rio's a big city, man."

Efrain rubbed his scar and ordered another chopp of beer. He gulped it and several more.

Maybe this guy just wants to see me leave. Maybe he's right, though. It wouldn't hurt to get away from Rodrigo's territory. I need to plan my new business so I can get back in Rodrigo's favor, get my job back. Otherwise, I'm in big trouble.

As he left the bar, Efrain thought he heard faint singing in the distance, farther up in the favela. It wasn't samba tunes, either. It sounded faintly religious.

No, he couldn't have heard music. It must have been the beers.

###

Sandra didn't see Pedro, his footrest, his stack of rags, and his grungy little sister for a week. But one boiling morning, Pedro reappeared on a side street near the Worldwide office, and Sandra nodded to his invitation to get her shoes shined. They were not her usual style; that blister on her foot still hadn't quite healed, so she'd slathered on antiseptic, covered the spot with a bandage, and had worn a shoe that didn't touch the spot. These shoes gave Pedro more to polish than her customary sandals, so the process took a while. As he worked, she acted like a reporter.

"Where were you?" she demanded as she looked up at the acacia, frangipani, and lilac-colored hibiscus along the street. The blooms seemingly poured out of the tall iron fences around them. The hot breeze was stirring the blossoms, mixing a heavy perfume scent with something less pleasant that she couldn't quite identify. Maybe it was the fruit on the jaca trees, which loomed high above the other foliage. Yes, maybe it was jaca fruit or the leaves that didn't smell very good.

She wished Pedro would hurry up with her shoes. The sun burned piteously on her very pale skin, and its force seemed to intensify the odor.

He gave the cloth a professional shake. "Business wasn't good. So I hitched a ride for me and Zaida on a gasoline truck, and we went to Praia de Vermelha. Business was okay for a few days, with the tourists around there going to the cable car or railroad to Cristo Redentor and Sugarloaf." He put more pressure on his polishing cloth. "But now that it's summer, everybody's wearing sandals down by the beach. Or they wear flip-flops or no shoes at all. So we came back here by the business buildings."

Sandra blanched at the thought of the children hitching a ride. She stared at Zaida, worrying about the possibility that some pervert might see his chance with an unprotected child. Unlike Pedro, Zaida had a chubby face, and her arms and legs were rounded.
Pedro looked grubby, but Zaida exuded waifish appeal.

"You go home at night, right, Pedro? You take the baby home?"

Pedro followed Sandra's gaze at his sister. "I take good care of her." But Zaida's short curls were tangled and dirty.

Could there be a mother in her life? Of course there could. They couldn't really be true street children, could they? They probably lived in a shantytown nest.

As Sandra had thought before, Zaida's hair looked coppercolored, but it was so grimy she couldn't tell. Probably, she reasoned, they lived in a favela with no running water.

While Pedro was identifiably African Brazilian, on a painter's palette, the little girl's skin was several shades lighter. Racist elitism still abounded in Brazil; Zaida might well have an easier life than her brother.

Pedro stopped polishing her patent-leather shoes for a second. He studied his cleaning rag. "You know, maybe instead of paying me for this, you could give me a comb and brush. I could make her look prettier then."

The American reporter wanted to get up and run away. She wished she could be on the morning flight to Washington right now, right this minute. Images of another child, a baby who never was, ran across her field of vision like a film on fast-forward.

Her long white fingers grasped the arms of the rickety cane chair she'd provided for Pedro. "Where do you live? Where are your people, Pedro?" Her voice sounded unnaturally loud and harsh in her ears, as though someone else were speaking.

Pedro didn't look up from Sandra's shoes. They were very shiny now. Still he kept on polishing, probably beyond the time when it was good for the leather.

"Tia, please. We used to live inside, and it wasn't good. Now we live outside." His tone was matter of fact, as though speaking of strangers.

"You're saying you live on the street?"

"No, Tia, not really. We live with a bunch of other kids, kids like us. We have a kinda village under an old factory awning. It's okay. There's shelter from rain, and the big kids keep a fire going at night when it's cold. We've even got a big friend, Georges. He makes sure nobody takes our money. And Maria's there. She's sixteen. She has a baby. She helps me with Zaida."

Sandra felt as though she'd been struck by a sandbag. Was there really no adult caring for Pedro and Zaida? Unreality gripped her.

"Did you run away from home? Your people must be frantic. Where are you camping, Pedro?" Her first guess was a sort of minifavela near the venue of some of the Olympic swimming competitions, not so far from the famous Copacabana Beach. "Or up somewhere in Botafogo? Where?"

He didn't reply, but just kept rubbing the cloth over her shoes.

When Pedro finally finished the silent polishing, Sandra paid him about four times as much money as he asked. She also left him the comb and small brush she dug out of her big straw purse. The bag was a birthday gift Charles had bought her while he was covering unrest in Aceh, Indonesia, years before. The purse was lined in plum silk. She knew she should carry another purse. Like her romance, the time for this one was over.

SEVEN

Next morning, Sandra drove from her apartment in the Leme district to her office an hour early. And, yes, in front of the building stood Pedro and Zaida. Sandra parked and hopped out of the Volkswagen. She nearly ran to seize Pedro by the hand to lead him and his sister toward a little coffee bar she thought was not too far away.

They dashed toward Rua Raul Pompeia, Sandra carrying Zaida, who seemed much heavier than she looked. Pedro ran in front of them, and they didn't notice a BMW going against the light as they started to cross the street. A man wearing a broad-brimmed hat and a turned-up collar piloted the car. Huge round-framed sunglasses hid much of his face.

The man sped up, narrowly missed Pedro, and started to pull over. Sandra waved her fists at the driver. When he spotted her, the driver shot away with squealing tires.

"Pedro, be more careful! That car almost hit you."

The boy jumped up on the curb and took a man-of-the-world stance. He brushed off the scolding and changed the subject as Sandra and Zaida joined him.

"That happens around here. This is Rio." He spoke as though proud of his recklessness. "And you don't have to buy us food. I get enough for Zaida and me."

But the macho mood didn't last long. Soon he was trotting along beside Sandra. Zaida, freed to toddle on the sidewalk now, frequently stopped to notice the coarse grass or a Beija-flor bird in the bushes. She also kept trying to pick up cigarette butts from the pavement and put them in her mouth. At one point, the little girl picked up an empty package of Lucky Strikes. She squealed when Pedro took it away from her.

"Want it, wanna play with it, want it," she chanted, her lips pursed in a pout.

"Pedro, how did you learn to take care of a little kid? She should be with your family. So should you. I need to tell someone in authority about you two so we can get you some help."

But Pedro shook his head forcefully.

"No! If you tell someone, they'll break us apart like Georges said. I take good care of Zaida."

They walked and walked, Sandra having misjudged the distance. Finally, she succeeded in getting the two children into the restaurant where she'd planned for them to eat. It wasn't really a restaurant, though—just a kitchen and a coffee bar with tables reaching out into the open air. A few scraggly palms drooped their fronds wearily over the sidewalk, which was broken in several places and marred with discarded drink cans. Across the street, an alarmingly sunburned shirtless man lolled in the direct sunshine.

Sandra and the kids were seating themselves at a white lattice ice-cream table when the proprietor appeared from behind the espresso machine. His hair was the color of Pedro's deepest cordovan shoe polish. But his mustache was white, and it hung perilously over a downturned mouth. The man rubbed his hands on his stained apron. Sandra saw yellow, uneven teeth as he spoke to her in Portuguese.

"Moca, lady, you can't bring those kids in here."

"You don't want my money?"

The man sighed and switched to English. "Missus, these kids look terrible. Drive away my customers, don't you see?"

Sandra caught Pedro's expression. Young as he was, she saw that he understood. Probably he had been through similar experiences in his short life. She rose from the chair she had just occupied and moistened her lips. She took a second to mentally rehearse her words.

"Don't mind that disgusting man, Pedro. Let's get out of here and go someplace decent."

Pedro followed her as they left the café, but Sandra had to pick up a squealing Zaida to loosen her from the glass-enclosed fooddisplay case. The little girl's face reflected real grief and loss as she spied the rolls and bagels inside.

"Don't worry, kids. We'll eat very soon."

But she wasn't so sure. Then she remembered another café just a block distant. All kinds of people ate there. There were workers from nearby buildings, men in overalls, women in very short shorts and sweaty T-shirts. Sandra felt sure no one would notice the kids.

Soon Pedro was spooning mushy oatmeal into his sister's small, pink mouth. Sandra thought Pedro was right; Zaida really was beautiful. Or at least she would be if she had a bath. Green flecks like little pieces of glitter tinged her wide-set hazel eyes. Dimples punctuated her chubby cheeks beneath a high, patrician forehead. She smiled between bites of the oatmeal. "Good, good, good, good," she piped.

While helping his sister eat, the boy stuffed his own mouth with pieces of scrambled eggs and bacon. He lifted the food from his plate with his left hand and shoveled it into his mouth. His bony fingers seemed disproportionately long for the rest of his abbreviated, childish body.

"Have you ever been to school, Pedro?"

"Sure, I went."

"What was the name of your school?"

Adding bacon to his scrambled eggs mustache, he ignored her question. "Food's good. Tia Sandra, could I please have some plain ice cream with chocolate–chip cookies in it?"

"I guess so, if they have some. It's early in the day for ice cream, isn't it?" But she left the table for a moment and returned with a cup of plain vanilla ice cream.

For a second, Pedro looked disappointed.

"Hey, wait." Sandra dug in her outsized purse and pulled out a small, unopened plastic package of dark chocolate cookies from the machine in her office building. "Crumble these into your ice cream."

Pedro grinned, a wide, toothy expression of sheer glee. He then ripped into the cup and spooned at least half of it into his mouth all at once. Zaida took a taste, but pronounced the mess "too cold."

"Where do you usually eat, Pedro?"

The big breakfast must have made the boy more expansive. "I take what I earn at the end of the day and go to the supermarket. Then I make our dinner, and we eat on our blanket."

Sandra pictured the dirty, ragged blue blanket she'd seen while having her shoes shined. She wondered where he kept it and his footrest and his rickety chair when they weren't in evidence. And how did he carry his stuff around to all the spots where he said he worked? Even those poor possessions could be stolen, after all.

"Tell me more about where you sleep. Where is it?"

Pedro just looked at her. His expression said, I like you, but I don't trust you not to tell the police or somebody else about us.

"Zaida, take a little more oatmeal," Pedro ordered in his best big-brother voice.

But Zaida had other ideas. One chubby hand reached into Sandra's purse and emerged with three or four coins. Quicker than Sandra thought imaginable, she hot-footed it to the checkout counter.

"Wanna buy Lacta Ao Leite," she told the clerk.

"Sorry, honey, you don't have enough money," A matronly woman looked expectantly at Sandra with a wide grin.

But before the reporter could react, the little girl whizzed back to her side and slipped Sandra's VISA card from her purse. Ridiculously fast, she reappeared at the counter.

The clerk laughed as Sandra paid for the big chocolate bar. Zaida smacked away while Sandra repeated a short morality lecture on the need to ask permission before digging into someone's purse. But she thought how smart the child was to imitate her actions when making a purchase, and Sandra giggled while she scolded.

Pedro frowned. "That wasn't funny, Tia. Terrible things can happen to kids who steal. You should have slapped her."

"But she's a just a baby."

"Not to the police, she isn't."

Sandra sipped her bitter espresso. She made up her mind that she must do something about the kids, and soon. Children weren't meant to lead lives like this boy and his sister. If Pedro was telling the truth, they were sleeping outdoors, protected only by an awning and bigger kids.

She'd seen dozens, maybe hundreds, of young children sleeping on dirty blankets by roads. She'd seen them in Sierra Leone, in Bangladesh, in other places she'd covered and, of course, in the barrios of the Buenos Aires of her teen years. But there were also adults around.

Where could she get help for these Brazilian children?

Pedro broke into her thoughts. He offered her a sticky hand.

"OK, Tia, gotta go to work." Then he swept up his little sister and disappeared toward some of Copacabana's tallest buildings.

Dr. Olivia Kattah left Wilson Azevedo Hospital by the emergency room exit after a shift she wouldn't soon forget. She was attending the two-year-old daughter of a Cabinet minister. It was one of those stories that doctors dread: a case of something that didn't follow the rules. The little girl had come down with what seemed a mild "bug" a week before, then gotten much better. And just as suddenly, she'd turned up in the emergency room with a frighteningly high fever, seizures, and a cough.

Hours passed when recovery seemed impossible. The pleas of the little girl's parents still rang in her ears: "Can't you do something?" Well, Olivia had done something, all right. She'd ordered the right medication, supposedly a drug way down on the effectiveness list for the child's illness. It worked where others had failed.

The tiny girl finally responded. She'd improved so much that she was now talking to her parents, demanding toast and her teddy bear. But it was the adults' earlier words that Olivia was hearing: "Can't you do something?"

The glass doors of the emergency room entrance opened for her. "See ya!" she called over her shoulder to a nurse's aide.

The woman, years older than she, waved and called, "Have some fun, honey. You've earned it."

It was nice that somebody thought she deserved some fun, she thought, some escape from heavy responsibility.

But the moonless darkness stifled her, made her feel short of breath. Some of the lights in the hospital's parking lot were burned out, and it seemed very black. Her high-heeled leather sandals from Rome made a clicking sound as she hurried to her car, shrugging off her white coat in the process.

In the darkness, the deep red of her BMW looked like blood. She turned the ignition key, gunned the accelerator, and shot through the loose gravel. Damn, the hospital trustees had been promising to repave the parking lot for several months. What was the matter with them?

Olivia wasn't concentrating much on her driving. Instead, she mentally reviewed the last few difficult hours with the Britto baby, who would make it now. But, Lord, she thought, what a night. She reached for the silver comb that held her curls in an upsweep. She breathed easier as her shining extravaganza of black hair cascaded onto her neck and shoulders.

Tired, I'm so tired. But I know I can't sleep, not as keyed up as I feel. I'm sick of being the responsible one, the drudge. No, it isn't sleep I want. It's a drink, and a little fun, maybe some real excitement. I want to see somebody besides sick children and desperate parents. Yes, a drink and some excitement, that's the ticket.

Olivia half-smiled to herself as the car purred along the quiet, palm-lined streets.

Her father, old-fashioned but forgivable for his vast wealth, had discouraged her from studying medicine. Senhor Kattah was a computer mogul, one of the first to bring the digital age to Rio. He'd questioned her decision to be a doctor and predicted difficult days and nights.

"Do you really want to work so hard, and be accountable for other people's wellbeing and even their lives? Think, Olivia!"

Maybe he'd had a point. But right now she thought about where she could find that drink and a little fun. Fun for someone with her looks wasn't hard to come by, after all. She'd check out the Zero Zero, or maybe the Melt. She was headed for Leblon when, quite suddenly, Olivia turned the car around. The quick change of direction sent her hair flying over her face. The tires screeched.

"I know," she thought aloud. "I know: that American bar near Rocinha. What's it called? Oh, yeah, The Breezes. Maybe it's full of crooks. They like it there. It's kind of chic. That's it. That's where to end this night, that's where to celebrate the Britto kid's living to be three. The Breezes."

###

After sobering up on lots of coffee, Efrain de Carvalho had left Misericordia in a hurry. He found himself almost all the way to another favela, Rocinha, when he decided he was thirsty again. He spotted a promising watering spot with a mural on the front of the building. It showed a huge sailboat with a billowing white sail.

He talked to his windshield as he parked the BMW. Miraculously, Rodrigo hadn't sent anyone to reclaim the car. In truth, after threatening Efrain when he learned of his bad judgment in killing the kids, Suares hadn't talked to him at all. Wouldn't take his calls, wouldn't have anything to do with him.

"But, damn it, I'm going to bring him a new business, a moneymaker that doesn't require much hassle." Big disappointment though it was, he was sure turning over the profits from the new business to Rodrigo would regain him a place in the Misericordia organization. Maybe he'd even get promoted.

Efrain felt stressed, but definitely not defeated. In fact, his mood moved up a notch as he walked into the nightclub. Soon he leaned over the brass railing of the bar. His head was cocked as though he were listening to the music. But it was just an ordinary samba tune. He wondered why all samba music sounds alike. But then, he thought, it didn't really matter. He was listening to his inner voice, not the music.

He called to the bartender.

"You there, give me something interesting to drink."

"Mojito, maybe?"

"Man, can't you think of something different?"

"OK, I'll make a mystery drink for you, my special caipirinha."

Efrain leaned against the railing, pushed his elbow onto the counter, and spoke as the bartender moved around to make the cocktail.

"You know, sometime I'm going to have to go home, back to Isobel. But not now, not tonight. I don't want that woman anymore, her and that kid that's not even mine."

He realized that it was the second time that day that he'd used a bartender as a confessor. But then, wasn't a bartender the world's best listener?

"I've never felt like this before. I'm... but what? Restless, I guess. Ma always said I was so restless, the most restless of the bunch."

Efrain sipped the potent cocktail and wondered what happened to them, his mother and the other kids, back in Buenos Aires. Couldn't call, couldn't contact them; he might have gotten caught. He'd fled the country. Brazil wasn't anxious to extradite. Or, more likely, he wasn't important enough to bother with. He wasn't anybody yet. It was here in Rio that he'd made it.

He remembered his last conversation with his mother. He'd come home bleeding from the face and neck and tried to lie about how it happened.

She'd spotted the lie immediately and shouted at him. "Efrain, what are we going to do? I have no money for a doctor."

"I'll find one," he'd said, grabbing a towel from her shaking, outstretched hands. His two youngest brothers, Carlos and Luis, stood wide-eyed and frightened behind his mother as he mopped the freely flowing blood. "The guys will know somebody that can sew me up." He'd talked as normally as possible, but the pain was maddening. "The guys will help."

"Stupid boy! You wouldn't be in this trouble if it weren't for those guys." Her voice quivered, a mixture of rage and fear for him.

"Will the police come looking for you?" Then she started to cry, her heavy breasts heaving in her blue printed housedress.

He'd run away from her sobbing, run out to the waiting gang. Efrain never saw his mother again. He never knew what became of Carlos and Luis or the others. Sometimes he thought of the littlest ones with an aching fondness. They'd dogged his footsteps—their handsome and street-smart big brother—while they all crowded into that hovel in a back alley of Buenos Aires.

Sometimes, with at least a little ripple of pain, he understood that those brothers might be the only people besides his mother who'd ever cared for him for something besides his money. There was Isobel, of course, but he'd just as soon she didn't.

Now, many years later, Efrain raised his slightly graying head to ask the bartender, his quiet confidante, for another fancied-up, specially mixed caipirinha.

Drink in hand, Efrain took a vicious stab at the mysterious piece of fruit in it. He looked up to see a woman entering the bar. Was someone with her? No. That seemed odd. Broads didn't usually turn up in a place like this without guys unless they were hookers, and this one didn't look like a hooker. Not at all.

She looked classy, and not from anyplace like this neighborhood, just a deep breath from a favela. Efrain nodded in response to his own thoughts. He understood. This was a rich woman, slumming.

She was trying to look nonchalant, he thought, like she belonged here. But he guessed that she probably was from one of those high-rises around the Rodrigo de Freitas Lagoa, Rio's famous lagoon, looking for a little excitement.

Efrain gulped down the mushy fruit and ice mixture in the bottom of his glass. His body tensed. He waited, a leopard about to pounce.

He watched as the woman approached the bar. Average height, shining jet-black hair, glowing sandy-colored skin, and my God, what a body. Smashing legs, well exposed by her short, tight black skirt. The top wasn't too bad, either. The low neck of her black blouse was decorated with silver jewelry; he could see the shine on her silver earrings as she drew closer.

Mustn't scare her away.

But he had the confidence of an extraordinarily handsome man, a man who usually got his way with women, and he didn't delay long. The woman stepped up to the bar.

"Oi, hello," he said. Efrain de Carvalho lifted his glass and nodded slightly to Olivia Kattah. "May I treat you to a special kind of caipirinha? They're very wicked here."

EIGHT

  Sandra had been sitting in the otherwise-empty Worldwide Rio Bureau for hours. She'd drunk a lot of coffee, and every so often she stood up and walked around a little. She told herself she was doing research, but until Nilda and Tomás showed up, she mostly stared at a stack of newspapers or looked up factoids on Google.

  Not many lines of copy found their way to her computer screen that day. She dashed out most of the world news first, almost on auto pilot. Aleppo, Cairo, Iraq, and Libya were erupting like geysers. ISIS and Al Qaeda wannabes were sprouting up in Europe, Asia and Africa. In the United States, deadly attacks by lone-wolf jihadists had terrified many people. On her current turf, there was a big fire in Belo Horizonte—several commercial buildings aflame under mysterious circumstances.

  Teachers in Rio were threatening another strike, and so were miners in Minas Gerais, up in the mountains. A record number of people had visited the Village Mall in Rio the previous few days in a buying bonanza. A woman in Leme had unexpectedly and suddenly given birth to triplets, and all were doing well, although the babies would have to stay in Prontobaby Hospital da Crianca for weeks. And everybody was worried about Zika, the disease that threatened pregnant women with giving birth to terribly disabled children.

As the Olympics approached, angry Cariocas were organizing more protests that sometimes became violent. They demanded to know why the government pushed poor people from their living areas, including native peoples, to build elegant athletic venues and veritable Potemkin Villages to impress Olympics visitors. They wanted to know why the government spent billions on the Games when some Brazilians were going hungry.

Back home in the U.S., the House of Representatives had passed a major education bill. But it didn't look like the Senate would follow suit. And in Iceland, that volcano with the name nobody could pronounce threatened to explode again. Sandra speculated nervously about her father's travel plans in case the damn thing fused off. An eruption of it had scrambled flights and stranded people all over the world in 2010.

Could Dad and Elizabetta make it back to Rome? Her mind wandered to the fact that she was a little jealous of the woman who held her father's attention when she, herself, got so little of it.

Almost done. No, wait! She hadn't written a word about the killings in Misericordia. Had the police identified any suspects?

Sandra called Delegado Carneira, part of Misericordia being his responsibility. But a youthful-sounding cop named Saenz told her Carneira was out and wouldn't be back before her deadline. Saenz said he himself knew nothing of the case. Sandra believed him because he sounded as though he would know very little about anything.

Again and again as she worked, her mind skipped to Pedro and Zaida. She mechanically checked the wire services and CNN, then hurried through her recorded telephone interviews as fast as she could. The local and international news she selected for her broadcast melded into a script of violence and sadness and, of course, that item at the end that was supposed to cheer people up.

Today, though, the only so-called comical item on the wires wasn't funny. She ignored it and finished with the discovery of a huge sea creature in Alaska. Scientists thought it had some of the characteristics of the prehistoric mosasaurus.

"Welcome, Nessie," she said aloud. "You're a long way from home." The exclamation earned her a quizzical look from Tomás.

Checking over what she'd written, she wondered if he'd noticed how superficial her broadcast sounded. And why hadn't he prodded her about the American missionary nun who was trying to help preserve the environment and aid the farmers and rubber workers of Pará State?

Verdant forests stood in the areas where the trees hadn't been razed. But the earth in the state was getting more and more scorched. Lumbermen were slashing and burning the forests. And there was big money in growing soy and corn on the land. Greedy cattle ranchers and investors in many places continued forcing out small farmers, sometimes violently, rocking food prices into crazed behavior all over the world.

Tomás, aided by Nilda, kept up with the daily bread-andbutter coverage of the support rallies for the crusading nun and the occasional interviews with the victims of the lumbermen's raids on their opposition. Blessings on Nilda. But somebody, namely Sandra, had yet to write a major piece on the nun and her struggles for the workers and farmers.

Sandra needed to think out loud about the subject, and Nilda was nowhere to be seen.

"Something like a hundred deforestation protesters have been killed or wounded, and hardly anyone paid attention," she called over to Tomás. "But this nun comes down here from Boston and even gets a little notice from the government."

"I noticed." Tomás sounded wry and far away from behind a copy of *O GLOBO*, Rio's most influential newspaper. "You know, a lot has happened since Sister Dorothy Stang was murdered years ago in Pará. But I haven't read any of your backgrounder broadcast on the subject."

Well, there it was. He'd withheld his wake-up call until now.

She hadn't written a single line of that broadcast, of course. Conscience twinging, Sandra decided to abandon her current story about a conference of ecologists in Sao Paulo. Instead, she resolved to make an outline of sorts about the Pará situation. But her efforts were fitful. All the while she wrote, Pedro and Zaida flitted through her mind, distracted her, intruded on her concentration. They danced onto her mental stage like a mini corps de ballet, leaping, performing jetes, in and out, up and down.

Whose children are they? Did they really live under the awning of an abandoned factory? Maybe Pedro was lying. Like Tomás said, maybe the kids had a mother who sent them out in the morning and took Pedro's earnings when they returned at night.

But I don't believe that. Every day I feel more sure that the children are truly alone.

After accomplishing nearly nothing on her broadcast project, Sandra called Heloisa Santos, a Brazilian she'd met while Heloisa was getting a master's degree in social work at Catholic University in Washington. Truthfully, so far Heloisa was Sandra's only Brazilian friend.

Heloisa administered several religious-supported daycare centers in Rocinha, maybe the most gentrified of Rio's favelas. The women decided to splurge on dinner at the French restaurant atop one of the biggest hotels in Copacabana, a place with a Paul Bocusetrained chef. The hotel offered a view of the ocean and the illuminated granite rocks that grow out of the earth in the midst of the ocean.

"Sandra, why do you want to involve yourself with these children?"

Heloisa fiddled with the swizzle stick in her cocktail. The Brazilian friend shook her head, rearranging her curls. It was a habitual gesture, combined with swinging hands that darted to and fro as she made conversational points. The look on her round face was concerned. Her eyebrows knitted and she took a gulp of her drink before starting to talk.

"Believe me, I speak from experience. These kids who have no home can wear you down. And no matter what you do, almost none of them have any future. For one thing, merchants get disgusted with them." Heloisa reached into her big straw purse for a pack of cigarettes. "They hang around and steal from the stores and scare away sales. Some merchants even pay cops to get rid of them—even kill them."

Sandra blanched.

"Geez, Sandra, don't you look at your own network's website? Just a little while back, your people ran a story about an anniversary observance of street kids killed by police in Sao Paulo."

Heloisa lit her American cigarette, a Marlboro. Smoking was a habit she had never been able to break since Washington. Sandra recoiled slightly, but Heloisa missed the hint or ignored it. Sandra hoped the waiter would delicately remind her friend that smoking wasn't allowed, but he didn't seem to notice.

The social worker inhaled deeply. "I doubt that the kids you've met are living entirely alone on the street. A kid shining shoes might get by alone, but surely not a kid dragging around a toddler. If they stayed in a favela, they might not be noticed. But these kids you're talking about are down here; the boy is working among mostly comfortable people. Surely they'd have been noticed and picked up and placed with foster parents.

"And even if they're truly homeless, you don't get it about street kids. In general, if these kids live to be teenagers, they're lost souls. By that time, they're into prostitution, stealing, or hard drugs. Suppose somebody snatched them off the sidewalk and gave them a good home when they're still fairly young, it's almost impossible for them to learn."

She paused for another long drag on her cigarette, waved her left hand in an oval, started again. "It's all right to have good-hearted notions, but I don't think the lives of those kids can be easily fixed. "You have street kids in America, too. When I visited Los Angeles and San Francisco, I saw lots of young people lying around the streets. No babies, for sure, but lots of young people." Down went the cigarette into her butter plate and up went both hands. They each described ovals in the exhaled smoke. Her voice grew louder.

"It's one thing to take in a stray animal and another thing to get mixed up with stray kids."

Sandra nodded. She looked out the window at a huge illuminated rock growing out of the street not far away. After the Christ the Redeemer statue and Sugarloaf Mountain, these rocks provided favorite targets for tourist cameras. Other lights of the city twinkled brilliantly. From here, the world was surpassingly beautiful. "God, Rio is indecently sumptuous."

"Relevance?" Heloisa scolded. "Stick to what's on your mind—those kids—until we can get through this dismal topic."

"Their situation is intolerable."

Heloisa gulped her daiquiri, made a face and a promise. "I'll use my contacts and inquire about residential schools, even some temporary shelters. But I'd have to present them in person. You'd need to get them to me." Her hands rose to her forehead. "We're not savages here. If the authorities knew about a street child as young as the little girl, they'd surely get her into custodial care immediately. I can't guarantee that she and her brother wouldn't be separated."

"Separation isn't an option after what they've been through!" Sandra's face flushed with the effort of making her point. "And anyway, there's no way I could round up the kids to turn them into the authorities. Some bigger kid told Pedro that maybe his baby sister would be taken from him, and that he'd be sent to school."

Heloisa took another deep drag on her Marlboro. "All right, all right. But I need at least their names and their history, for goodness sake. One of these times, that boy's bound to give you a hint about who he is and where he came from."

Sandra smiled, relieved.

"Come on, now, Lady Bountiful, let's talk about something else"

To Sandra's astonishment, she found out very soon that Heloisa's guess was right on target. While Sandra got her shoes shined the next morning, Pedro offered a confidence—a splash of light into his short, shadowy life.

He buffed Sandra's bone pumps as he spoke. "I used to hang out inside a church. It's okay in there. The bigger guys can't beat you up like at school." There was no self-pity in his words; Sandra thought he sounded like he was talking about someone else, as he had the other day. He continued: "The priest was OK. Sometimes he played futebol with us. Near Flores."

"Is that a village?"

"Dunno."

"What church was that? What was the priest's name?"

Pedro ducked his head. "Tia, do you want me to put some water-proofing on your shoes? I bought some yesterday." He looked up at Sandra, then down again.

Sandra raised her voice. "Where's your mother?"

"Dead." Pedro spoke to Sandra's shoes. A few seconds passed.

"Where's your father?"

"No father."

Sandra heard herself say, "Would you like to go to a futebol match with me at the Maracanã?"

The child leaped several inches into the air. His bony bare feet made a "whoosh" as he landed on the pavement. He grinned, though the concrete should have hurt him. Sandra noticed again how very far his ears stuck out from his head. His dark hair spiked rakishly from his scalp, the strands parting in various directions. Sandra thought Pedro had a hairstyle that would cost big bucks in Georgetown or Manhattan.

Later in the day, Sandra tried to reach Heloisa on the phone, but found that she was attending a social workers' conference in Belo Horizonte. For lack of anyone else to share the news that Pedro and Zaida probably had no parents, Sandra confided in Tomás Mello, taking the risk that he might just scold or mock her. To her surprise, he half-smiled when he heard about the futebol game. But the expression lasted only a second.

"Don't you realize that the kid is just working you? He could snatch your purse at any time and disappear forever."

Sandra tugged at her braid, pulled it from her back to the front of her shoulder. A few wanton strands of hair escaped from their rubber-band prison.

"He's already had plenty of chances to steal my purse. He'd lose his best shoeshine customer and have to change territories, and he's doing well in all those places he mysteriously turns up. I'm safe."

"Listen, my American naïf. You're old enough, and a reporter who has seen all sorts of shit and suffering all over the world. Don't you know you're never safe?"

Sandra blinked and gave her braid an extra yank. Tomás often struck her as a leering goof. Was it possible that this man actually was concerned for her as a human being?

She dismissed the thought and sat down to write a broadcast about the drug trade in Rio. It reminded her ruefully of how close, and yet how far, she'd gotten from the story just days before. It seemed that the drug gangs still had strongholds in many of the city's hundreds of shantytown neighborhoods. The narcotics groups had created what one sociologist called "a third way" of government.

For years, in some places, the gangs operated almost entirely without police interference.

Some favelas, like Misericordia, had evaded attempts at reform. Many drug criminals in Rio had fallen before the fierce invasions of law and order, and they'd remained down because of occupation by those forces. But that hadn't happened to Misericordia. It still had its internal "law," not much hampered by conventional legal code.

Sandra had researched the drug trade within the favelas. Inside Misericordia's territory, she knew, gang members followed the strict rules of "the third way." But the police were uniformly silent on who might be responsible for the spectacular executions of the young men in Misericordia. It was getting close to deadline time, and she was having trouble writing her broadcast. Reluctantly she consulted her boss.

"I'm having brain-freeze, Tomás. This story has too many statistics for a listener. The web version's OK, but all these numbers won't do for the radio. And what do I write for the video?" She handed him the hard copy of her draft version.

Tomás raised his thick reddish eyebrows. "What's the matter with leading with what you saw the other day? That'll lighten the load of numbers. And if those shootings weren't gripping, what is?" She turned—more like slunk—away with a murmured "obrigada," thank you. Sandra felt a blush rising beneath her paperthin white skin. She'd been so distracted that even her most basic journalistic skills went dormant at times. This, embarrassingly, was one of those times.

She made a quick call to Delegado Carneira, who sounded far more cooperative on the telephone than he had in person. Maybe he'd heard that she and Nilda had been threatened while he was off the scene. Maybe he was taken aback that they'd been endangered.

More likely, he wasn't anxious for a lot of media attention to the Misericordia killings. That would mean more pressure on him to make it seem that a part of the favela was under at least some control.

Sandra yanked her mane loose from the braid and began writing:

"They could not have been more than eighteen or nineteen years old. The young men who lay dead in Misericordia the other day were victims of the 'third way' of life of the favela's drug culture. Had they lived, they looked forward to an existence shortened by drugs and in-fighting...."

She nodded as she read over her work and was pleased to see that Tomás made few editing changes. She was writing better today. She arrived in the studio in good time, even got a smile from Mario, the grumpy engineer.

Sandra voiced her script about terror and loss in the favela and, on her way back to the office, made a decision. "One way or another, I'm going to make things right for the children," she told Tomás. Then she caught herself, but not fast enough.

"You sound like Don Quixote." He grinned. "You have fantasies of rescuing those kids—just you, all alone. Lady, you have quite a grandiose notion of your own power."

For once, Sandra wasn't upset by his sarcasm. For the moment, she'd settle for getting Pedro to a futebol match. And the kid needed to be decently dressed for the Maracanã, after all. She checked out shops in two tony neighborhoods, Copacabana and Leme, but drove away in a hurry when she saw the prices. She wondered how Brazilians could afford to clothe their kids. After a while, her lemon-hued Volkswagen found its way to Botafogo and its many vendors' stands. These places were pricey enough, but maybe not so much as the others. In a tiny shop with an open front, she found a T-shirt bearing the name "Flamengo," Rio's most popular futebol team, and a coordinated pair of shorts, size P for pequeno.

Then she hesitated over a pair of flip-flops after trying to picture Pedro's bony bare feet as he'd leaped from the sidewalk. What was his shoe size?

Her other, more important duty, she realized, would be to make plans for Zaida's care while she and Pedro went to the game. A phone call to Heloisa solved that problem; her Brazilian friend said she'd take Zaida for the afternoon at one of the crèches she supervised.

"I'll do it," said Heloisa into her cellphone. "But remember what I said about getting too involved."

Sandra thanked Heloisa and pushed the disconnect key before her friend could back out. Good, Sandra thought, obstacle overcome.

NINE

The next morning, Sandra found Pedro and Zaida only a block from the Worldwide offices. Brimming with pleasure, Sandra showed Pedro the outfit she'd bought. His deep cocoa eyes enlarged, lightened. But when she explained about her arrangement for Zaida, he waved his polishing rag wildly in the air and started to yell. "No, no! I can't go to the match if she can't come along!" Sandra took a step back on the scalding pavement. "Pedro, a good friend, Heloisa, will take care of Zaida for the afternoon. Your sister will be in a safe place with a good person. She doesn't have anything to do with the police."

Pedro kept waving the grungy polishing cloth and shouted even louder.

"Zaida has to stay with me."

Sandra spent several more minutes trying to reason with the child.

"Zaida has to be with me!"

"Pedro, I'm going to be late for work. Please, think about this calmly. It's your chance to see a real futebol game." She had another big feature to write, and she knew she couldn't make the afternoon deadline if she delayed any longer. She started to move away. But as she took a few steps, Pedro followed, holding her gifts. He handed her the T-shirt and the shorts.

"Here."

Sandra reached down and pulled the child close to her.

"Pedro, please keep the clothes. And we'll take Zaida with us to the game." Instead of rebuffing her half-embrace, as she expected, he let her hold him for a few seconds. How thin his body felt.

Then he broke away to run over to Zaida, who was playing with a water-filled shoe-polish bottle on the tattered blue blanket. He grabbed the little girl's chubby arms and pumped them. He said something Sandra couldn't understand, but she caught the word "Flamengo."

Each day that week, Sandra parked the Volkswagen around the corner from the spot where Pedro sometimes operated his shoeshine business. And every day he asked the same question. "How many days until we go to the futebol?" he'd ask, and Sandra would count on her fingers.

Finally, the weekend arrived. Sandra's hands shook as she and the children rode the packed metro train to the Maracanã. What if she got separated from the children in the mob? How could they return to their makeshift home on the street, his and Zaida's community of the lost? But then, how did they ever get around to so many places as they did?

Why had she taken on this responsibility? What was the matter with her? Tomás' comment about her fantasies of rescuing the children drummed in her head, not even silenced by the incomprehensible brother-sister jabber of Pedro and Zaida.

At the ticket window outside the stadium, she smiled gratefully as the seller said she wouldn't have to pay for Zaida. The other two tickets came to 200 Brazilian reais, and she planned to buy refreshments and maybe a souvenir or two. The little party left the line, and she thought she had never seen so much of her fellow humanity.

The Flamengo fans with their brilliant red shirts looked like a single moving serpent. Everyone seemed to shout, the sounds reverberating in the stadium's interior as though in a tunnel or an indoor swimming pool.

The crowd moved toward the distant patches of light that beckoned to the seats, causing the reporter to look down constantly to make sure Pedro was still next to her. Zaida seemed happy to be carried on Sandra's shoulders.

"Giddeup," Zaida chirped.

Before finding seats, Sandra bought cachorro-questes, a Brazilian version of hotdogs. The trio waited in a separate line for Guaranas, soft drinks something like ginger ale. Sandra realized that Pedro had managed to find a place to wash himself.

She wondered where, and how. The layer of dust that almost always covered his skin wasn't there today, and his spiky brown hair was slicked down neatly. Sandra thought he looked like other Brazilian children in the throng, well-loved and cared-for children.

In some places back home, she thought people might look curiously at the dark skinned boy-child, the caramel-colored passenger on Sandra's neck, and her very white self. But Brazil was different. Lots of people were lots of colors.

"What a cute little girl," gushed several futebol fans admiring Zaida. She wore a yellow sun suit with a white rabbit on the front and a bonnet that almost matched. Heloisa Santos had contributed this outfit from the donated clothing box at one of her daycare centers.

No one commented on Zaida's brother, however.

Most seats in the center of the stadium were occupied already—expensive tickets bought in advance—but Sandra headed for a row in the less expensive upper section that still had room.

They moved to the far end of the row, Zaida on Sandra's right and Pedro on her left. Almost instantly, the row filled up. So tightly were the people packed in that Sandra could hear the breathing of the man beside her, who seemed to be suffering from asthma.

"Do you understand the game, Tia?" asked Pedro. "There are eleven guys on each team, and the idea is to move the ball down the field and score a goal."

Sandra opened her mouth to say that she once was a pretty fair substitute goalkeeper at Saint Helena's Secondary School for Girls in Buenos Aires. But instead, she listened and nodded.

Zaida quickly climbed into Sandra's lap. Sandra turned her head to the right and noticed a man a few rows down who seemed to be staring at her. He had the profile of a Hollywood movie star, but a white line ran down his cheek and disappeared under his T-shirt collar. Hadn't she seen him before? But shouts and waving pennants diverted her as the players trotted onto the field, and she forgot the man.

Besides, it wasn't unusual for Sandra to be stared at by men.

Soon the play began. Sandra and Pedro were yelling for the Flamengo. Sandra had been sure the noise would frighten Zaida, but the spirit of the match captivated the little girl. Every time her brother shouted, she joined in with an excited squeal. "Flamengo! Flamengo!" People chanted. Drums thumped and vuvuzelas shrieked into the humid air.

Luckily, Sandra wore a hat to protect her skin, which was the color of a bleached white bed sheet. The sun seemed to beat with special ferocity this afternoon.

She caught herself wincing as one of the Flamengo players returned the ball with a rapid-fire header. As a player long ago, she did what was needed, but she'd never entirely lost her fear of whacking the ball with her head. Maybe if she had, she thought she might have been St. Helena's first-string goalie instead of the substitute.

The Flamengo forward took control of the ball and worked it skillfully past the opposing Boa Vista team and kicked a goal. Thousands of people leaped to their feet, bawling and screaming with glee or grief. The game continued with Flamengo steadily dominating the play.

The team won easily. Pedro jumped up and down, Zaida squealed, and Sandra felt as though she'd won the lottery. As they were leaving the stadium, Zaida again rode on her shoulders, and Pedro didn't protest holding onto Sandra's hand.

Here we are, three against the world, she thought.

As she and the children wove through the now-shadowed stadium, Sandra realized that today, for the first day in weeks, she had not longed for the way things used to be.

Later that day, Efrain de Carvalho had to admit to himself that he'd drunk too much again. His recent reconnaissance trips and his failure at the soccer stadium had taught him an unwelcome lesson. The incidents showed him that starting his new business wouldn't be as easy as he'd thought. And his maddeningly many telephone calls to Rodrigo had gone unanswered. He'd had no chance to explain the killings or beg to get his job back. Still, he nurtured hope. Nobody had come to take back the BMW, after all.

I gotta just keep trying to show Rodrigo that I can help the organization. Hey, I've done a lot with my life since coming from B.A.— and I ain't done yet.

The air conditioner in Sandra's apartment wasn't working very well, and her nightgown kept bunching and tangling around her perspiring body. Marmalade, her no-longer-homeless orange cat, kept hopping into the bed, its furry warmth adding to the heat. She kept meaning to get up, throw the cat out, and close the bedroom door.

But somehow, the energy she needed failed her.

Tired from the crowds and the screaming at the Maracanã, she'd fallen asleep almost immediately, only to wake up a half-hour later. Then she started her familiar pattern of wondering if, how, and where she could transfer within the Worldwide network—or get another job right away. Surely freedom from the remote office managed by Tomás the womanizer would renew her energy and skills. So far, though, a couple of phone calls had gone unanswered.

She began to review the day, to relive the way she felt while dropping off Pedro and the little girl after the game. She had left two defenseless children to fend for themselves on the streets of Rio. How could she have done such a thing? She wouldn't even put out her cat at night.

Still, if there really were safety in numbers, she had left the kids with perhaps two dozen others. They formed a colony under an awning of their abandoned factory.

"It's OK, Tia." Pedro had dismissed her objections as they'd pulled up next to the awning. "We kids all stay together. My buddy Georges protects us in case anybody tries to take my money. He's tall. Georges will be here soon. Georges got a job cleaning streets, and he even bought a sleeping bag and backpack. No one can harm us with him around. And Maria's always here. She's a grown-up girl. She's sixteen. She has a baby, and she shows me a lot about looking after Zaida. It's like I told you. Georges and Maria help us."

Sandra asked Pedro if she could meet the two older kids. He said Georges was probably working late, but he guided her to Maria, who was holding her infant as Sandra approached. Maria's skin was the shade of light sand, while the baby looked whiter. Another of Brazil's rainbow of racial mixes, Sandra had thought. She looked up at the young woman, who was considerably taller than she and probably still growing.

"I hear you take good care of my friends Pedro and Zaida," Sandra had said. "I worry about them sleeping out here because they're so young."

The girl made a face. "They're better off here than in lots of places in Rio. I've been looking after them a little ever since they got here, right straight from wherever they came from. It was a long time ago. I hadn't had my baby then." She patted the infant's head. "A fruit truck from the country brought them, dropped them here and drove away. Pedro never says where he came from. Nobody here does."

This was how the kids were living, Sandra had thought with a start. For a second she considered taking the kids home. But she knew she'd have to all but kidnap them to do it. Instead, Sandra reached for her purse to offer Maria extra incentive to watch over them until arrangements could be made.

Maria shook her head.

"No money. I don't need money to be a friend." At that, she turned away.

A boy of about seventeen stared curiously at Sandra, at her car. "Moca, babe, are you on a slum tour?" But he laughed and waved at her. No one else moved from their dirty blankets piled with backpacks or plastic bags. One girl lay seemingly fast asleep on a mattress.

This camp of the forsaken, Sandra had reflected, was Pedro and Zaida's home. Their babysitters were other, bigger street kids. Before Sandra pulled away, she renewed her resolution. She'd bought Pedro a Flamengo banner to take home. But her mental monologue stumbled on the word "home."

At least today, though, she thought as she tossed in her bed, Pedro and Zaida had a Saturday like other, luckier Brazilian children

"But how could I have left them under that awning like that?" she said aloud, startling Marmalade. He'd wound himself around her feet in a kind of pretzel configuration. But then, her other voice replied, the children were that way before. And soon, very soon, she would find a happy solution for them. The kids might have to stay where they were for a while, but it wouldn't be more than a few days. Somehow she was going to see that they had a more normal life.

The resolution quickly yielded to rationalization.

If I were home in Washington, she thought, I'd have gotten this little boy and his baby sister into juvenile care the minute I first realized they were unsupervised. It's just going to take a little while longer here.

"Are they really alone, though?" She mused aloud for perhaps the 100th time. "Surely there's some relative back where they came from." Then Sandra patted the cat and returned to her muddled, contradictory thoughts in silence.

She asked herself again if Pedro's story were true. Or had Pedro run away from home because he hated school?

Things are tough here now. There's not much hope for street kids. Nobody wants them; they're dirty and diseased. People say most of them are thieves. If I report Pedro and his sister to the authorities immediately, Heloisa

says it's possible they'll be split up, and it's obvious that the little girl is Pedro's purpose in life.

Some life.

Sandra rolled to one side, then the other. She pushed her long hair, liberated from its daytime imprisonment in the braid, away from her face. The room seemed hotter. She checked the clock. It was three a.m., and she had to get up at five to cover a presidential speech in Petropolis about the very troubled Brazilian economy.

Must go to sleep, she told herself. Must get some sleep to do this job. She thrashed around some more in bed. Then, at last, she fell into a fitful doze.

Soon she was dreaming. Most nights Charles starred in her dreams, and the background showed the narrow, overpriced condominium in Georgetown, a historic and trendy section of Washington. But on this boiling night, she dreamed of the boys from her teenage years, the boys in Buenos Aires, the boys and the flashing knife. Even after so much time, the scene still recreated itself. She often thought that therapy would have helped, but the teachers at St. Helena's—the nuns—showed little interest in her traumatic experience. They'd urged her to let it pass, not talk about it, study hard, forget it and forgive her attackers.

By day, she always told herself philosophical things about this dream. She told herself the incident happened a very long time ago—more than twenty years. She told herself that she was perfectly all right now. The bad time had lasted just a few moments, was over forever, and everything was all right now.

But tonight, when she awakened from the dream alone in Rio de Janeiro, she realized that it was easier to be brave in the daytime than after dark.

###

That same night, Pedro was dreaming his recurrent dream about ice cream. Tonight, the dream ran much the same as usual: He was smaller, younger, lying on his mattress in semi-darkness, covered by a real sheet. His mother entered the house. Her full cotton skirt swished as she bent over Pedro.

"Are you asleep?"

He sat up, a little startled. He felt her cool hands on his face. She whispered so as not to disturb the others in the hot room. "Baby, I wouldn't wake you up, but my boss Senhor Baumgartner gave me some ice cream. It's your favorite, plain vanilla with chocolate cookie chips. Can you wake up enough to eat it before it melts?"

Pedro knew it was a pretty long walk home for her from the general store where she worked. He understood that he must eat the ice cream right then, before it melted. He wanted some badly. But he was so sleepy. As his mother turned away to get a dish, he fell back down on the mattress. Within a few seconds, he was asleep again.

In the morning, he found the ice cream she'd scooped out for him the night before. Their refrigerator didn't work well, and now it was too soft, just a puddle of goo in a chipped pottery dish. It took him a moment or two to control his disappointment, but soon he mustered himself to action.

He searched the room where he'd slept, stepping over the fast-asleep bodies of a man and woman he didn't recognize. After a while, among the mostly empty boxes on the floor, he found some cereal, some rolled oats. He poured the cereal into the bowl with the sloppy ice cream and ate his breakfast.

Now, on this night in Rio, Pedro half-awakened on a corner of the worn blue blanket. He heard a little whining noise next to him and realized that Zaida was starting to cry. He wondered if she was hungry, but their food was gone. As in the dream, he felt so sleepy. He didn't want to get up to tend to her. Maria often helped, but she was asleep, her baby tucked under one arm.

Other kids were around him, including some he didn't know. Pedro thought that if he didn't keep Zaida quiet, somebody bigger might get mad and punch him. Where was Georges, his much older friend who always protected him and Zaida? But Georges was not in his accustomed spot next to them.

A very noisy motorcycle passed by, the racket cutting through misty heat. He saw the rider, a man with a kind of stripe on his neck. A light flashed and Pedro could have sworn that the man had taken a picture. Pedro started to stand up to see better. But then, Zaida's cries grew louder. The motorcyclist turned a corner and faded.

Pedro forgot the biker. He lifted Zaida off the blanket and cradled her. On this night, his sister felt very heavy in his arms.

Efrain de Carvalho drove out of the driveway at the Barra da Tijuca home of Dr. Olivia Kattah. He sailed past the red BMW in her driveway, recalling how they'd laughed when they left the nightclub to discover they had matching cars. Naturally, he'd failed to mention that his wasn't exactly his.

Efrain had not felt this full of himself for a long time. He'd been with a beautiful, exciting woman. And she's respectable, he thought.

A gorgeous, respectable woman. How about that for a change?

On the strength of his euphoria, he made another of his many calls to Rodrigo Suares. To his surprise, at last he got past the boss' caller-identification device. He heard Rodrigo's voice instead of the message machine.

"Whaddaya want? I told you to beat up those kids and you killed 'em. You're through and you know it. You're lucky to be alive."

"Rodrigo, you don't know how it was. Don't hang up. I had to kill those kids. I got one alone and was starting to hit him when the other one turned up with a gun and fired and…" He blathered as fast as he could, mixing a little of his native Spanish with the Portuguese. He heard a distinct snarl on the other end of the line, but rushed on.

"And, boss, I've got something special for you. I've been investigating a new business. It's much easier than the drug operation. No rough stuff, no worries about enforcement. Lotsa money."

"You're takin' up my valuable time." Rodrigo cut the line.

Efrain's good mood now evaporated, and he headed home to his dreaded Isobel.

Efrain realized that if he ever were to win his job back, he would need her help.

TEN

Sandra and Heloisa Santos met again for dinner. This time, they were sipping margaritas under a Technicolor umbrella at Angela's Cafe near the Copacabana beachfront.

"I'm doing my work," Sandra told the social worker, "so Tomás can't object to the time I spend with the kids." She knew he did object, but she thought it wasn't his business so long as she completed her assignments.

Of course, she wasn't doing her best; instead, she was marking time until she could reasonably ask the main office for a transfer or apply for a job with another news agency. She suspected Tomás knew that, too.

"He's a distinctly funny duck," she told Heloisa. "He doesn't like it that I'm independent or that I won't play his flirtation game. I know he's disappointed that I keep him at bay. But I have to admit that he hasn't taken it out on me in the office. He seems more annoyed by my interest in Pedro and Zaida."

Heloisa shook her head, then reached to get a cigarette from her purse. "I think you're suffering from rescue fantasies." Seeing her friend's expression, Heloisa quickly added, "OK, that was a low blow. But I haven't even gotten anyone to return the calls I've made about the kids."

Sandra nodded, swinging her braid. "You're telling me. I've spent hours on the phone trying to get information from government offices about what can be done for street kids. But the authorities can't help because I can't provide any particulars."

"Course not. What did you expect? You can't even prove that they're orphans without other relatives. The boy doesn't have a chance for adoption unless some family would take him to get the little girl.

"The rule here in this state is that to adopt a child who has siblings, you've got to take the other children, too. And what're the chances of that? You say the boy's way behind on schooling and almost to puberty."

Sandra folded her paper cocktail napkin in quarters. "But these children need to stay together. Any kid as young as Pedro who cares that much for his sister deserves to grow up with her."

Heloisa waved her hands around, then lit her perpetual Marlboro. The brand had been her favorite in Washington, when the two women met at a conference at Georgetown University. Heloisa, the very bright master's degree candidate, had been part of a team researching juvenile justice, or lack of it, in America.

Sandra had interviewed her while covering the story. Ever since, the emotive Heloisa had been a favorite friend, even though thousands of miles had separated them 'til Sandra was sent to Rio. "Have you gotten any more information from the boy?" Heloisa asked.

"Not much, but he let it slip that he came from way out of the city somewhere, somewhere near a place called Flores. He mentioned that he played soccer at a church there, but wouldn't give a name. But I'm hoping to check that out soon. How many churches could there be around there?"

People at the surrounding tables were talking loudly as they drank, and Sandra had to strain to hear Heloisa's next words. "Oh, my gosh, plenty. There's a saying that there are more churches in Brazil than there are people. You'll get a list, of course, but it may be hard to call out there. Communication over that way is sometimes bad."

"I've done some calling already, and I just got curt or puzzled answers from church secretaries who weren't anxious to put me through to the priests. I think I need to drive around in the hope that

I can find the right parish. I'll just fill up the gas tank and go on the weekend...."

Heloisa tossed her black hair, which today hinted of an auburn rinse. "Alone? It's a long way, and you won't know where you're going. I seem to remember that in Washington, where you lived for quite a while, you had a bad sense of direction. You were always getting lost when you showed me around. Didn't you search for landmarks like the Capitol and the Washington Monument to get your bearings?"

"That's why I bought a GPS."

"I have to attend a social workers' forum this weekend. Wait another week and I'll go with you."

"Thanks, Heloisa, I appreciate it."

I can't wait any longer, though. Sunday. I'll go Sunday.

###

The following morning, Sandra found Pedro and Zaida on the sidewalk near her office building, as usual.

"Hey, big girl!" She picked up the toddler and flopped herself and the child in Pedro's rickety shoeshine chair. Fortunately, it held, and Zaida felt rounded and warm in her arms.

"San-dra, San-dra, San-dra," the child chanted. She patted Sandra's face, pulled on her bangs, swung her braid back and forth.

Sandra wondered what it would be like to be a mother. She'd been pregnant once—one of those strange accidents that was hard to explain. Charles had said they weren't ready for marriage, for a child. Both travelled continually, after all.

"We're getting there," he'd said, "but we're not quite there yet."

Not that he had that much influence on her decision, of course. She was an adult, making an adult decision, wasn't she? She worried about the career slowdown that would be necessary if she were to go through a pregnancy and take care of a baby. Her colleagues with children had a hard time balancing the demands of work and kids. They virtually trembled when an assignment delayed them from picking up the baby from daycare, or quite literally mourned when required to work twenty-four-hour shifts on some big story.

So she'd taken care of her situation quietly, just a few weeks after her condition was confirmed. What was removed from her body wasn't anything like a child, after all—just a zygote, a blob of tissue, nothing at all like a human being.

She'd felt depressed afterward, but only briefly. She was younger then, with the prospect of marriage and children before her. There was plenty of time. She and Charles would have children when the time was right, when their careers were better established. But that time didn't come.

"Tia, tia, tia," chattered the little girl.

If I can't have Charles, if I can't have children with Charles, I don't care about having children. I have my work, a life that counts, or at least it would count if I could get out of this frying backwater.

Still, as she held Zaida, she thought a child, this child, could be very appealing.

"Tia Sandra, please let me polish your shoes." Pedro's voice sounded listless. Sandra glanced up at him, startled. She realized that in fussing over Zaida, she hadn't really looked at Pedro this morning. His peach-pit skin looked faded. His face seemed washed out, especially around his eyes, which were ringed in circles.

"Something wrong?"

"No." But he turned his face away as he ducked down to work on her patent shoes. Sandra shifted uncomfortably in the chair.

"Pedro, did something happen?"

Pedro closed his eyes, squeezed the lids tightly together. "Georges died."

"Georges? Who's Georges?"

Pedro stood up. "I told you before, Tia. He's a kid, lots bigger than me. He sometimes shared his food with us when he had a lot." Pedro still didn't look at Sandra, but stared down at the hot pavement. "He usually slept next to us. I told you. He kind of protected Zaida and me. I told you before."

Sandra controlled an urge to leap up from the rickety chair. "What happened to Georges?"

"He was away from our place for a while, and when he came back, he was sick and he didn't say much to us like he usually does.

He went right to sleep. And this morning, this morning..." Pedro stopped, shook his head, started again. "When we got up this morning, he wouldn't move or sit up or anything. Maria's a big girl. You saw her. She has a cellphone. She called someone to come. Then they came and said he was dead and took him away."

"What do you mean 'they'? Who came? Who said he was dead? How long was he sick?" Pedro didn't answer.

"The kid who sleeps near you on the street is sick for a day or two and just up and dies? How can that be?"

"San-dra, San-dra, San-dra." Zaida pulled on Sandra's sunglasses.

Pedro's voice went toneless again. "It happens, Tia, it happens. Another kid died in the spring."

Sandra put Zaida down on her blanket on the sidewalk. "Have you had your shots, Pedro? Have you and Zaida been to a doctor? Where was your home? Please answer me."

But he just replaced his polishing cloth in the new backpack Sandra had given him the day before. If he knew the answers to her questions, he wasn't sharing them. He packed their things, grabbed Zaida, and off they ran, quickly leaving Sandra behind.

Later, upstairs in her office, she confronted Tomás Mello.

"Where do your children get their medical care?"

Tomás turned from his computer screen and looked at her. He was creating a file about an international business conference in Sao Paulo.

"We have a good pediatrician, Dr. Gomes. He's the pediatrics supervisor at the Wilson Azevedo Hospital. Why do you ask?" He made a face. "As if I didn't know..."

"The kid who was sleeping under the awning next to Pedro and his sister was found dead this morning. Pedro said he was sick, but I don't know any more about it."

Tomás rose from in front of the computer. He scowled at Sandra, a motion that seemed to lift his red beard.

"Are you careful not to touch the kids?" he asked. "As you've just found out, street kids can be unhealthy."

Sandra gave her braid a fierce tug, then pushed a wayward lock of her bangs out of her eyes. How could a man like Tomás, a father himself, seem so indifferent to the suffering of children?

He read her expression. "Yes, you're right. I'm not concerned about these menores, these kids. It's you I'm worried about. You seem so caught up with the brats, and I can't understand why. Like I told you, they're dangerous."

"Tomás, they need help. And I admit I'm fascinated by the why of their situation, the mystery of it. How did they come to be alone?"

"Sandra, I get discouraged with you. I've offered you friendship at the office and would be glad to extend that." He watched her face closely, then changed his tack. "I could introduce you to my wife's and my friends." He pronounced "wife" rather sanctimoniously, she thought. "We," he said, emphasizing the "we" at the same time he leered at her, "could get you started in Rio society."

Playing it straight and respectable, was he?

Sandra moved closer to her more youthful boss, putting them nearly on eye level. But she ignored his remarks and pursued her subject instead.

"Pedro isn't saying how he came to be on the street, but he's dropped a hint or two. I'm going to find out."

Tomás jerked his head quickly from side to side. "What is it with you, Sandra? Do you have fantasies of rescuing them or what?" The comment stung. He'd said nearly the same thing before, and her friend Heloisa had echoed that same thought.

"Listen to me. You've been here several months. Do you ever have any fun? Have you done anything except work here and worry about these brats?" Again, he read her expression. "I'd like you to enjoy this country—my country." He shook his beard, spoke more slowly. "Next thing you know, you'll have those kids in your house. How many times do I have to ask you to have a drink with me after work?"

"I just don't think that's a good idea,"

"OK, all right, adopt those dirty little kids. And pay no attention to the more interesting life you could have here in Rio." *Interesting for you, maybe.*

She walked to her desk, sat down, yanked open a sticking drawer. She turned on her computer, simmered for a few minutes, then raised her voice to him.

"And why do you think it's so odd when I'm just trying to help kids who desperately need it?" She drummed her fingers on the desk. "I'm certainly not trying to adopt them, or take them to my apartment. Pedro wouldn't let me, anyway. He trusts me only insofar as I haven't brought the authorities down on him."

"For God's sake, they're not like the stray cat you've taken in."

A few minutes passed, during which both typed frantically. As she fumed, Tomás looked up at her from behind his screen.

He sighed, eyebrows knitted into a V. "I never answered your question, did I? I'll give you the phone number for my kids' doctor." Instead of sending an e-mail, he rose from his chair and walked over to her with a small notecard in his hand. He dropped it on her desk, then bent and kissed her on the side of her forehead.

"You've got a good heart, anyway, Ms. Shelton, even if you are some kind of ice princess. But I'm not going to give up on the thawing operation."

Sandra made a quick decision. She wasn't quite ready for this battle. She had another struggle to pursue. She thanked him for the telephone number but never looked up at him.

To her dismay, she realized she was doing her schoolgirl blush, and not from rage. She recognized that she'd enjoyed Tomás' gesture. Her next thought was also unwelcome: Sandra Shelton, always supportive of feminism, had been without a man in her life too long.

Suddenly, the tight braid she almost always wore seemed constricting. She pulled off the band and the shining copper comb that kept it in place, tossed her newly freed mane. Golden hair touched her ears, her neck, her shoulders. She smiled.

Sandra started punching in the number for the doctor's office on her cellphone. Then she realized she couldn't even provide a last name for Pedro and Zaida. She put down the phone.

She would search immediately for the church where Pedro played soccer. Her targets were churches outside the maelstrom of sprawling urban Rio.

The time for action had arrived.

ELEVEN

Sandra began her quest for the children's village with a book of maps and a list of churches provided by the Catholic Church office in Rio. It seemed that "Flores" was a rural whistle stop hours distant from her apartment in Rio.

She thanked the VW manufacturers for the strength of the little car's air conditioning as she flew west over steaming roads. She followed her GPS religiously until the highway gave onto a bumpy, poorly maintained, narrow two-lane affair. After about twenty minutes, the directional device led her into the driveway of a large church complex off a dirt road with the iconic name Rua John F. Kennedy.

"Church number one, here I come." She hummed as she pulled into a parking lot between two white vans. A big sign above the open gate announced that the church was called St. Francis Xavier. To her surprise, the lot was about two-thirds full. The Brazilian morning had simmered past noon, and masses should have been over.

The sanctuary was of gray brick that seemed to reflect and intensify the sun that beamed from a mercilessly cloudless sky. She felt a shock of increased temperature the moment she started to get out of the car. She had only one foot on the ground when she heard a hoarse, disembodied voice.

"Bom dia." Then a body materialized. Sandra saw a short, white-haired man wearing a black cassock with a white clerical collar.

He seemed out of breath; he'd probably run to meet her arrival. The man squinted up at her through dusty eyeglasses.

"Oh, but you haven't brought the goat," he said. "But of course you wouldn't have. You couldn't fit a goat in that puny car. Where's the pick-up and where's the goat?"

"Uh, Father, I think you're mistaking me for someone else. I don't know anything about a goat."

"But of course you do. You're Senhora Parker, from the Gandoloifa Farm, aren't you? Why haven't you brought our goat?" She wasn't sure if his hoarse voice resulted from age or annoyance.

"No, my name is Sandra Shelton. I'm here to ask if you might know anything about some children I'm trying to help in Rio."

"You must go back to the farm for the goat. The children are getting very anxious." He gestured toward the cars in the lot. "Everyone's here. The pageant is about to start."

"No, no, I'm here to ask if you might know a boy about ten and his little sister, a toddler, maybe going on three." Sandra looked down at the man and tried to sound normal. "Their names are Pedro and Zaida. Pedro said they came from around here. He won't say a last name. He says he hung around a church a lot." She licked her lips, feeling dust on them, then pushed back her bangs, which were heavy with sweat and drooped into her eyes.

She fixed her gaze on him and continued to blather.

"I can't imagine how they got to Rio alone, but they're in trouble. The little boy is trying to feed them by shining shoes, and he says his mother died. He doesn't seem to have anyone. That's why I'm here, to ask if you know anything about two children like that who might have been in this parish." She stopped, out of breath. The little priest frowned and looked puzzled.

"The boy calls himself Pedro," she repeated. "He said the parish priest played futebol with the kids. And I don't know anything about a goat."

"Dear lady, are you really not Senhora Parker from Gandoloifa Farm?" It was his turn to stare. "You look like her, I mean, she's tall as a building and light-haired like you and she promised to have the goat here by noon."

"No."

The priest rubbed his high, deeply wrinkled forehead. "Oh, all right. I've mistaken you for another, er, blonde beanpole. But those names don't sound at all familiar." He added, "I never played futebol. And you're surely no help to me because you haven't brought the goat."

Sandra waited, and after a few seconds he modified his tone.

"You know," he mused, "Santa Teresa de Avila is only about twenty minutes from here. You might try that."

"But the next closest place on my list is Saint Finbar."

"Finbar is closest, but I think Father Mulroy at Saint Teresa's might be your best chance. He plays futebol. As long as you're no help with the goat, go there." He turned away. "Yes, go there. Now I must call about that goat."

Sandra felt tired already as she urged on the yellow Volkswagen. Quite suddenly, the green of a forested area seemed to melt into a severely dry landscape. After a few minutes, she swerved into a wide cinder alley by Santa Teresa de Avila. She stepped out of the car and studied the church. Railroad tracks loomed in the distance, and she heard a haunting train whistle, surely the loneliest sound in creation.

The church stood alone on a barren strip of land. Why was this land so empty? Where were the palms, the jaca trees, the flowering bushes of Rio? Where were the sounds of the small chattering toucans and the little 'mico' monkeys who danced and frolicked in the canopies of Tijuca?

Sandra saw clay-like earth, broken with the orangish hives of termites. The ground looked like it suffered from measles or chickenpox.

The sanctuary building was a dirty burnt Sienna, and a stack of bricks of a different shade sat next to it on the roadside. Some of them looked broken. Either she was having visual aberrations, or the building tilted ever so slightly to the left. So Santa Teresa was tipsy, Sandra thought.

As she trudged up the cinder driveway, she giggled and mumbled, "There I go again, acting like a twelve-year-old because I'm nervous. Good thing nobody's around."

But she hadn't taken more than five or six steps toward the church when she found herself surrounded by young men. Half a dozen teenagers stared at her. Where had they come from? They wore tattered shorts and shirts, or no shirts at all. Their feet were bare on the burning earth.

At first, they talked so rapidly that she wasn't sure what they were saying, but it didn't sound friendly. She stepped back.

"What's up, pale lady?" The tall boy looked her up and down as he spoke.

Another boy said, "Maybe she's coming to mass, except there isn't one. They're over." He was much shorter than the first. His tone sounded pleasant enough, or at least neutral. But underneath his ragged T-shirt, his muscles looked formidable. And Sandra had rarely seen so many tattoos on anyone's arms and neck. Dragons, slogans she couldn't read, and the inevitable heart with an arrow through the center wiggled as he flexed his biceps.

He walked backwards, whirled around a couple times, and stared up directly into her face as she tried to move quickly toward the church door. He kicked dust with his sandaled feet.

Sandra hoped her tone was level.

"Let me pass, please."

"Hey, moca, we're not trying to scare you," piped a much smaller kid. "We're protecting you. Somebody might try to take your purse. We'll walk you to the church."

Sandra moved resolutely, but she knew her pale complexion had gone even whiter. Suddenly, she was sixteen years old again, back in Buenos Aires, just a few doors down the street from Saint Helena's Secondary School for Girls.

She'd stayed after school for a piano lesson and left the building alone. The sun was setting, and dusk was coming down. And there appeared a gang of boys, teenage boys, shouting obscenities. They'd surrounded her. After a moment, one pulled out a knife from his blue-jean pocket.

Now, decades later, movement in the middle distance cut off her flashback. A side door opened in the listing church, and a man in black pants and a white shirt approached. He said something to the kids she couldn't pick up. The little knot of boys frayed out in separate directions.

Sandra found her voice and croaked, "Good morning." Then she remembered it was well past noon. She extended her hand and hoped it wasn't shaking.

"I assume you're the priest here, Father...."

"... Mulroy." The man took her hand in his much larger one. "I'm sorry about the kids. They're perfectly harmless, but it may not have looked that way to you. And you are...?"

Sandra identified herself and stumbled through her prepared speech in Portuguese about the children and how she needed information.

"So you're American. Well, come on in," he said. "Let's sit down in my quarters and speak the mother tongue. I'm Irish myself." He led her over a hot cinder path toward the back of the church. The smell of dust and her own nervousness filled her nostrils.

Before long they were seated at a scarred table in the kitchen at the rear of the church building. Presumably, the kitchen served as a kind of parlor—a reception area for a poverty-stricken parish.

"Coffee?"

"Please."

It's the last thing I need, she thought, being this nervous. Why am I still so nervous? For a moment, she considered the irony of her comparative nonchalance with high-level politicians, business titans, and well-known academics. Why, then, did she feel so queasy and uncertain now? Hope, she reflected, did strange things to people.

But at the moment, drinking coffee sounded like a good remedy for the shakes. It would give her something to do with her hands.

She wished for a cigarette, though she hadn't smoked since graduate school.

"Could you please tell me again who you wanted to know about?" The priest cleared his throat. "Frankly, I didn't quite catch all of what you said outside. After twelve years in Brazil, there are times when I'm still not totally comfortable in Portuguese."

Sandra frowned. His brogue was heavy, and she had to strain to understand his English, too. "Maybe the problem's my Spanish accent. I lived a while in Buenos Aires. I'm not super-fluent in Portuguese, either."

The priest handed her a chipped cup filled with coffee so strong that Sandra thought it could stand up alone. He puttered around several more minutes, but didn't offer sugar or cream. Sandra launched into her story the moment he sat down.

"I've become friends with two street children—a boy, Pedro, and his little sister, Zaida. The boy shines shoes near my office. He's about ten going on eleven, I think, though he doesn't seem so sure. He won't say much of anything. I want to get information I can use with the bureaucracy to help the kids, but he doesn't cooperate." Sandra watched the priest's hands finger the coffee cup.

"Last names?"

"That's what I came to find out, and I'm hoping to find some family."

"But he's given you at least some information. Otherwise you wouldn't have come way over here. What did he say that made you come to me?"

"He said something about a church out this way, and a priest who played soccer, I mean futebol, with the kids. I got a list of churches in this area and…"

"The description is pretty vague, miss. And unfortunately, there have been other kids who have taken to the streets of Rio from around here, though I know of no others so young." He let that thought hang in the air for several seconds. "But, come to think of it, there was a young woman in this parish who died and left a couple of children. The kids disappeared from here many months ago. So, maybe…." One large hand brushed his hair the wrong way. "Did you bring a picture?"

Sandra shifted in her chair and restrained an urge to tug at her braid or fiddle with her bangs. "Just this one."

She handed him a photo taken from her phone. Why hadn't she used the office's aged Nikon instead? It was a relic but capable of excellent portrait work.

The picture she'd brought showed Pedro staring soberly into the camera, his polishing cloth in hand, on a morning when he'd set up his stand around the corner from Worldwide Broadcasting. Zaida had moved slightly and seemed indistinct.

Sandra cleared her throat to hide her embarrassment at the quality of her photograph. Meanwhile, the priest rose, went to the stove, and found a pair of round reading glasses on one of the burners.

She spoke into his silence. "I've tried to get a last name out of him, but I couldn't. But he did tell me he hung out in a church and described the place as being near Flores."

Mulroy thumbed the picture and swallowed a mouthful of hot coffee. "The name of the family in this parish with the disappearing kids was de Andrade." He pronounced the name as "Ahn DRAHD juh. Still, the boy in the photo looks quite a bit older than the boy I remember. But then, he would. Time's passed."

The priest spoke more slowly now and stared at the table as though searching the scarred surface for faded images. "It seems like I recall a boy who hung out here a lot. Liked to play futebol." He checked the picture again. "But Pedro's an extremely common name, miss, and the game's every kid's favorite here, boy or girl.

"Still, the Pedro I'm thinking of in my parish had a baby sister. This could be her, though it's been quite a while. She'd be bigger by now, of course. We told the policia when they went missing, but they got nowhere."

This isn't real, Sandra thought. I couldn't be this fortunate. Not on the second try.

"Pedro, Pedro de Andrade," the priest said. "It just might be. He played around the church a lot. The little one would be close to three by now." His eyebrows crept up on his high, wide forehead. "I believe it's possible that I knew their mother."

Sandra leaned forward in her chair. "You know them? Whose children are they?" She realized her voice had gone up half an octave.

The priest studied the cigarette burns on the wooden table. "I think these actually could be the children you're talking about." He hesitated. "But I'm sorry to tell you that there are no parents. No close family at all that I know of. The children disappeared from here after their mother died." Sandra thought the priest's brogue slowed his speech, and he left maddeningly long gaps between phrases.

At last he continued, "Camila...Camila de Andrade was her name. The mother's name, I mean. Camila was a nice kid. She was left alone early, though. Her mother died young." He looked up at Sandra. "Lots of people die young here." He paused again.

Sandra stifled an urge to say that she'd spent some of her girlhood in Argentina, had lived for years in Washington D.C., had seen poverty in a number of other places in the world, and would he please, please get on with it? She wondered what his homilies must be like, this hesitant and slow-spoken priest.

"Anyway," he resumed at last, "Camila married at sixteen, probably so she could have more to eat. She got married right here in the church, but the man turned out to be a poor sort. He didn't work, ran around for years—wasn't in the home enough for Pedro to even know who he was. He left this area permanently after she had the second child—left her with the little boy and the infant. I heard later that he'd died after a fight in a bar somewhere." He hesitated again and took another gulp of coffee.

"Camila had a job in a food store, but the wages were so low that she couldn't pay much rent. She was living in a group home. Then there were other lovers, other men who could help feed them. Sometime after the girl was born, Camila got sick." His voice trailed off, and there was a maddening silence before he resumed.

"She got an especially virile pneumonia." He cracked the knuckles of one large hand as his memory sharpened. "There was a cousin, a young cousin of Camila, who was supposed to take care of the kids until the social workers could sort out their placement. But the cousin was young and irresponsible. The boy and the baby lived in what sometimes seemed more like a flophouse than a group home."

He coughed, cleared his throat, and started again. "I tried to find a better temporary caregiver, but nobody wanted to be around the kids. People wrongly suspected that Camila had AIDS, because she died so young of pneumonia. The social workers I contacted were just stepping in with some kind of guardianship arrangement when I lost track of the situation. I was told that the children were safely placed somewhere else."

Sandra realized she must have looked as taken aback as she felt.

"Have no fear, the doctor tested Camila and the kids. Neither she nor the kids carried the HIV virus."

"It's not my health I'm worried about."

The priest shifted his large body in his chair, causing it to creak. "My people here are sometimes superstitious and frightened by baseless talk. Sometimes I think they're closer to Condomblé and Umbanda than to Christianity, no matter what I do or say. Some like to come to church, all right, but I'm not convinced that their Catholicism is anything more than cosmetic." He furrowed his brow, which was deeply lined. Above his forehead, his thick mop of black hair was succumbing to gray.

"Condomblé and Umbanda—those superstitions are hard to root out. Not so far from Voodoo, in my opinion. You can't imagine how primitive some of these beliefs are."

"But aren't Condomblé practitioners supposedly doing so much for the environment?" Sandra instantly regretted speaking, fearing she'd diverted him from the subject. "But back to the children…"

The priest swished his coffee in the cup, then inhaled the steam. "So, you're saying these kids are on the streets?"

"Near where I work in Copacabana. I met them when Pedro chased another child who'd stolen my money."

"I see." The buzzing of a fly was the only sound in the hot kitchen. He coughed. "I'm sorry I let them get away from here…."

Sandra winced. The man sounded as though he were speaking of stray dogs, not human children. But she caught herself. Of course, he'd faced the same bureaucratic slowdowns and mix-ups that she and Heloisa had not even begun to experience.

He half-smiled. "I saw your eyebrows goin' up, but social services out here can be very complicated, very complicated indeed. It's sometimes better to try to find another local family for orphaned kids and then worry about the legal papers and proceedings afterward."

Sandra studied his face. The skin around his nose and mouth was deeply lined from the Brazilian sun, and finer lines ran down from his deep-set gray eyes. The eyes seemed tired. Still, he was middle aged rather than old. At first, she'd thought he was elderly. She recalled that he limped or hitched slightly as they'd walked into the church.

"Otherwise," he continued, "kids can get stuck in orphanages we're not so sure of, or they can be moved from foster home to foster home."

"I was hoping you'd say there were other family members, an aunt, a grandmother, somebody who could take care of them."

Sandra was about to return to the details—what little she knew of the children's current circumstances—but he spoke again before she could begin.

"Children so young can't live without adult care. I need to go to Niteroi, but after that I'll drive into Rio and we'll visit some orphanages, or maybe even a temporary shelter. Everything around here's full.

"These places I'm thinkin' about in the city aren't ideal, but anything would be better than them sleepin' rough. It's much better to do these things in person, y'know. Saves time."

Sandra felt a throb of relief. Now someone would help her with the kids, someone who knew Brazil and knew what to do. It would no longer be her burden alone. The kids might be off the streets. Pedro might even be on his way to school. And maybe then she could think of something else.

Still, Sandra had to admit that her concern for the children had reduced her rage with Charles—and, better yet, her longing for him.

The priest walked the American reporter to her car, followed by the gang of kids who'd greeted her. They were chattering and laughing and now didn't seem the least menacing. She wondered why she'd been scared. But of course she knew the answer. That day so long ago in Buenos Aires had followed her to Brazil.

TWELVE

When Mulroy returned to his overheated kitchen in the back of the church, it seemed oddly quiet—solitary, really. He sat down in his tippy chair and stared at his coffee, which was still quite warm. He ran his hands through his hair and leaned forward as he thought. He knew he should believe that this woman turning up with her story was providential. Instead, it seemed fraught, loaded with his own guilt over his failure to make sure that Camila's children had a safe home.

There isn't much use trying to excuse myself. It's true the social workers misled me, but...

He feared he'd essentially allowed two young children to become lost— after promising their dying mother he'd watch over them. Anger and guilt competed with each other in his brain. His head began to ache fiercely as he put the coffee cups in the sink.

He heard a bark, and he opened the back door to let in the parish dog, James Joyce. The priest began to mumble, suspecting that hearing his own voice aloud would help sort things out, as it sometimes did when he was trying to write a homily.

"I neglected them long enough after their mother's death so that the boy somehow got them away. I wonder how in the world he did it—with an infant, yet. And how did he take care of the little one?"

Mulroy went to the sink, poured cool water into James Joyce's drinking bowl. But memories of the children forged on in his mind and he continued to mumble.

"A stranger drives up and hands me another chance to help the kids I've failed. But I don't appreciate this blessing. I dread seein' those kids again." He rinsed his cup and poured himself another little bit of the coffee, now cool.

"Pedro de Andrade. The bigger kids around here taunted him, probably 'cause they had families and he didn't. So I let him hang around the church."

His thoughts drifted to another child, a child in Portadown long ago. Even in his backwater parish in the Brazilian countryside, he was aware that some priests had committed crimes against children, fondled and raped them, in fact. The thought turned his stomach. Well, he'd sinned against a child, too, but his was a different kind of crime.

Those molesting priests had scarred some lives, downright ruined some lives, caused suicides. His own conscience, though, carried the life of a child back home, a child whose life he might have saved—and did not.

Peter Mulroy reached for a last sip of the coffee. A fly landed on the rim of the cup. The priest made a face and dumped the last drops into the sink. He washed the cup, put it in the drying rack, and started to work on the parish books, always a chore he dreaded. Then someone knocked on the door.

Mulroy admitted a woman in a noisy print dress adorned with purple and chartreuse toucans and what looked like crocodiles. Or were they caimans? She had a tattered shawl around her shoulders and looked like she was well into middle age, but he knew she was still in her early thirties.

"Father, please help me. My youngest boy, Xanviero, is fooling with Umbanda. He's turning his back on all he's been taught." The woman's lined sepia-toned face reflected something between horror and shame. "You've got to do something."

Mulroy wanted to ask her what she expected him to do. He knew the boy, knew how the kid had been on the edge of rebellion since about the time he said his first word. Now he was involved in a cultic thing that combined elements of animism with some

Catholicism. Well, the priest thought, so far as he knew, at least the kid wasn't robbing people or shooting dope or getting into fights like so many others his age.

"I'll try, of course," he told the distraught woman. To himself, he thought he would try, but he would probably fail. It seemed to Peter Mulroy that his days as a priest too often held problems of children, and he couldn't do much to help.

As he had so many times before, Mulroy wondered if he might have done better had he never entered the priesthood—or if he had just been a chaplain in an old people's home.

###

Sandra cursed the elevators in her office building for not running at this pre-dawn hour. Zaida had balked about walking, so Sandra carried the little girl up the back stairs to the Worldwide Broadcasting office on the fourth floor. Zaida chirped loudly, words that Sandra didn't recognize. Her brother tagged behind, far behind.

"Pedro, please hurry."

But he slid his hands along the banister, occasionally hopping down a step and back up again. Obviously, stairs were a new toy. Sandra felt her face redden with the effort of holding the little girl as she climbed. Somehow, despite the children's questionable diet, Zaida probably weighed close to thirty pounds. Well, soon they'd find out. Sandra was taking the children to the pediatrician for examinations and shots today. But first, she'd have to clean them up.

She looked into Zaida's small face, which bore the dirt of days and nights on the tattered, dusty blanket.

"Honey, it would be so much easier if I could just take you two home." She spoke English so the children wouldn't understand. "I just don't want to show you how normal people live until I find a way for you to live normally."

She recalled Tomás' words, "Soon you'll have them in your house." The words resounded in her head like a curse.

Finally, they were on the fourth level and almost to the bathroom. The radio network's office shared restrooms with half the floor, perhaps twenty other journalists who worked in foreign news bureaus. Still, it was only 5:30 in the morning. She figured it was too early for even the earliest early-birds, too late for the night-writers.

She wished she had the key to the men's room so she could send Pedro off to wash up by himself. She remembered that he looked slicked up the day they went to the soccer game, so he somehow knew how to make himself look fine. But she didn't have the key. She set Zaida down, fumbled with the other key, and plowed into the women's room with the two children.

The mirrored walls and rococo ceiling of the room seemed out of sync with the utilitarian building. Zaida toddled in, took one look around, and began to scream. "No, no, no hurt Zaida!"

"Oh, Zaida, I suppose you've never seen a mirror before." Sandra picked up the little girl again and carried her to a panel of the elaborate glass, which was bordered by a kind of etching in gold paint. Sandra waved at their reflection and made a funny face. "Kids are supposed to like mirrors, aren't they? But obviously you haven't read that book," Sandra told the wailing little girl. "See, there's nothing to be afraid of. That's just you and me. See, Zaida..." The child only raised her decibel level.

Sandra caught sight of Pedro. He had advanced to the back of the room and was standing on tiptoes. He was trying to pee into one of the hand-washing basins.

"Pedro, no!" In that instant she heard a key turning in the ladies' room door. There stood Marilyn Evans, a newspaper correspondent from New York. Marilyn had a strangely flat face, as though someone had poked holes in a pancake to form her features. Her mouth seemed too big and too red, and, at the moment, it had fallen open.

"What are you doing in here? Who are these kids? Why is that ragamuffin fouling the sink?"

Marilyn's tone made Zaida scream even louder.

"Oh, for heaven's sake, Marilyn, they're just children."

Marilyn stared at the kids. "Wherever did you get them?" Somehow, Marilyn's cultured, upper-class accent made her words all the more offensive. Sandra hugged the screaming little girl closer and stared down, way down, at the much shorter woman.

She yelled at Marilyn, using a word she would have bleeped from any broadcast.

###

Two hours later, Sandra was sitting in the waiting room of Wilson Azevedo Hospital, waiting for her appointment with Dr. Gomes, chief of pediatrics. Instead of the four-month-old periodicals that usually populated doctors' and dentists' waiting rooms at home, here were current, expensive full-color fashion and sports magazines. On one wall was a bookshelf stuffed with children's books. An enormous television screen blared a video starring a talking hippo and a goldfish.

A young woman with a wild mane of black hair walked by. She wore a white lab coat with a physician's name label on the breast pocket. She slowed her pace, glanced at Sandra and the children, then stared openly. The woman seemed about to say something. But she moved on when a nurse appeared and spoke to Sandra.

"Senhora Shelton, Dr. Gomes will see you now." The nurse also gave Sandra and the kids a long look. "The doctor speaks Spanish and English, too, if you prefer." She led them down a hall covered with a thick Persian carpet. The hospital windows had cutglass tops with what looked like carved sandalwood at their oldfashioned transoms. Sandra noticed how slowly Pedro was walking. Zaida stopped toddling altogether, and Sandra had to pick her up.

Obviously, this hospital was intended for upper-class Rio. But then, what was she expecting? Tomás, who'd sent her here, belonged to exclusive clubs and took expensive vacations. Nilda had said his wife's family was wealthy.

The nurse ushered Sandra and the children into the examination room. A tall, portly man of middle years wearing a blue lab coat greeted her. He looked friendly enough as he shook Sandra's hand. But like the black-haired doctor in the white coat and the nurse, he failed to hide his curiosity. Sandra decided to explain herself, explain the children, in English so Pedro wouldn't understand.

"Pedro often shines shoes near the office building where I work," she said. "The little girl is his sister. They're orphans, and they live on the street. A priest from their old parish out past Flores is helping me get them into care. Meanwhile, another kid who sleeps quite near them just up and died of unknown causes. Pedro says they haven't been to a doctor."

Gomes nodded as he donned a face mask with a blue whale on it.

"Oh, they don't carry HIV," Sandra said. "They've been tested."

Frown lines appeared over the doctor's mask. "If you're referring to the precautions, Miss Shelton, this is just routine hygiene. I suspect you haven't taken children to a pediatrician before?"

"This is all new to me."

"Yes. Well, I try to start by making friends with the kids." Sandra looked down. Talking to the doctor, she hadn't noticed that Zaida had crawled under the examination table. Pedro was trying to open the door to leave the room. Sandra sensed rather than saw the doctor's grin under his mask.

He switched to Portuguese. "Young man, if you let me look in your ears and eyes to see if there are elephants in there, I'll give you candies."

"No." Pedro's tone was polite, but he was still trying to turn the door handle to escape. "People don't have elephants in their ears." Sandra fiddled with her braid. She knew if Pedro wouldn't cooperate, Zaida would scream and fight.

The doctor switched to English. "I think a little bribery is in order. What do they want?"

"A mother," blurted Sandra.

"Ah, but it would seem you're playing that role, at least for the moment, wouldn't it?"

"Just trying to help." She wondered bleakly if the doctor was about to accuse her of rescue fantasies.

Gomes switched back to Portuguese. "Young man, this kind American lady is trying to make sure you don't get sick."

Pedro pulled himself up to his full height and exhaled a little frightened sigh. "Zaida and I don't need any doctors. I take good care of us."

"I'm sure you do," said Gomes. He stooped to ferret out Zaida from under the table. She looked dubious, but didn't cry.

"Your sister seems well fed. I'm sure you've done a very good job of taking care of her."

The doctor plunked Zaida on the table and started to hum a Portuguese nursery song. To Sandra's surprise, the little girl joined in. Did the homeless kids sing nursery songs? Good grief, Sandra mused, was it Disneyland they lived in under the awning? She'd have to ask Pedro later about how Zaida knew the song. Could she remember her mother?

Pedro let go of the door handle and stepped closer to his sister, as if to protect her. Amazingly, the kids cooperated as they received a whole batch of shots. Thanks to the doctor's benign personality, they gave no major opposition to modern medicine.

Needles aroused no comment from Pedro, now clearly determined to be manly, and only one momentary little shriek from Zaida. Clearly, the doctor's offer of a lollipop helped her cooperate.

"I have good news for you, Ms. Shelton," said Dr. Gomes when he finished his ministrations. "These kids are hardy little devils. They're both of very sound basic health. The boy needs more nutrition, and they both need vitamins. The little girl has fluid in her ears, and I'd like you to give her something I'll prescribe...." He hesitated, apparently remembering the situation.

"Well, perhaps you can see to it that her brother gives her the medicine for a couple days until you get them into care." At his words, Sandra swallowed hard. Could she let even a couple more days pass without getting them out of possible danger on the street?

The doctor picked up his prescription pad and began to write. "And then, please bring her back in a week so I can make sure the fluid is gone. Otherwise, she might get an infection, and ear infections hurt a lot."

As they walked toward the lemon-colored Volkswagen in the parking lot, Pedro asked, "So why did we have to get all those shots? Why did you take us there?" As he complained, he licked at the purple lollipop given to him by Dr. Gomes.

"So you'll never get sick like Georges did." As Sandra spoke, she caught sight of the black-haired doctor who had looked at them so curiously in the waiting room. Again, the young woman stared at the threesome. She passed them, sailing fast on extremely high heels toward her car, shrugging off her white coat in the process.

Sandra realized she and the kids might look out of place in this rather elegant hospital. But she mulled over the doctor's news with pleasure: The children are healthy. Now all I have to do is get them off the streets. That's all. That's an incredible lot. Still, I'll have some help now.

"Hey, Zaida, do you like your lollipop?"

"Yum. Yum, yum, yum."

Sandra decided that the syllable must be universal.

The following morning, Olivia Kattah stopped in to see Dr. Gomes, her superior. She passed the big comfortable chair in front of his desk and stood in front of it.

"Coffee, Olivia?" He turned to reach a silver coffee pot standing on a mahogany table behind the desk.

"No, thanks, I've only a minute. I came to satisfy my curiosity."

"How so?" Dr. Gomes gave Olivia a long look. He was twice her age, but he could look, couldn't he?

"I'm curious about the two children you saw yesterday with that tall, terribly pale gringa woman. The kids looked like charity cases—buffed and polished charity cases, for sure, but they stared at the surroundings and seemed so unusually scared. You usually see charity patients in the clinic, not in your office."

"Oh, that tall, terribly pale woman, as you put it, is a paying patient, all right. She was referred by another patient of mine, the journalist Tomás Mello. She's a journalist, too. She's American, trying to do something for some homeless kids she ran into."

Dr. Gomes grinned, basking for a moment in Olivia Kattah's beauty. "Olivia, do you ever feel guilty about being so wealthy?"

"You're thinking that I'm Brazilian, I'm a kids' doctor, and I do nothing extra for poor children." She watched as the portly Gomes stirred spoonful after spoonful of sugar into his coffee.

"But then, I only do the clinic, and call that enough, when it's clearly not enough. What you do is your own business. As long as you're as excellent at your work as you are now, I won't complain."

He watched her smile her confident smile. The expression seemed to start from her slightly pointed chin and climb toward the high arches of her black eyebrows. As she left, the older doctor reflected that perhaps Olivia's curiosity meant the beginning of a social conscience. But then, he thought that was probably just wishful thinking.

THIRTEEN

Efrain sat in a café perched over the ocean in Ipanema. He was sipping a cappuccino and watching the nearly naked women on the beach. From his white wrought-iron table far above the shoreline, he could still smell the saltwater.

Great asses, he thought, looking down at a row of young girls wearing thongs and nothing on top. But these women couldn't nearly be as amazing as the one from The Breezes nightclub, the woman called Olivia. Even her name seemed classy. He thought of the women some other men preferred. They liked the so-called fruit women, girls whose bodies supposedly were shaped like bananas or melons. They cavorted at funk dances in the favelas and other places, and Efrain thought they were crude.

He sipped his coffee and stared at the waves. He wondered why the water looked so choppy on such a calm day. The little swells couldn't seem to make up their minds if they were a brilliant sky-blue or a briny green, and they slapped crazily at one another.

The ocean's all stirred up today, exactly the way I feel.

He shrugged as though in conversation with someone else. There was only one other occupied table on the balcony, and the couple seated there were blond—tourists, maybe. The lovers sat close together, staring deep into each other's eyes, looking moony and stupid.

"Good thing I'm not like that," Efrain mumbled aloud, tapping his head in the universal gesture for crazy.

"But that Olivia is something. Who would think? A rich and educated woman being so hungry... I don't know... What happens now, though? It's hard to stay away from her, but I don't want to seem too anxious." He thought more about some of his associates in crime, those lowbrows who patronized the funk dances and the fruit women. He picked up his folded cloth cocktail napkin and unfolded it, folded it again, kept on mumbling aloud.

"Olivia and I had a great night, but what's she thinking in the daytime? What if she found out about my business? I'm not so sure she believed my story about running an import-export agency. But then again, she didn't seem too interested in details, either."

Efrain signaled for the waiter, who seemingly had disappeared. Efrain's voice rose: "A kids' doctor she is, of all things. That's ironic. I can't stand kids. I'm putting up with one, too—that Ana, she's not even mine. I don't care for her mother, anymore.

"Kids. That was my mother's trouble, all us kids. Too many brats, too many mouths, not enough food. But it'll be kids that will give me my new business and save my job in Misericordia."

The blond couple looked up at the man talking to himself and stared. He glared back, but returned to conventionally silent meditation.

Any other day I'd go tell you to quit gawking. Emphatically. Not today, though. Gotta think about this. How do I proceed with the elegant Olivia? Maybe I can't proceed. Maybe I was her one-night stand. But sure as hell, I'm going to try.

His reverie was interrupted; across the café patio he spotted Rodrigo Suares. Within a blink or two, the fat man stood close to his face, breathing hard.

"Quit calling me, you moron. And give me back my BMW. You don't work for me no more."

"Rodrigo, I got away clean. No witnesses. The cops haven't contacted me at all, and the shootings can't be traced to you."

"I told you before, you're history."

"C'mon, let me tell you about an idea I have for a new business. It'd be so easy. I'd run it, and make a lotta money for you. American dollars, even."

"You always bore me."

"Listen, Rodrigo. Don't you ever get tired of working so hard? Sit down and I'll tell you...."

To Efrain's amazement, the fat man pulled up a chair and looked around for a waiter. Spotting one in the distance, he yelled, "Amaretto for me." But the waiter just scurried back into the interior of the cafe.

Rodrigo made a snarling noise in the back of his well-larded throat. His double chin wiggled as he spoke. "So what is this business you're going on about?"

"Kids."

"What the hell—"

"Kids are big money nowadays. All kinds of people want kids, can't have 'em and can't adopt 'em through legal agencies." He dragged hard on the cigarette while Rodrigo bellowed for a waiter. "It can be a pain to adopt in Brazil—takes quite a while. And there're rich Americans and Argentinians that'll pay almost anything for a healthy little brat. But a lotta people want just one kid, and a very small kid at that.

"Foreigners can't get kids under five years old from here in Rio State unless they take the kid's siblings. The best way for foreigners to get just one newborn or one small kid is to do it under the radar. That's where I come in. I've had some very good deals, and I've only just started in this stuff."

"No shit?" Rodrigo was still snarling, but he'd lowered his voice.

"Yeah, I've already launched and am doing great."

So far I've lined up only one couple, but even if I have to give you ninety percent, there's still a nice chunk for me.

Rodrigo's large, mostly bald head swiveled again. "Jesus, what do you have to do to get a drink around here?" Again, he roared for service, and this time a waiter came on the run. He was a teenage boy with very pale skin and, at this moment, a deeply red face.

The two men were silent until at last a small, gilded tumbler of amaretto sat before Rodrigo. He took off the hat and fanned his sweaty, gleaming head.

"Rodrigo, if you're interested, I could put you in the loop."

"Where would you get babies, anyway? Sometimes the girls on the game around here get pregnant, but they get rid of the kids. And who'd want a slut's baby?"

"Lots of people would, as long as the kid hasn't inherited clap or some other crud."

"OK, you foreign moron. I've listened to your scheme. I still don't believe you could organize anything and carry it out right. But if you can show me you're making money for me, OK. Otherwise…" He finished his amaretto in one gulp, stood and walked away. Then he turned back and yelled, "And goddamnit, return my BMW!"

Olivia Kattah sat up in bed with a start and a gasp. Lord, she thought, it must be afternoon! Was she supposed to be at the hospital? Then she remembered it was Sunday. Sleepily, she reassured herself: *You don't have to go anywhere today, Olivia. You don't work Sundays. Go back to sleep.* She looked at the bed and remembered something else. She remembered the man from The Breezes and this very same bed.

Olivia got up very slowly, like a woman thirty years her senior. She put her feet carefully on the inlaid rosewood mosaic tiles, as though her soles were sore. She rubbed her smooth, unlined forehead and slapped at her cheeks. She told herself that maybe she ought to stop thinking about that night, that night with the strange, exciting man who called himself Efrain de Carvalho. His first name seemed more commonly Spanish than Portuguese; she'd asked him about his Spanish accent, but he'd changed the subject.

Her maid, Thais, called to Olivia in the bathroom. "Would you like breakfast on a tray, Olivia?"

"No, thanks. Hey, I had a great date last night."

"Oh, what was he like?" Thais was twice Olivia's age. She wore a blue scrub suit with a white apron around her ample waist.

"He was scary, kind of, but so handsome."

"Scary? That doesn't sound good."

"Damn, coming right down to it, my behavior was weird." Olivia's back was to the maid as she stared at her reflection in the mirror. "But then, I'd been with the Britto child night and day and was really spacey afterward. I picked up this stranger, this handsome guy, and we danced and talked and I brought him home."

Thais charged toward the bathroom door. "No! Did you really do that? He could have been an axe murderer."

A smile teased Olivia's lips as she dashed cold water on her face.

"No, he wasn't an axe murderer. But he isn't quite presentable, either. Still, what a night it was. Wonder if I'll ever hear from him again. It would be better if I didn't, of course."

"Well, you end it if you hear from him again," huffed Thais.

"Oh, don't be such a fussy old grandmother. Take the rest of the day off, by the way."

"Obrigada," thank you. Thais retreated, muttering about her employer's safety.

Olivia went back into her huge, oak-paneled bedroom. She studied the Picasso prints on the wall and the Picasso sketch that wasn't a print. She looked at her Louis the Sixteenth dresser, its top cluttered now with tangled strands of extremely high-grade Mikimoto cultured pearls.

Her father had bought her this house when she graduated from medical school. He didn't want her to live away from home. He thought it was improper. But as long as she insisted, he said he wanted her to have someplace decent.

Decent it is, she thought, within view of the National Park of the Tijuca Rainforest. From the patio she could see for miles when the weather was clear. How lovely it looked in the morning, the trees especially green and inviting, several small favelas colorful in the distance. And again, she looked at the inlaid mosaics on the wood floors of her room, the white lace curtains billowing in the breeze.

After a while she heard Thais slamming the back door on her way to a free Sunday, humming a sprightly tune. But the song died as Thais moved away. The only other sound was a dog barking in the distance. Olivia was alone in her Spanish-style home, alone and free.

Sometimes, though, she had to admit that the beautiful house seemed a little empty. Last night, though, it wasn't lonely. Olivia smiled again.

She slipped out of her white satin nightgown, pulled on a turquoise bathing suit that was hanging on the shower door and headed for the swimming pool, a straightforward 25-meter expanse. None of those heart-shaped or tiered or fountain pools for her. From about eight months of age, her parents told her, Olivia had been a swimmer.

She backstroked a half-mile, then another, her body powerful but quiet in the sapphire water. As she swam, she breathed the perfume of the blooms that surrounded the water—azaleas, quaresma, acacias. Occasionally, the palms around the sunken brick pool bowed a little in homage to the breeze.

At last, her energy used up, Olivia pulled herself out of the water. As she reached for her aqua terrycloth towel, she looked up toward the fence that separated the pool from the verge of rainforest growth. There stood the man from The Breezes.

Efrain greeted her with a toothsome smile, and Olivia noticed the long scar that began at his eyebrow.

"*Olá!*" He pulled on the iron bars of the fence, imitating a prisoner in jail. "Let me in?"

"I appreciate that you're asking for an invitation, since I didn't exactly expect you." Olivia kicked at a Brazil nut on the pool deck, looking down to hide her smile.

"Bad manners, I know. But could I please come in? You realize it's pretty hot out here. I'd certainly like to take a swim."

Olivia went to the gate, unlocked it, and found herself in the embrace of Efrain de Carvalho. A half-hour later, sans clothes, the two embraced again—in the deep end of the pool.

FOURTEEN

Sandra was sitting at an outdoor table at Angela's Café overlooking the water. The scene in front of her looked like a poster in a travel agency office—the ocean azure, with little breakers lapping gently at the shore. The Atlantic was making whispered background to the conversation at the tables around them. The air smelled of the water. But Sandra wasn't thinking of the beach.

She was waiting for Mulroy. He'd told her that telephone inquiries about resident children's homes were likely to fail. He thought that if they appeared in person, they might have a better chance. He didn't say so, but Sandra was sure that Mulroy thought a Catholic priest might command more attention than a foreign woman.

And she suspected that he was determined to look around for living facilities before meeting the children again; she thought he was probably anxious to have something hopeful to suggest when he saw them. But the priest was late, twenty minutes going on a half-hour, and she began to wonder if he were coming. A call to St. Teresa's produced only static.

"Oh, there you are." She rose to meet him.

Mulroy sat down heavily. He wore a bulky black cassock, and sweat poured off his forehead. Again she noticed the many etched lines on his face and on that unusually high brow, which jutted out a bit over tired gray eyes. Still, she decided he probably wasn't much more than fifteen to twenty years her senior.

He called the waiter in his husky throated, heavily accented Portuguese and then sat down, saying nothing. Sandra bit her lip to quell her impatience and decided she'd better open the conversation herself. She reported the kids' visit to the doctor, at which he laughed heartily.

He accepted a chopp of beer from the waiter with a cheerful, "Obrigado, thanks." He gulped it thirstily, ordered another, then turned his attention back to Sandra.

"I'm relieved to hear that the kids are healthy, though the Lord knows how, considering how they've been livin'. Have you finished your coffee? We should get to the business at hand."

And you should have come on time, Sandra thought. Aloud, she said, "Realistically, what are our chances of finding a place for them?"

He shrugged. "In truth, Miss Shelton, I'm less optimistic than I was when you came to Santa Teresa. I've had some telephone conversations with the archdiocese children's office and some other institutions." He scratched one eyebrow, which was turning gray. "Foster care takes a while to arrange. During that time, there's a good possibility the two might be separated. A solution for the little girl could be relatively easy. But placing a twelve-year-old boy who has been homeless for a while, living by his wits on the street, is something else."

"Ten, he says he's ten."

The priest nodded.

"You're right. Come to think of it, we have his birthdate in the parish records. He's almost eleven, though."

Sandra recalled the way the boy ate, his use of the hand-basin as a urinal. "But rough edges can be smoothed. A young child can be taught."

"In all honesty, miss, if I were a prospective adoptive parent, I wouldn't want to try it myself. And lots of other people wouldn't, either. People want babies or very little ones. They want a chance to mold children in their own image, to teach them their own ways. Surely it's the same in the United States."

Sandra nodded. She knew that, of course, but she continued to long to find someone to disagree with her. Futilely.

The priest gulped his beer, paid the waiter. "But I've got a long list of places that wouldn't take telephone queries. So there's still a chance we could at least find a shelter with some regular childcare, if not an orphanage. Let's go."

They arose from the table at Angela's and he led her to his dusty van, parked illegally lengthwise at the curb. Sandra studied the battered, muddy vehicle, shook her head. Two hubcaps were gone, and the front tires both looked low.

"Uh, how about if we take my car?"

Peter Mulroy's lined face creased slowly into a grin, each line moving a little as an ironic expression took over. "I see. You don't trust my limousine. Very well then, but let's get on the road."

"I'm very sorry," said the woman behind the desk at the Amalfia Creche and Boarding School. "We'd like to help, of course, but there's just no more room. It's true that every child is eligible for school in Brazil, but the reality is that we just get too many applications here. Our residential school is always full.

"And I strongly, strongly suggest that you contact children's services so the kids can be taken into custodial care immediately."

Sandra stood and started for the door. The priest followed her more slowly, thanking the woman in his Portuguese, which sounded curiously more lyrical than native Portuguese because of his brogue.

A moment later, they stood outside on the cracked stone steps of the creche, a grey brick building that absorbed and redirected the sun unmercifully. Her bare head felt so hot that Sandra thought her hair might catch fire. The building smelled burnt, as though they were near a kiln. The jacaranda shrubs near the iron fence drooped in the three o'clock sunshine.

"Don't be disheartened. That's only the second place we've been this afternoon. There are several more on my list." But Sandra noticed that the corners of Mulroy's mouth were turning downward.

She looked up at him, way up. Somehow, until now, she'd failed to notice his height. "I'm just glad you're not losing interest."

"I'll help you, miss, as I said I would. I sympathize with the boy's need to keep his sister with him. It seems she's his reason for being. And from what you've said, they're experiencing safety in numbers where they are. Perhaps it's all right for a few days more." The two were scooting through the Rio streets to their next destination when they heard yelling from the sidewalk. Sandra slowed the car, saw gangs of kids in a tangle of fists. The priest jumped in his seat, then shouted, "For Lord's sake, don't stop! Guns! Move on."

Sandra paid no attention. Instead, she gawked at the combatants. They moved so fast she thought she might have been looking through a kaleidoscope. But he was right; she glimpsed a handgun shining in the sun. She heard a retort, an unmistakable shot, quickly followed by the siren of a police car. She moved quickly back into the flow of traffic and turned off the troubled street. On her right, she saw the priest grasping the armrest.

"Just a little gang warfare." His face reddened. "But I never get used to it."

"Are you from Northern Ireland?"

"Portadown."

"I see. Quite a history, that city. So do you have some memories of conflict between...."

Mulroy took a wrinkled white handkerchief from his pocket and patted his face. "None I like to dwell on, miss."

She blinked, took the hint and changed the subject as they left the gang rumble far behind.

"Could you stop calling me 'miss'? Sandra would be better."

"Sandra, you say? Sandra, then."

She avoided using his priestly title; she thought tartly that she already had a father. And "Peter" seemed too familiar. So for a second, she elected not to call him by any name. But she changed her mind. "How did you come to be sent to Brazil, Mulroy?"

He acknowledged the absence of his title with an ironic grin, wondered why he felt no offense. "I asked to come to South America, and eventually my request was granted."

"You have something to say about it?"

"It can happen. I've been around a bit—a coupla places in the Six Counties, you see, and in the Irish Republic and then here. They said I had a flair for languages, and that figured into the decision. I know the accent's not so good, but I'm a quick study."

"This seems a very long way from Northern Ireland, and very foreign for an Irishman."

He smiled again. "Oh, and isn't Rio a long way from home and very foreign for you?"

Sandra manipulated the little car through a clot of traffic. Her petite VW was surrounded on all sides by vans and trucks. "Actually, South America isn't so foreign as all that. My father was a diplomat before he retired, and I spent my teenage years in Buenos Aires. That's one of the reasons Worldwide Broadcasting sent me down here."

"You don't sound thrilled."

"I'm not." Sandra surprised herself by speaking blunt truth to this near-stranger—a priest of the church that she'd long ago rejected.

"Oh, I like the Brazilians a lot—unusually good-hearted, friendly people, it seems to me. But there are so many poor people here in some parts of Rio. And..." She stopped, steered away from a taxi caroming crazily along the road. "It's not just my concern for the poor, either. I'm not that altruistic. This was a career blow for me. I thought I'd be assigned to cover the White House, and instead, here I am. But I'm going back to Washington just as soon as I can get a transfer."

"And I wanted to serve as far as I could from the Six Counties." He laughed. "This is pretty far, at that."

"I wouldn't think you have much cultural life."

"Not unless you call our celebration of Carnival cultural life. Still, there wouldn't be much time for that sort of thing, anyway. My parish keeps me busy. The people are so—what do they say nowadays in psycho-babble—needy, I'd guess."

Sandra meant to ask questions. Who'd have thought this man, exiled to a backwater parish with a poverty stricken congregation, would have anything interesting to say? But the traffic was becoming increasingly hectic. Besides the big vehicles, other Volkswagens and Fiats, so popular in Rio, seemed to be aiming for her. Probably she should have let him drive his van. Then if they got smacked, at least they'd have had the protection of his tank-like vehicle.

The priest gave more directions, and Sandra wound around labyrinthine blocks until they arrived at the next place on his list. It was a small, one-story, pink-brick structure next door to a lumberyard. She noticed that it was the only place in the neighborhood that lacked flowers on the fence.

Considering the way things grew and spread in Brazil, someone surely had worked hard to remove the flourishing greenery of Rio in this location. Odd, she thought, to fight nature that way.

Noise greeted them as they opened the front door. It was barely cooler inside than outdoors. Children raced pell-mell around the visitors, shoving and yelling. Some of the girls' blue uniforms looked worn out and ragged and the halls smelled of urine and disinfectant.

"This doesn't look all that much better than the streets," Sandra whispered. They'd been told to wait in a breathless little anteroom.

"It's that they don't have very much money," he said. She watched him noticing her look. "Yes," he said, "I'm defensive 'cause it's a church orphanage." Score one for his candor, Sandra thought.

When they finally were ushered into the headmistress' office, the middle-aged woman behind the desk didn't immediately acknowledge them. Her hair was the harshest shade of red Sandra had seen in a while, the hard lines of her face unwelcoming.

She continued writing for a full minute or two, then finally looked at them. "I suppose you wish me to speak English?" She did not invite them to sit down. No matter, thought Sandra. The hardback chairs looked punishing—seats for recalcitrant children summoned for scolding, maybe.

"And what do you want, Father?" The woman ignored Sandra. But Mulroy wasn't halfway into the story when the headmistress shook her head.

"Homeless children? Out of the question. We have only orphans here."

"But Pedro and Zaida have no family. They don't even have any extended family," protested Sandra. The woman still didn't look at her. Instead, she continued speaking exclusively to Mulroy. "That's not what I meant. These are orphans whose parishes have applied for their admission."

"Madam, I've told you. I'm their parish priest at Saint Teresa's near Flores." Sandra watched the priest as the red crept up his neck. "And I'm applyin.' Can you give me the application papers?"

She nodded slowly. "Oh, yes, I can give you the application papers, but the waiting list is over two hundred for just a few places. Frankly, I believe it would be a waste of your time."

"Give me the papers, then, and let me judge how to use my time."

Outside again on the stewing and parboiling street, Sandra asked, "Why should we bother with the papers? It's plain that there will never be room. Besides, except that this place is enclosed, I'll bet the kids are happier under their awning."

"Well, it's like this." He walked almost too fast for Sandra to keep up, despite his odd, hitching gait. "Everything in Brazil is supposed to be about clout, as you Americans say, about power and influence. She's the headmistress, but that place is a Catholic institution. And I'm still a priest."

Sandra wondered why he said "still."

The day dragged on, the heat singing the pavement as Sandra and Mulroy repeatedly climbed in and out of her car.

Several superintendents of other institutions told them the same thing as the hostile faux redhead. The others spoke far more politely. They sounded sympathetic, but the message remained the same.

After the fourth refusal, the reporter and the priest stopped talking. The business day was over. Sandra drove in silence until they reached the traffic of Avenida Atlantica at sunset. They pulled up to the nearby street where his ancient van was parked.

"Do you have any more ideas, Mulroy?"

"Not at the moment." The dying sun illuminated the wrinkles in his tired face as he got out of the car. For a moment, he looked well beyond middle age. "But, don't worry. Rio's a big city. Brazil is a big country. There's got to be somebody who says something besides, 'There's no room in the inn.'"

He turned away, then turned back again. "Give me another one of your business cards, will you? I'll call you tomorrow and we'll try something else."

FIFTEEN

Tomás arrived early in the Worldwide office, a rarity since he liked to play handball at his club before coming to work. Sandra wondered if he ever helped his wife with their twins.

Still, the Mello couple probably had a nanny and maybe other servants as well. Nilda had told her about attending a Christmas party in the Mellos' luxurious high-rise building near the Lagoa, the Rodrigo de Freitas Lake, prime Rio real estate.

Tomás greeted her when she passed his desk. "Okay, beautiful, no more delaying. Get with the Pará story!"

Sandra sat down to write another broadcast about Sister Jean Hightower, the latest of two American nuns to fight the lumbermen who were slashing and burning the trees of the Amazon rainforest. The first, Dorothy Stang, had been murdered. The situation now merited media attention.

Nilda was constantly gathering facts about events in the huge state of Pará, working the phones and visiting the state. But she'd never reported from Sister Hightower's lair. Tomás had written the broadcasts before from Nilda's notes; then he'd gotten busy with other things and assigned the story to Sandra. But she'd just deleted the second and third pages of her broadcast in disgust. It wasn't Nilda's fault that the story didn't flow.

"Why do I have to write about the nun who doesn't have sense enough to know she's going to be murdered, just like Stang was killed?"

Tomás whistled a samba tune. "I'm so glad to have you here, Miss America, so I don't have to deal with the crazy nun and her death wish."

It seemed to Sandra that no Brazilian could go a whole day without hearing or singing or dancing a samba. She mumbled a complaint that she thought was inaudible.

"Hey! I hear you talking to yourself. Do you think the sun in Rio is making you crazy?" He crossed the room, pulled over a squeaky chair and sat down next to her workstation.

"How're you doing?"

Sandra decided to be honest. "Not so good. I can't seem to work up the proper inspiration for this Amazon rainforest story."

"You know," said Tomás, tugging his red beard with one freckled hand and passing the other over his forehead. "I've thought of a remedy for that."

"Oh?"

"Nilda's tired of tracking that story, and so I'm going to send you up to the do-gooder's fiefdom. You'll pick up details for yourself, and you can write the stories firsthand." He smiled wickedly.

"I've read some of the broadcasts you wrote before coming here, from Syria, from Louisiana during the oil spill. I know what you're capable of. But I think you need to get out of town and stop brooding about those street brats for a while. You'll catch fire up there." He leaned very close and stared into her face. Sandra opened her mouth to protest that she hated the story.

Still, she knew she'd never been at liberty to protest that way to earlier editors, and she had no right to refuse an assignment from this one. But he kept on blurring the line between editor and reporter, between boss and employee. Sometimes their relationship seemed to her more like hunter and prey.

"When would you want me to go?" Sandra stared at the stack of disorganized papers on her desk, her notes and Nilda's on what she had come to think of as "the Pará affair."

"Well, today would be good."

Tomás smiled so widely that she thought the outer corners of his lips might meet with his earlobes. She uttered a syllable of dismay, but he amended his suggestion.

"Book your tickets and arrangements now for tomorrow. Get somebody to explain how to get there—it's something of a pain." If anything, Tomás' grin got even wider as he turned away.

Oh, no!

"I can't leave town."

"What do you mean?"

"I can't leave the children."

"My God, are you refusing an important assignment? Are you a reporter or a frustrated mother?"

"They depend on me."

"They were in danger before you came here. They're still in danger."

"But I'm checking on them, seeing them regularly."

"Listen to me. You know the network neglects this office—sometimes ignores our stories. I'm trying to build up our reputation. If you don't want to help, I'll find someone else. I like you, but I can live without you." He took a ferocious tug at his beard and walked back to his desk.

She swallowed hard. Somehow, the fact that she slept in the same city as the kids, though in far different circumstances, made her feel that she was helping to protect them. She knew it didn't make sense, but she thought as long as she stayed in Rio and kept an eye on them, the children seemed at least relatively safe.

But, that's absurd. It's magical thinking. It's like Heloisa and Tomás say. I'm fantasizing that I'm so strong and effective as a person that I can keep the kids from harm until I rescue them, come up with a new future for them.

But how can I make this trip? Something terrible could happen to them while I'm gone. Something terrible could happen to me *while I'm gone. What if my plane crashed? And that nun's center could be in danger.*

She realized that Tomás was standing at her desk.

"Look, you can do this assignment in three or four days, including the travel. But you have to do it. My position is clear." Again, he walked away from her.

I can't go. I can't. But I dare not lose my job until I get another one in this city, or I'd lose the kids. And it's true that they aren't any better protected than when I first saw them. Maybe three days won't make any difference.

She argued with herself for several hours, then regretfully picked up the office landline and called her neighbor. Could the nice lady with the orange hair across the hall from her apartment feed Marmalade while she was away?

She hoped that the woman wouldn't notice that she was crying as she made the request.

Pedro's chin trembled a little when he heard that Sandra was leaving town for several days. He stood in front of the Worldwide building, leaning one bare brown foot on his footrest. Then he drew himself up manfully and asked about the mountains and the jungles of Pará.

"Is it hot up there? Are there big cats, those pumas?"

Sandra picked up and rocked Zaida, who seemed very fussy that morning. She also felt heavy; there was no arguing that these kids were growing daily, despite their privations.

"Pedro, I won't be near any pumas. And I'll only be gone a short time. And I'll be thinking about you two when I'm away. Worrying."

"Nobody'll hurt us 'cause my friend Maria's great at capoeira." He took a few steps to demonstrate the Brazilian combination of martial arts, dance, rhythm and movement that Maria had mastered.

"Of course," she said again. "I'll send you postcards…"

I'm losing my mind. Like they have a street address under that awning? I can't do this. But I have to do it. Otherwise, I might have to go home to Washington for work and leave them for real. None of the other media down here have responded to my job inquiries.

The same fears that had rocked her after Tomás' order ran through her mind. It seemed like a piece of audio that was looped to run again and again.

Come on, Sandra. Behave normally, for Pedro's sake.

"I have to go, Pedro. You understand, don't you?"

"OK, Tia, but promise me you won't forget to come back!"

SIXTEEN

Sandra was still thinking of the children while trudging up the hill—it felt more like a mountain—to the aerie where Sister Jean Hightower held court. The journey had been exhausting, a trip that reminded Sandra vividly that she was thirty-six and not sixteen.

She'd taken a plane that surged over a huge stretch of Brazil to a patch of the rainforest. Then came a smaller plane and a hired car, a sort of Jeep taxi. It had no air conditioning, and it bumped and jounced nauseatingly through miles of flat, raped earth.

She'd seen bruised land, some patches still smoking from the fires of land-grabbers. She also passed unviolated spaces—huge, lush green clusters of trees spread out for miles towards the horizon. The relatively few people living in the thousands of sprawling hectares of Para´ had small houses and big trucks. Roadside bars dotted the countryside, their business lucrative. After navigating some of the roads there, it seemed to her that people would need a drink.

At last, the beat-up, wheezing vehicle dropped her off at the bottom of a hill, next to a mailbox that proclaimed the Peace Community Center. But the center itself was still up, up, up.

As she climbed to Sister Jean Hightower's lair, the reporter wished her boots weren't so heavy; the Reuters correspondent in Rio had warned her to pack hiking boots for this last leg of her journey. But as she climbed, it seemed that they weighed five pounds apiece. And darned if she weren't getting another blister. One foot, one heel, seemed to know when she was most vulnerable.

With each step, she nursed her resentment at being forced to come here. Sister Jean had been curt on the phone. It was clear that she would allow Sandra to invade her territory only because she understood that media coverage might help her people fight illegal loggers and land-grabbers. *This woman isn't one of those activists passionate to talk about her cause. I'll have to work extra hard to get a story.*

A few soldiers, or government-hired paramilitaries, guarded the brick community center on the hilltop where Sister Jean both worked and lived. The glare of the sunshine prevented Sandra from counting the camouflage suits. The soldiers, all men, served there because of the press given the murdered activist nun and the very recent threats received by Jean Hightower

Still, in a memorable gesture, two of Sister Dorothy Stang's convicted killers had been given home leave from prison to celebrate Father's Day in 2008. And the ringleader in Sister Dorothy's death was sentenced only in 2010, five years after plotting the deed. Then, in May of 2013, the Brazilian Supreme Court annulled the last trial of Vitalmiro Moura. He had been convicted and sentenced to thirty years in prison for plotting Sister Dorothy's death.

Sandra huffed and puffed as she climbed, especially dreading the time she would be following Sister Jean's footsteps. Some days she felt that all her journalistic expertise had deserted her in Brazil; she no longer felt like the seasoned correspondent of the Haiti earthquake or the earthquake and tsunami in Japan that had melted down nuclear reactors.

She whispered to herself, grumbling with every step. It seemed Charles' leaving her had taken so much of her self-respect— even her confidence in her skills. She could almost feel her feminist genes imploding with shame. How could his rejection have so deeply damaged her professional poise?

When Sandra finally reached the top step, she was panting. Her bangs, wet with sweat, clung to her forehead. The rest of her blonde mane hung in a limp tangle. She felt like she'd arrived at the sprawling Potala Palace in Lhasa, Tibet, upwards of 12,000 feet.

Sister Hightower's Peace Community Center proved to be a long, squat building of yellowish brown brick with startlingly yellow window frames and shutters. It sat precariously on a hill, topped by a cross that seemed to Sandra to lean a little to the left.

It reminded her of Mulroy's Saint Teresa Church, which also leaned. But Saint Teresa's emerged from a dun-colored field without vegetation, with only an occasional termite hive and weed patch to break the monotony of the land. Here, the building was carved from the jungle, surrounded by a dense growth of leafy green thickets. What were the trees and bushes called? Well, she'd have to learn pretty quickly. A feature broadcast needed details of the setting. Otherwise it was like an egg or a tomato without salt.

Monkeys, bigger ones than the little micos she'd seen in Rio, chattered at the top of the canopy. What looked like enormous ferns and tightly interlocked palms thatched the horizon.

Sandra saw a small woman in a denim skirt and white blouse standing on the portico. On either side of the door, two soldiers stared straight ahead like the Beefeater guards at Buckingham Palace. But where were the other guards?

The nun wore street clothes. Her gray hair was cropped into a short, straight pageboy that emphasized startlingly green eyes. Her face was lined and square, with jaws no longer sharply defined. Yet without any make-up, and definitely not young, she looked comely.

Great, thought Sandra, one small woman well into middle age, encamped in a remote site, versus men who threatened, beat and sometimes killed their victims. Some lumbermen craved more wood and simply took it. Some plantation owners who wanted more space for crops also simply took it, burning and destroying whatever was on the land they desired.

Together, the criminally greedy hurt not only the local forests and smallholders. The trees they felled for lumber provided oxygen that helps clean the atmosphere. Their crimes against the environment harmed people oceans away. And there was yet another element of danger for the nun and her center. Some ultra-radicals had turned to lawlessness against any and all landed people, whether guilty of anything or not. Sandra knew Hightower, who preached gaining human rights by peaceful means, had had a threat or two from those who found nonviolence abhorrent. It seemed to Sandra that the woman needed a lot more guards than those she saw standing around woodenly. Surely, Sister Jean's vulnerability merited a platoon.

Hightower nodded to her as Sandra caught her breath.

"Quite a climb, isn't it?'"

The reporter reached the building's porch, trying to pretend she wasn't nearly gasping for breath. Sandra blushed, thinking that Hightower was at least twenty-five years older and probably made the climb without even a tiny pause.

"I haven't been able to jog much since arriving in Rio." She bit her lip.

Why in the world would a stranger care about her shortness of breath, unless she collapsed in a heap? But nuns seemed to have an unsettling effect on her. Maybe it was the memory of Sandra's teenage years in Catholic school in Argentina.

Maybe it was the way her teachers there had viewed the ordeal she'd had with the boys in the street at age sixteen. Seeing that Sandra was unhurt after the attack, the relieved principal, Sister Benedicta Anne, had warned her after a week or two that to talk about the boy with the knife was well… bordering on whining.

"We don't want to constantly call attention to ourselves, dear," she'd cautioned, softening the words with a smile. "You must forgive those boys and forget what happened."

But the other girls made a fuss over her ordeal, found it an exciting adventure, even asking if her attackers were "cute." Sandra's math teacher scolded her in class for trying to attract attention. All the adults brushed off the nightmares that haunted her.

The worst of it was her confusion over the stabbing she herself had done. The attack had taken place under the curtain of dusk. She'd wrested the knife from her assailant. But then, had she lunged at that person or the boy behind him? Most of the time, trying to remember, she was sure the person behind him had tried to pull back the attacker, tried to protect her from harm. And that's the one she accidentally stabbed.

Maybe, as her classmates suggested, she should have been proud of putting up a fight and escaping harm.

I don't see it that way. I acted to defend myself, but what did I do?

Counseling, or at least talking with someone with expertise about teenagers, might have helped. But, she realized wryly, trauma therapy was not exactly practiced in an Argentine Catholic girls' school twenty years ago.

Now, so long afterward, Sister Jean Hightower smiled at Sandra, revealing startlingly white teeth. As she took Sister Jean's extended hand, Sandra wondered vaguely if nuns in the Amazon got their teeth whitened.

"How was your trip?" Sister Jean spoke first in Portuguese, openly studying Sandra. Then she switched to English. "You're American, of course. I've had a number of reporters up here, but you're the only woman so far. I don't imagine that you enjoyed the ride on the last lap."

Why did nuns always act as though other women were not strong, not willing to endure discomfort? Sister Jean's words were pleasant enough, but Sandra suspected she heard irony in the tone. A wisecrack formed on her lips, but died there. She needed the woman's cooperation if she were to succeed in this assignment. And Tomás was obviously testing her.

Much more importantly, she needed to show a strong performance to her next prospective employer when she escaped Tomás' clutches. She hadn't done much that was unusual or notable since arriving in Rio, and, in journalism, it was a truism that you were always judged by what you had done lately. Her prizes for features about the difference in living standards in Haiti and the Dominican Republic or the savage corruption facing honest law enforcers in Mexico no longer counted for much.

Leading Sandra out of the boiling sunshine, Sister Jean ushered her through a community room with bare gray linoleum floors. Folding chairs were stacked against every wall. Made of gleaming metal, they looked forsaken, as though waiting for some anxious bottoms to settle on them. Well, thought Sandra, people who'd made the climb to Sister Jean's den deserved a place to rest.

The nun opened a side door of the open porch and led her into a tiny sitting room. It had a pretty flowered settee festooned with a dahlia pattern, a matching chair, quickly occupied by the nun, and a floor lamp with a shade that looked like a lantern.

Hightower looked at Sandra expectantly as the reporter fumbled in her huge raffia purse and withdrew her mini-laptop and the small hand-held recorder she'd insisted that the Rio bureau buy for this trip. Sister Jean asked a polite question about what network Sandra worked for; she said she'd forgotten the name. She thought a woman named Nilda-something had called her repeatedly from that network.

"You know, I'm amazed about the interest in our work here," she said in answer to Sandra's opening question. "I'm American, so I expected to hear from *The Catholic Reporter* and the newsletter of my order, but I'm stunned by how many writers and camera people have made the climb."

Sandra pushed some buttons on the recorder. "What, exactly, are you hoping to accomplish here? I mean, after the other sister was killed?" She was surprised at the obvious skepticism in her tone. The question sounded challenging. For a second, she felt like one of Fox News' golden-tressed anchorwomen going after a liberal guest.

"Ms. Shelton, someone needs to speak for the workers here, and for the defense of land reform in Brazil." The nun frowned, deepening the furrows in her brow, several of which crossed in an unusual pattern. "The suffering of these workers is almost unspeakable. They're worked until they can hardly stand up and then just get thrown away. And there's now a lot more land that was cleared in earlier years so people can make a lot of money growing soy without pushing out small farmers.

"The greed is amazing."

The woman looked her age, at least for a second. *Come on, tell me something I don't know.*

"Some big landowners can be brutal. The government encouraged people to move for arable land. Some have moved over and over again. They deserve to keep their property." She shook her head, a motion that slightly moved the chain that hung around her neck, a plain wooden cross. "True land titles are often just not respected here. Corruption and Old West-style land seizures are the thing. Someone must help the people stand up to these criminals. Surely you can understand that."

"But, Sister, let's face it, you're in danger all the time. The government sent a few guards here. But that's for show. You've been threatened and the danger you're in has been well publicized. But people lose interest after a while. You'll be virtually alone and vulnerable. Aren't you scared?"

The nun shook her head more energetically this time. Her answer sounded exasperated. "I'll bet there are things in the world that would make you step out of your comfort zone."

That, Sandra thought, was the most quotable thing the nun had said.

Clearly danger could be looming around the yellow building on the hill, yet as the day passed, Sandra was struck by how normal and tranquil life in the aerie seemed. The soldiers in fatigues, the Brazilian Beefeaters, as she thought of them, looked out of place in the hot stillness. Except for their stoic presence, the place might have been in Florida or California.

The resident dog in the community center seemed much more lively. The nun announced very precisely and unsmilingly that his name must be spelled Xoquian if he were to appear in Sandra's script on the Web. But the nun called him "Ouch."

Sandra trailed Sister Jean all day, and so did the dog, a very large animal with outsized paws. He seemed to be mostly yellow Lab, yet his height made Sandra wonder if he should be measured in hands, like a horse. But when she asked Sister Jean his breed, the nun said, again with a straight face, "He's a miniature poodle."

Encouraged by this hint of humor, Sandra persisted with her microphone and her questions. Ouch and the reporter followed Sister Jean as she rushed around her office organizing papers and trying to talk on her cell phone, although the reception was poor.

Occasionally the nun would fall into the chair in front of her computer and type out a few lines of the remarks she planned to make at a rally that night. The protesters expected to show up had several complaints. Rubber workers labored for extremely low pay in dangerous conditions and could be beaten or worse if they protested. Farmers lived in fear of confiscation of their land, or being forced to surrender it for a pittance. Still others lived in danger from illegal loggers.

Sandra tried hard to get a solid interview with Sister Jean. But the nun was willing to say only that her order wanted to maintain a presence where it was most deeply needed. She said Sandra would understand better at the rally.

"It's about basic human rights. Don't you get it?"

Sister Jean dismissed Sandra to consult with Nana, a very dark-skinned woman of middle years who lived in the center. They talked about what they would have for dinner. They elected churrasco, barbecued meat on skewers, and then everything went on fast forward. Nana cooked while the nun chopped vegetables for a salad. Three other women bustled in and out so rapidly that the reporter could barely get their names straight. Their families had suffered at the hands of the lumber thieves, it seemed, and they were now bringing evidence of the injustices to the nun.

"Sister, won't some of them be hurt or even killed if they protest? What's to protect them?"

To herself, she thought sourly, God?

"Young woman, do you imagine that African Americans in our country would ever have gotten anywhere had some of them not risked injury and death? What movement for justice ever prevailed without suffering?"

Good quote, thought Sandra, and she cranked up the volume on the recorder. But she could draw out the nun no further. Between talking and doing, the woman was definitely a doer—and a very tough interview.

Each of the visitors to Sister Jean's center carried papers or notes of some sort for the nun. She accepted the papers while she mixed a salad dressing heavy with Brazilian olive oil. She didn't engage in much conversation with the visitors, except for a hurried "obrigada," thank you.

Sandra tried to stay out of the way but still within earshot as Nana wrestled the beef onto skewers. Ouch stood by patiently, clearly hoping she'd drop a piece.

"Damn dog." Nana bent to pet him and give him a large bite.

Eventually Nana brought their dinner to a big oak table in what Sister Jean called "the front room." Sandra couldn't imagine why, as it was not in the front of the community center. Maybe the use of an old-fashioned name for a room made the place seem more like a home. Still, Sandra recalled that her grandmother had talked about a front room, and that room was not used for anything.

At dinner in the Brazilian rainforest, Nana sat with the nun and the reporter and talked animatedly in Portuguese. She spoke so fast that Sandra's head began to ache with the effort of trying to understand. She caught enough to learn that within an hour farmers and laborers would come to the front of the center's long, open porch. Hightower's role would be to hear their stories and urge them to form unions, to find safety and power in numbers. Whoever built the center must have envisioned a stage, for the porch perfectly fit that description.

The speakers would stand near its edge, where light and sound equipment had been placed for the nun's frequent meetings and rallies. They would appeal to the demonstrators to try to fight the bulldozers, earth movers and tractors off their land.

Sandra asked questions between bites of the churrasco. Nana said she'd come here because rubber plantation owners wanted her to clear the trees on her land for their own purposes. She said they'd offered her far less for her farm than it was worth.

"When I said I wouldn't sell, first they scared off my workers. I hung on for months, doing some of the work myself. I didn't give up until men came at night, carrying torches. They gave me twentyfour hours to get out or they'd harm the kids."

Sandra leaped up from the skewered beef, ran for her recorder and put the microphone in front of Nana's face, asking permission by tipping her head.

"You stood up to them." she prompted. "You were brave."

Nana showed a missing front tooth as she spoke. "I lost everything. Maybe I was brave, and maybe I was stupid. If it weren't for Sister Jean and the community here, I'd have no place to go. But they didn't kill me, like they did da Silva. The loggers got him."

In her research, Sandra had come onto the name of the activist Jose Laudio Ribeiro da Silva again and again. He and his wife had been fatally shot in 2011. He'd known he was in danger and asked for police protection, but didn't get any. Sandra realized that he had been murdered not so very far from where she sat in comfort, eating tasty churrascos in a house protected by men with rifles—too few men with rifles, she thought.

Sandra helped remove the dishes from the table, hoping the gesture might get the women to think her less an outsider. She stood in front of the long, antique-looking scarred porcelain sink and started to rinse their plates, glad for a chance for normal activity in this building where violence always threatened. But at least the Beefeater Boys were on duty.

From the kitchen window behind that venerable sink, she saw an aberrant sight. Instead of falling, the darkness seemed to rise from the steep hill. Profound blackness arrived in what seemed like five minutes. Clouds hid the stars, and the moon peeked out only occasionally from the cloudbank. She recalled only one other time in her life when the world had seemed so dark.

Power had failed totally on Martha's Vineyard Island, where her parents had an A-frame summer cottage. She was maybe seven years old and had been put to bed in the top level of the cottage. She awakened when a generator boomed the message that it had failed. The stillness was absolute, the darkness impenetrable. She'd shivered despite the August heat.

Now, so many years later, Sandra was also shivering in the heat. She'd put on a sundress to cope with the humidity. And she felt alternating waves of heat and chill on her skin as she faced the darkness from the kitchen window.

Sandra returned from grabbing a sweater from her room, and in that time the clouds had rolled back. She stepped onto the front porch. It ran the length of the house, like the back porch at George Washington's home at Mount Vernon. And like the Mount Vernon porch, it looked over a grassy lawn that rolled down the hill.

A few people began to gather on the grass, and then a few more on the steps. The night was so humid that she felt she was breathing through a wet washcloth. And gradually from a lighted porch she saw dozens, maybe hundreds of people swarming up the steps, holding torches that melted the blackness. Most moved in front of the porch and to the right side. As they picked their spots, flies and insects with huge wings flitted and danced, making a ballet in the shadows.

Ouch wound himself around Sandra's feet, snatching at the cords of the center's sound equipment with a big yellow paw. His mistress, Sister Jean, stood at the edge of the porch, waiting to speak to the crowd.

"Stop, pooch!" Sandra wondered at trying to talk a dog out of normal dog-play in these unreal circumstances.

The nun turned to Sandra. "Why are you talking to him in

English? He speaks only Portuguese, for goodness' sake."

Sandra batted down Ouch's paw. *What do you know? Another flash of humor. Maybe Sister Jean was nervous, joking a bit to dispel her tension. She certainly ought to be nervous. Anybody could be in this crowd, anybody at all.*

At the sight of the nun, the people grew quieter. Sister Jean pointed to a man wearing torn khakis and a white undershirt.

"Paolo Mendes," she introduced, and Paolo hopped up next to her on the porch. His last name recalled Chico Mendes, the hero of the movement to unionize rubber workers and arguably the first to warn the world about the effects of deforestation. Chico was murdered in 1988. Now, another man named Mendes addressed a crowd of workers in need of just treatment. "I want to remember my brother in our movement, our friend Theodoro. I want justice for my friend, my brother in the struggle. He was laced because he fought the bosses. Laced!"

Sandra blanched. Of all ways to die, being placed in a tire that's set afire seemed to her the very worst. Paolo was just beginning to explain how his friend had tried to organize other workers. But as he spoke, a cry went up from a man in the crowd. "Look out!"

Paolo ducked. Sister Jean ducked. Sandra, stunned, just stood still for an instant. Ouch bit her leg at the knee, pulling her down. She sensed, rather than saw, a grenade whisk through the air over her head.

One of the soldiers standing woodenly at the back of the porch dropped his rifle and leaped up to field the grenade. But where could he possibly throw it? Sandra held her breath.

Time stopped. The soldier let loose a very long throw, past most of the crowd on the left of the porch. People ran back. The grenade detonated, unleashing a small cloud of earth. The smoky mess, unloosing grass and dirt, rose for a few feet in several directions. As some of the smoke cleared, Sandra saw a body on the ground.

Breathless moments went by. Miraculously, the body moved. Indeed, it stood, and brushed itself off, but blood flowed. As more smoke cleared, Sandra could see that the man's shirt and pants were in tatters. A woman sat on the ground, rubbing the top of her head.

Instantly, the nun was on her phone, and a siren sounded from the road at the bottom of the hill. The crowds parted for medics with stretchers. After a few minutes, the medics waved a thumbs-up. Apparently, the victims' injuries weren't life threatening.

Time started up again. Soldiers ran in pursuit of the grenade thrower. Sister Jean murmured a brief prayer for the injured and urged anyone in the crowd who saw the attacker to come forward and tell what they'd seen. She wished everyone a good night and urged the people not to lose hope of improving their lives.

Hightower was all cool efficiency as Sandra approached her. "Well," the nun said archly. "We've had some excitement, haven't we?"

"Your dog probably saved my life."

"Heavens no, you're not that tall. The grenade flew well over your head. It was lucky that the attacker made a bad throw—and that the soldier made a good one. Otherwise…"

Sandra pulled up her microphone and placed it in front of the nun.

"Oh, all right, I'll say something about what happened. You've got your story now."

Sandra rushed inside the community center and filed her account from her laptop.

> *"On a boiling night in the Amazon rainforest, activist American nun Jean Hightower and a speaker at her rally for the environment and human rights became the apparent targets of a grenade attack…"*

She also sent two related stories. Paolo Mendes gave the reporter a very articulate interview. In addition, she also wrote eloquently of Nana's rebellion against big corrupt landowners.

At one point, she caught Sister Jean looking over her shoulder. "Come on now, Ms. Shelton, don't overdramatize. The attack was frightening, but nobody died. In that way, it was just another night in our struggle."

"Just another night for you, Sister?" Sandra pictured the words as a headline for the web.

The nun frowned. "Just you remember what I told you about Ouch. You promised to spell his name right on the Internet."

Sandra suspected that the moment she sent her story into cyberspace, the nun would be fielding questions from media all over Brazil, perhaps internationally. She wondered if the woman would demand that other reporters also spell the dog's name correctly.

The trip back to Rio seemed to go faster than getting to Pará. But the presence of the nun and the violence at the community center had somehow thrown Sandra back to her days as a student in Buenos Aires. The nuns at school had swept away discussion of the attack on her with a light broom.

It seemed to the reporter that the car was actually bouncing on the road, but it didn't stop her from writing on her laptop.

"This is about twenty years too late," she told the driver, who smiled uncertainly.

Sandra made a quick and successful online search for the school's e-mail and assurance that Sister Benedicta Anne was still in charge. Then Sandra wrote the note as though penning a letter. In the subject line, she wrote "URGENT."

Sr. Benedicta Anne Merriweather
Principal
St. Helena's Secondary School for Girls
Buenos Aires, Argentina.

Dear Sister Benedicta Anne,

I wonder if you remember me—Sandra Shelton, class of _____. Many years ago I was attacked on the street by a gang of boys after leaving a music lesson with Sister Mary Augustine. I was nearly stabbed—and I stabbed someone else to defend myself.

You and my teachers counseled me to forgive the boys, forget the incident and not draw attention to myself. In doing so, I believe you failed to understand the possible long-term effect of such an experience. And of course, you as principal knew that my mother had died recently and that I was far from my home and friends in the United States.

You acted in good faith, with every good intention—but I believe you gave me poor advice. I am still, at age thirty-six, occasionally haunted by nightmares about the incident, and especially by the fact that I think I struck and wounded a boy who seemed to be trying to help me. To fend off attackers and draw blood on the street was a heavy burden for an ordinarily sheltered teenager.

Should something like this ever happen again—and I surely hope it will not—I believe you should consider professional counseling for the victim.

*Sincerely,
Sandra Shelton*

She pushed "send" before editing or rewriting, a rarity for Sandra. She pulled a handkerchief from her purse and wiped the sweat off her face.

One decision led to another: The next time she came face to face with her father, she would also tell him how his extravagant outrage about the gang attack had made her feel even worse.

Howard Shelton had reacted with emotional canon fire. He kept demanding that Sandra do a better job of describing her attackers for the police. When she protested that they were indistinct, he turned some of that anger and frustration on her. But the worst came when she told him that the person she stabbed might have been trying to help her. Howard Shelton started shouting.

"How can you say such a thing? How could you possibly know which person you were defending yourself against in that crowd of thugs? Even if you did strike the wrong person, my God, Sandra, you were fighting for your life! And that person was in a gang that was trying to disfigure or kill you! Don't ever let me hear you feeling sorry for anyone in that lot of criminals! That's idiotic. You could have been killed."

She sighed at the memory. The taxi took an especially rough turn, and she spoke to the driver in English.

"I guess I have something in common with my friend Pedro. Had my mother not been dead, if she'd been around, things might have been different."

The driver looked puzzled. No doubt wondering what the foreign woman was talking about, he decided on a broad grin.

SEVENTEEN

Sandra went directly to the office on her return two days later, complete with matted, fuzzy hair and a black and blue mark on her leg from Ouch's bite. She got a hug from Nilda and an all-toopassionate embrace from Tomás, replete with a slew of compliments in Portuguese, which he'd never before used with her.

"I guess you liked my stories?" She broke away quickly from the hug, but she had to admit that she enjoyed the moment.

I showed him, didn't I? But I have to admit that it was his forcing me to go to Sister Jean's center that caused all these accolades.

Nilda told her that her telephone hadn't stopped ringing during her absence. Taking the messages, she learned that France 24, Reuters and AP all wanted to interview her for their own stories about Sister Jean's work. They hadn't followed the story very closely lately, it seemed. But now that violence had occurred, they acted like lemmings. After all, she'd been on the spot when someone had targeted the nun and her worker-activist.

The most important call came when she was still taking messages. Luckily, she interrupted her note-taking for a live call. A voice said, "Sandra Shelton? One moment please for Michel Temer."

Sandra had been sure that if she ever were to speak directly to the country's interim president, she would be asking him about the accusations of government corruption that had caused the impeachment of his predecessor, Dilma Rousseff. This call, though, was about Sandra, not corruption. Temer's voice was warm and congratulatory. He told the reporter that because of her stories, many more soldiers would be assigned to Sister Jean Hightower.

Sandra longed to ask Temer why more wasn't being done to protect the rainforest and its people. But the politician ended the call before Sandra could do more than thank him.

Tomás was satisfied, though. "God, this is wonderful. Sandra, you've put Worldwide radio and web on the map in Rio—in South America! We've made news that isn't about sports!" He suggested a staff luncheon with Nilda to celebrate.

The three repaired again to Angela's Café on the Avenida Atlantica. Before the women could decide what they wanted, Tomás ordered champagne for everyone. They talked about Para´, about Dilma Rousseff, about former President Lula da Silva. Then the conversation moved to Nilda's husband, who owned flower shops in Leme, and her married daughter, a newly minted doctor serving a fellowship in plastic surgery at a hospital in Manhattan.

"Why so far away?" Sandra said. "Brazil's known for plastic surgery. Movie stars and CEOs come here for their lifts and tucks."

"Finishing off her education in the United States should get her some of the best-heeled patients when she comes back." Just as Nilda spoke, an orchestra began playing Beethoven's 7th in her blue leather handbag. She excused herself from the table for a few moments to take the call, then returned with an anxious smile.

"That was Edivaldo Schatz from the Chamber of Commerce. I've been trying to get an interview with him all week, and he can see me now."

"Then off you go," said Tomás. Sandra saw that sardonic smile again. "We'll manage somehow without you."

Tomás and Sandra faced off over the white tablecloth in the icy air conditioning of Angela's. When the drinks arrived, he stirred his cocktail and stared at her.

"A personal call came for you while you were gone. Fellow named Charles-Something in Paris. Said he couldn't get through to you on your cell, and that you don't have a land number."

Sandra fought the urge to throw her glass at Tomás. Shoot the messenger, that was the idea. She took a big gulp of her drink, didn't reply.

"He sounded kind of desperate to talk to you. Gave me his new phone number to pass along." Tomás reached into the breast pocket of his expensive silver-and-blue striped suit coat. "What's the matter?"

"Just give me the phone number, will you?"

He passed the paper across the table. Sandra crumpled it up. "Old boyfriend?"

"History." Sandra was amazed to hear herself say the word.

"I see."

But she could tell from his expression that he wasn't sure he did.

"So he's out of your life, then?"

"Right."

Tomás stirred his caipirinha very deliberately. "Then do you think there would be perhaps a bit of room for me in your Brazilian experience?"

Sandra shook her head. He'd stated his goal, directly and boldly. "You have a wife, Tomás, and two little girls."

"So?"

Sandra took another gulp of her drink. The man was incorrigible. But she realized that if she had to work for him, she'd better be careful how she dealt with his very male ego.

"Look, I don't have affairs with other women's husbands. It's a game that isn't fair." She mustered a giggle and a light tone. "It ain't sisterly."

Tomás sighed and stared at the tablecloth. "I don't know what to say to you. You have something against fun, don't you?"

"How do you know what I'm doing when I'm not in the office? I've been dating a very nice Italian diplomat."

"No, you have not." He pronounced each word separately and heavily.

She decided not to pursue her lie.

"Tomás, don't you love your wife? Your family?"

"My wife loves the babies. For the last year, she's loved only the babies. I'm not in her life. The babies and her charities—that's it."

Sandra wondered what she could possibly say. Should she play advisor to the neglected husband? She tried it.

"Sometimes new mothers are overwhelmed and forget to pay attention to their husbands. It's a stage, a phase that will end."

"What would you know about it, anyway?"

"You're an attractive man, Tomás, I don't deny it. But I have somebody, and you're married."

He lifted his cocktail glass.

"Okay, Ice Lady. You are clearly a lonely woman getting over a bad affair. Until you change your mind, I salute you."

Sandra shook her head again. All she could think about was how anxious she was to see Pedro and Zaida.

EIGHTEEN

The compliments and comments on Sandra's work in Pará were still flying through the airwaves and the Internet when she was back at Wilson Azevedo Hospital with the kids in tow.

This time, they entered the long, thickly carpeted halls of the hospital's pediatric section with less fear. Indeed, Pedro even swaggered a little, having lived through his first experience in the place. And Sandra repeatedly assured them that there would be no more shots—just a one-minute ear exam for Zaida.

Sandra told the same staring nurse at the reception desk that they were there to see Dr. Gomes.

"Dr. Gomes is on an emergency upstairs. His associate, Dr. Kattah, Dr. Olivia Kattah, will see the little girl. Here she is now."

Sandra turned to recognize the black-haired young woman who had gaped so openly at them in the waiting room and on the parking lot on their earlier visit. Today, though, the doctor looked friendly instead of baldly curious as she greeted them. Her first words were in English.

"Dr. Gomes told me about you." She extended a hand to Sandra. "It's a very fine thing you're doing." She hesitated ever so slightly, then bent to shake hands with Pedro and pat Zaida's plump arm.

"Come with me, and we'll see if she has elephants in her ears."

Pedro tugged at Sandra's arm.

"Why are these people always talking like that? What do they think we are, babies?"

A few minutes later, Olivia found no elephants. But she said Zaida still had fluid behind her eardrums. The doctor put the little girl back on the floor, and she toddled around the room, humming and chortling to herself. This time, the attention she was getting in the luxurious hospital was clearly not frightening.

"I wonder if the child really got the medicine," Olivia said as she sat down at a desk in the corner of the room. "It should have dried the fluid." Both women looked at Pedro, Sandra wondering at the irony of depending on a ten-year-old to administer medication.

Pedro stood up taller. "I never missed. It tasted like grape, so she drank each teaspoon like Sandra showed me."

"How did you tell the time to give the medicine?" the doctor asked, voice heavy with suspicion.

The pupils of Pedro's eyes seemed to shrink into cinders. "I kept asking people what time it was—my customers and other people with watches."

Dr. Kattah looked up at Sandra. "Dr. Gomes was telling me that you were looking for a place for the kids to stay. Have you had any luck?"

"Not yet, but we're working on it."

Dr. Kattah frowned. "It's possible that I might be able to help." Sandra exclaimed something, but Olivia talked over her. "I know a businessman, Tonio Campelos, who is quite interested in street kids. Ever heard of him?"

"Is he the guy who made all that money in the mines?"

"That's the one. He's over seventy and mostly retired now. He's a friend of my father's. Since he hasn't been working so hard, he started a couple of shelters for street kids.

"One's under a viaduct, enclosed, and loosely supervised, and the other one's actually inside what was an unused gasoline station. It's in a quiet spot sort of near Leme. It's fully enclosed and has some meals. They're nothing elaborate, mind you, but they're shelters, at least a temporary answer."

"No orphan place," Pedro said. "They'll separate us because I'm big and Zaida's little. That's what Georges said."

Dr. Kattah wrinkled her nose, sounded snappish. "No, no, these aren't orphanages." She turned her attention to Sandra.

"In the one that was a gas station, Tonio's company provides one big meal a day, and he strong-arms all his friends for contributions."

Sandra instantly began proclaiming joyful interest.

Dr. Kattah cut her off. "There's no schooling involved—just cots and some food and a safer place to stay at night. Tonio pays somebody to guard, so the kids don't get into trouble. It's not heaven."

"Oh, but that's much better than sleeping rough on the pavement as the kids do now." Sandra controlled an urge to twist her braid. "I've spent hours on the phone and driving around Rio looking for childcare facilities. Everything was filled. Isn't this place filled, too?"

Dr. Kattah smiled. "It won't be filled if I ask."

Sandra looked closely at the younger woman, heard the pride and resolution in her voice.

She's probably rich and influential to have friends like Tonio Campelos. As long as it didn't hurt, it's a good thing Zaida had ear problems and Dr. Gomes didn't show up.

"Will you speak to Senhor Campelos?"

"Of course. Why would I have brought it up, otherwise? I'm sure he'll order that the kids be given a place in the better facility. I'll let you know when you can take them there."

Dr. Kattah patted the silver, turquoise-studded comb holding her upsweep and freed the raven mane. The dark hair, liberated, seemed to explode into the white of the room. Then she looked at her prescription pad. "Well, that's that. Now let me deal with the fluid in the little girl's ears."

Afterwards, Sandra nearly floated out onto the scalding parking lot with the kids, but Pedro kept tugging at her sleeve and trying to hold her back.

"What are you doing, Tia Sandra? I don't understand. What about my business? My shoeshine stand?"

"I'm sorry, Pedro. You must feel like people are making plans for you without talking to you about it. Please come into the car, and we'll discuss it when the air conditioning is running. The sun is making me sick."

Soon the Volkswagen was moving fast down the Praia da Botafogo. "Pedro, the doctor's offer is wonderful." She turned her head toward the kids in the backseat, seeing Zaida wiggling in the child's car seat she'd borrowed from Heloisa. "It means you'd have a better place to sleep and something good to eat that's free, and you can still work." She glanced at his face and saw his tense frown ease. "You'll need to work to earn your other food. And you'll still take care of Zaida. There are no caretakers there, only guards at night to protect you."

Pedro still looked cautious, but she thought she saw the faintest beginning of a smile. She reflected on how few times, except at the futebol match, she'd ever seen him smile. The Fiat back of her tooted, the horn angry in the afternoon traffic, and Sandra returned her attention to the road.

She dropped off Pedro and Zaida at his most recent shoeshining spot in her office's neighborhood. They removed his supplies from the trunk, and the new medicine Dr. Kattah had prescribed was in Pedro's hand. Sandra watched as he grudgingly demonstrated how he followed the doctor's orders. The reporter had to agree that he'd done it perfectly. *Age ten going on twenty, this boy.*

Then she hurried off to get to work. Sandra put a heavy foot to the accelerator during the four-block trip to Worldwide's headquarters. Bursting into the office, she streaked by Tomás' desk.

"Whew, you're certainly in a hurry," he said. "What happened? Your President is coming to visit Rio to dance the samba because he did the tango in Cuba? Brasilia has been bombed?"

"Tomás, I think your pediatrician's associate, Dr. Kattah, is going to help me get the kids off the street."

He combed his unkempt reddish beard with his right hand. "Pedro and Zaida, huh? Let me guess. You're adopting them, right?" He grinned. "Bad idea. They'll be hard on the furniture." He reached for a cigar that lay cold and dead in his big metal ashtray.

She returned the grin. "Nope, not adopting them. But I think we've found them a place to sleep where they'll be safer. A shelter run by Tonio Campelos."

"Oh, yeah? I've interviewed him once or twice. He's a big guy in mining up in Minas Gerais. Workers have died in his mines, so he assuages his conscience with good works. What makes you think you can get them into his place?"

"I told you. Your pediatrician's associate, Dr. Kattah. You must know her."

Tomás considered for a moment. "Yeah, she saw my kids once when Gomes was out of town. She's beautiful, quite young, with long black hair."

"Right, and she apparently knows this Campelos from the social circuit. Dr. Kattah told me she can get Campelos to take my kids."

"Your kids?" Tomás repeated, drawing out the "your." He stared at Sandra. "Have you ever been married? Did you live with that guy who called?" He leered at her as he spoke.

"No, yes, and you can't ask any more questions because I'm busy."

She punched in the priest's number on her cellphone and hoped for the best. Heloisa had been right. Telephones in Mulroy's area could be iffy. After a moment, though, he answered, sounding out of breath. Sandra again noticed how heavy his accent was, a curious combination of his lyrical English and the cadence of Brazilian Portuguese.

"Are you ready for good news?" she asked in English, forgetting to identify herself. "I took the kids back to the doctor—a different one, this time. This one's a woman who knows a rich guy who runs two places for street kids." Sandra explained about the shelters, stuttering as she did so. "She says she can get them into the better one."

"Well, praises be! That's a stunner, if not a miracle. What's the next step?"

"I think it's to wait for Dr. Kattah. She promised to speak to Campelos immediately and try to make arrangements. Will you come if this works, if I can take the kids there?"

"Let me know when and where to meet. We've got to approve it, after all." His voice soared. "Can't let the little ones go any old place."

NINETEEN

After Mulroy hung up from Sandra's call, he went to the stove. He decided to make more coffee, although he'd already drunk three cups that day. He knew he wouldn't sleep very well that night, but drinking coffee was his way of vegetating, meditating, praying, mourning, and celebrating.

And this is a definite cause for celebration, he thought as he leaned over the ancient black coffee pot.

The children are on the street because I failed to make sure that safe arrangements had been made for them. And now it seems they'll have at least a little precious security.

Then he began to share his thoughts aloud with the coffeepot. Mulroy noticed that he was talking to himself more often lately. Maybe it was because it was good to hear English instead of the rough Brazilian Portuguese of his parishioners. Talking to the American woman, it seemed, had awakened his preference for his native tongue.

"This shelter isn't really any permanent answer for the kids, mind you, for there's no school involved. But at least it's out of the rain and out of danger from drug dealers and pimps."

Still, much as he knew he should want to see the children again, should want to help deliver them to this promised relief of their homelessness, he wished he didn't feel obligated.

The priest poured his very strong brew into a chipped mug and sat down at the cigarette-scarred table, wishing he could have a smoke. But he'd tried to educate his church members to the dangers of tobacco, so he couldn't very well indulge himself.

"Nuthin' like a cuppa coffee," he told the rectory's venerable gas stove, "unless it's a fine dark Guinness." He couldn't buy his favorite beer unless he went to fancy hotels or pubs in Rio, and except for meeting the American woman to go on their quest, he hadn't done that in a long time.

It had also been a while since he'd seen Pedro. As he stared at the scrapes and burns on the table, Mulroy tried to picture the child. After a minute or two he called up an image of freckles, ears that stuck out and spiky hair. And somehow he'd let that child disappear to the streets of Rio—with an infant, yet. He winced and took another sip of the black liquid. It burned his offended throat. Just then, James Joyce trotted in, and he could have sworn that the dog looked at him with sympathy.

The priest pictured the house where Camila de Andrade had once lived. There were always other people in and out, relatives of the husband, it was said. But when a new baby came and the husband took off for good and Camila died, it became more like a flophouse.

"I should have moved much more quickly," the priest said aloud, ruffing James Joyce's ears. Long ago, he should have taken a trip similar to the one he'd made days before with the American reporter.

So many people in his parish had so many needs. And there was one of him and not enough time or energy or money. Yet rationalize any way he could, the result was still the same.

"Lord!" he exclaimed into the coffee mug. "How did they ever survive—a young kid and a babe like that in that city with its dope and theft and murder?" He covered his eyes with his hands to blot out the image of the children on Rio's streets.

An even more sinister image replaced it. Like a slide on a screen, it showed a boy about Pedro's age lying on the street back home in Portadown. The child's body was twisted and covered in blood. Strangely, though, the bomb that had drained the kid's life blood hadn't distorted his face. It was very white, dotted with freckles, with a small nose and a rounded chin. His lips were chalky, but their expression was relaxed, peaceful.

Mulroy remembered that image well. He would always remember that image. Many years had passed since the child was killed. Many years had passed since a young Mulroy had seen terrified, screaming people surrounding the boy's dead body. But the priest's memory of the scene remained vivid.

It was lunchtime, the mid-afternoon lunchtime fashionable among many of Rio's wealthiest citizens. Olivia Kattah sat across from Tonio Campelos at The Palms, among the city's most expensive restaurants. Tonio was buying, but of course, he should. He was one of the city's richest men, a close friend of Olivia's father, also far from poor.

As Olivia read the menu, she felt Tonio studying her carefully. He always marveled, as he often had said in recent years, at how the squiggly baby he'd once held as his godchild had turned out.

"Olivia, I can't tell you how happy I am that you asked me to get those poor children into my shelter. How wonderful that you've developed an interest in street children."

"What? Isn't taking care of sick children good enough?" For a moment, she looked beyond Tonio to the palms that grew right in the middle of the restaurant, some now surging through the skylight.

"Now, my dear, you know what I mean. I'm terribly wealthy and a little guilty about it. Sometimes I wonder if I couldn't have done better by my workers." He closed his eyes for a moment.

Olivia stirred her martini, wondering at how many pre-lunch drinks Tonio had had before arriving. She respected how swiftly alcohol can loosen the tongue, even the tongues of extremely sophisticated men like Tonio. She hoped he wasn't going to cry in his mojito.

He spoke softly. "So I started shelters for homeless kids, and I give to every charity I can think of. You're rich, Olivia, and now you're reaching out to the poor. I approve. I must tell you, though, that there was very little space left in the shelter for those kids you wanted to help. But we've made room."

"You're wonderful, Tonio." She watched with pleasure as he basked in her praise. The man across from her was old, older even than her father, but Tonio still had a full head of silver hair, and the wrinkles that darted downward from his slightly slanted hazel eyes simply added to his attractiveness. She knew she should disapprove of his obesity. But she reflected that the fact that Tonio weighed a lot more than he should have only made him seem even more substantial and impressive. He was shaped something like Luciano Pavarotti had been, and exuded a dash of the Italian tenor's charisma. "I'm very proud to know you, Olivia. You've turned out so very well." He spread the dazzlingly white linen napkin over his ample lap. "To tell you the truth, we used to worry about you sometimes."

"You mean when I was a crazy teenager? All teenage girls are wild like that."

"Well, you worried your parents sometimes. That pink spiky hair and the metal chains you sometimes wore, and your choice of friends. Boyfriends especially, as I recall. But that was a long time ago. Now you just date people of your own sort." He stated this observation as fact.

"Certainly."

With just one exception.

But she wasn't about to share that information with her old family friend. Once more she regaled Campelos with the full radiance of her smile.

"Tonio, what would you think if I ordered the lamb? I know you've said it's delicious here."

###

The following afternoon, Pedro spent a few minutes polishing the shoes of an elderly man in a white suit on Rio Branco. The suit reminded Pedro of an ice cream vendor's. Pedro was buffing hard because the patent leather didn't seem to want to shine.

"Take it easy, kid," said the old man. "You'll damage the leather."

Pedro thought, no, I won't damage it, but he nodded and mumbled, "Yes, sir." Last month he'd argued with a customer, and the man not only failed to pay, but kicked him. The pointed toe of the man's cordovan and white saddle shoe had sliced into Pedro's bare leg and left a pinkish, raised scar.

Like the scar, the memory would stay with him a long time. And, he thought, you never, never wanted a customer to get mad at you and report a complaint to a policeman. Georges had told him what could happen to street kids who drew the attention of the police.

This old guy grumbled as he paid, but he gave Pedro a handful of reais. Pedro accepted the folded, dirty bills. The price of the crackers and milk he bought for Zaida at the Rio Sul supermarket had gone up. And, she wasn't eating little jars of junior food anymore. She was eating the same, more expensive meat and cheese that he ate, cut into little pieces for her, of course.

Pedro knew how to take care of his sister, even if other people didn't think so.

He was still a little mad at Sandra for taking the two of them to those doctors. All those shots stung, though he thought he'd done a good job not to show it. Sandra said getting shots was a good thing. But he wasn't sure. The other kids at the awning didn't have any shots, and they're okay.

Yeah, he thought, but Georges died…

Pedro turned to his sister, who was playing with a plastic tube of shoe color that he'd closed tightly.

"Zaida, I'm not too sure about moving. I know the streets, feel okay here now. My business is growing. I don't know where we'd sleep." He rubbed his left eye, which felt like there was something in it. "There might be lots of other kids shining shoes. And the place for kids might well be where all the people are poor. How could I get over here in the business district during the day? Would the buses run at the right time?"

"I'm thirsty," said Zaida.

"Wait 'til we can go to the water fountain." Pedro yawned, which he often did in the afternoons. "One good thing, though; Sandra said there was no school with it. Can't go to school anymore. I haven't been to school in ages. I'd be way behind the other kids by now. They'd put me in with babies. Georges told me what school is like.

"Still, this place Sandra and the priest found should be better than sleeping on the pavement. And it would be safer for us at night. And having someone else fix some of our food would be good.

"Maybe it will be all right. We can try it, anyway."

I have to take good care of Zaida. Mamá died. There were other people in the house, but they didn't take good care of my sister.

"Hey!" he said. "This place may be all right. If we don't like it, we can just walk away."

"I'm thirsty," said Zaida again, pulling a hank of her curls. "Take me to fountain. Now, now, now, now." He grabbed the little girl's hand to grant her wish, concentrating on her steps.

A group of school children appeared from around the corner, and Pedro and Zaida were lost in the crowd. Pedro didn't notice the blue van that passed slowly by. The driver had half his head out the window.

He had a long scar that ran down under the open collar of his shirt.

A few minutes later, speeding without a destination, Efrain had a serious talk with himself. Several attempts at starting his new business had failed. He could almost feel the money from his first clients in his hands. But nothing could happen until he found a better method of gaining his goal.

New strategy needed, he told himself.
Think, Efrain, think!

Isobel Kwenten sat in the living room of Efrain de Carvalho's pink-brick house just inside Misericordia. She was reading *Vogue* in Portuguese while keeping an eye on her daughter Ana, who was moving tiny figures in a dollhouse.

Usually Isobel kept toys in the playroom, where Efrain wouldn't see either the toys or her daughter. Long ago she'd learned that he didn't welcome Ana's presence. But he hadn't been home in what seemed a long time, so on this day, she wasn't careful.

Then she heard the Rhodesian ridgeback dogs barking in back of the house.

"Oh, no," she said, "not now." She hastily started picking up the dolls, but Efrain bounded into the room before she could remove the evidence.

She decided that offense was the best defense.

"Efrain, where have you been? You've been gone for days."

"I've been so busy with work."

"Work! You don't work all night." She noticed how startled he looked.

Wait! What am I saying? I love him—and he's come home to me.

"Querida amor mía, I've been working so hard on my business." He flopped into a tapestried chair. He looked right over Ana, who continued to play with the dollhouse.

Isobel realized it had been a long time since he had used Spanish endearments to her.

She honeyed her voice. "Why didn't you call? I was so worried."

"You know I sometimes have to travel around Rio for days. Look, I've brought you a present." He reached into the hip pocket of his Levis and pulled out a necklace.

Not only is my man home again, he's brought me a beautiful necklace. I was a fool to fuss.

He rose, walked over to her, lifted her hair off her neck, fastened the necklace with amber stones that matched her hair. "I know I disappear sometimes, but you're my woman, Isobel, my only amor."

She touched the stones carefully, as though they might disappear if she handled them too energetically.

"Querida." He repeated the endearment. "I wanted to remind you of how much I care for you. I want you to help me celebrate the new business I'm starting so you'll understand why I'm away so much."

"What business? Isn't selling for Rodrigo and driving him around enough work? I mean, it's brought us so many nice things."

She looked around the room at the Louis Sixteenth desk, the Persian carpet, the heavy French drapes.

"Kids."

"What?"

"They're my new business. I'm going to be an agent who places babies and very young kids with families who want to adopt them."

"But isn't that very different from what you do now?" She hesitated a second. "Everything's going well with Rodrigo, isn't it?"

"Of course. But let's have a glass of champagne to celebrate the new work."

Isobel walked over to the wet bar. But before she handed the bottle to Efrain to uncork, she hugged and kissed him. And realizing that he hadn't scolded her for having Ana in sight, she reached down and hugged Ana, whose green eyes lit as though illuminated from some invisible inner lamp. Efrain patted the child on the head.

Isobel's eyes moistened. While he poured the drinks, she recalled how she and her baby had come to live in his house.

It was not long after Ana was born. She'd known she had to have some new clothes so she could resume taking tricks, indeed, so she could continue to feed Ana. After buying things for the baby and paying what room and board she could, she'd had little money left. She's worn a free-flowing caftan from the last days of pregnancy as she entered a high-end store in Copacabana.

"May I help you?" asked the saleslady majestically, looking her up and down. Isobel had thought the woman definitely looked snobbish. As she spoke, she tilted her head back slightly, as though smelling something not quite nice. An old bat, Isobel thought, returning her disdain.

"Please show me dresses for an elegant party. I'm invited to the French Consulate." Take that, snob, she thought.

"Really?"

"Yes, the party's tomorrow."

Under all her heavy makeup, the woman's cheeks still showed many lines, and a roll of fat undergirded her jaws. She hesitated, then showed Isobel to a fitting room and brought her an armload of dresses in her size.

In the mirrored room, Isobel spent a rueful moment looking at her stretch marks from the baby. But by dint of sheer starvation during her pregnancy, her figure looked good. It was actually better in a way. Her breasts had grown even more ample.

She tried a long teal gown and a green silk structured dress, a Louis Feraud original—but it seemed matronly to Isobel. Then she slipped into a pink silk shift that was just tight enough to send her desired message, but not as tight as the girls in the streets wore.

That was the one. Perfect.

She put on her roomy caftan over the dress, hung the other dresses back on their hangers and headed for the saleswoman, who was rehanging a rack of overpriced sweaters.

"None of these fit." Isobel dumped the rejected dresses over the saleswoman's arm. "I'll have to look elsewhere."

The saleswoman's brown eyes narrowed as she looked down at the armload.

"Where's the pink silk shift?"

"Oh, I left that one in the fitting room." Isobel walked quickly toward the exit. But the woman moved fast for an old girl. She hurried into the fitting room and returned just as Isobel neared escape.

"Wait! Stop! That dress isn't here!"

Isobel threw herself outside the door and ran directly into a man walking by.

"Stop her!" came the shriek.

The man caught Isobel in his arms, moved her away for inspection, gave her a long once-over. The saleslady surged through the door, continued to yell. But the man grinned at Isobel. He wore a blue pin-striped suit that seemed to illuminate his striking electric blue eyes.

"I'm sure there's been a mistake," said Efrain de Carvalho. "My wife wouldn't steal anything, would you, darling? Good Lord, what a misunderstanding. But let's try again. You certainly need some new threads, sweetheart."

He and the saleswoman traded remarks, but Isobel was so terrified that she didn't register a word they spoke. The man pushed her inside the store, swept over to the dress rack and announced that he'd buy all the dresses in her size.

Isobel and Efrain watched the woman's expression as greed overcame her rage at the nerve of the duo. The man had money, and lots of it, and he plunked many bills into her anxious grasp. The woman's eyes nearly left her head.

"Come on, lovely girl," Efrain said as he plunked the heavy purchases into Isobel's arms.

Outside in the boiling air, he said, "You look like someone who could use a drink of tea, maybe laced with a strong shot of bourbon."

Even though he'd rescued her, surely saved her from jail, Isobel was wary. She'd seen some very bad men in recent months. But this one was so handsome, and he talked so smoothly and comfortingly that she accepted his invitation to his house

Before long, Efrain was driving Isobel to her friend's apartment to pick up the baby. Even though he told her that he didn't care much for children, Efrain took her and the infant Ana to his lair in Misericordia. Efrain took her home.

And now on this afternoon, three years later, he popped the champagne cork and yelled "Olé," then poked her gently in the ribs.

"Hey, you seem very far away. Come and toast an exciting new adventure for you and me."

TWENTY

"Do you think I should call her?"

Back of his computer in the Worldwide Rio bureau office, Tomás Mello looked over at Sandra. "Hillary Clinton? The Duchess of Cambridge? You've gotten so famous that they might take your calls."

"Come on, Tomás."

"No, I don't think you should call Dr. Kattah, if that's who you're talking about. She promised, and from what I recall, she seems very determined and confident. If she said she'll help you, she'll do it."

"It's just that I'm so anxious that Pedro and Zaida be in safer surroundings."

He regarded Sandra with his customary leer. "No kidding. I could never have guessed."

She turned back to her own screen. It was half-filled with lines about the latest changes in the price of Brazilian coffee and the country's stalled economy. Would there be more riots? She stared at her notes, plunked loosely on the desk to the left of her word processor. Then she pecked out a few more lines. Over the top of her computer screen, she could see Tomás still staring. Damn, he did look rather handsome today, not that the wolf's appearance interested her.

Her phone rang. Sandra wondered if it was Dr. Mirabella, the agriculture minister. She'd been trying to reach her for days to get comments for the coffee story. But the caller was not Mirabella. The woman's voice on the other end of the line sounded clipped.

The caller didn't identify herself, but said in English, "Okay, Ms. Shelton. It's all arranged. Bring the kids tomorrow at noon to this address."

Sandra wrote the address and began a barrage of questions, but Dr. Kattah cut her off. "Just bring the kids." She hung up.

"My God," exulted Sandra as she replaced the receiver. "Dr. Kattah did it. I can't believe it. That woman must have incredible clout."

Tomás crooked his neck to call to her from the printer across the room. "Clout, huh? I think that was one of the first slang expressions I learned in English, Sandra. You sure need it in Washington, don't you?"

She agreed but didn't speak to his point. For weeks and weeks, she'd longed for news that the children would have at least a measure of comfort and safety in their lives. And she'd just heard the news that should help her sleep at night. But, illogically and unexpectedly, Tomás' mention of Washington broke the balloon of her elation. A pang of deep longing and regret coursed through her.

How she'd love to be among the politicians in Washington these days, writing about their moments of glory and their peccadillos. Presidential elections would take place soon—almost surely without much written about them from down here.

Maybe, if she were lucky, she'd get fifteen minutes on the air about how Brazilian politicians and other citizens viewed the American candidates. She'd write something like, "*A poll of 1,000 Brazilians shows that they favor the candidate of the United States' Democratic Party to follow Barack Obama as president. In the November election, Americans will select…*"

For a fraction of a second, she pictured home, her last home—the narrow townhouse in Georgetown. She ran a hand over her straw-colored eyebrows and pushed up her bangs. Mentally, she traveled the miles to Washington and watched the scene unfold:

It's Sunday morning. She and Charles are sitting together—close together—on the big overstuffed couch with its slipcover pattern of bamboo thatches and some sprigs of flowers they never could identify. For the last several hours, they've been making love on the king-sized bed in the sunny bedroom. Now, they've moved from the bedroom, nursing a more mundane kind of hunger.

Wearing bathrobes over bare bodies, they're stretched out before the gate-legged coffee table that didn't go well with the rest of the furniture. But they both liked it. On it are cut apples and several kinds of melon and a metallic container that keeps their coffee hot. On the other side of the table are many Sunday papers—the *New York Times*, *The Guardian*, papers from nearly everywhere. They'll delve into them after the meal.

Magic illuminated those mornings, at least in her memory. But then came that other Sunday morning, their last Sunday morning. On that day, there was no lovemaking, no elaborate breakfast. Instead, while pouring a cup of coffee, Charles announced that he'd decided to take a job in the Paris bureau of a London newspaper.

"It's better this way, Sandra," he'd said to her astonishment, for he'd never, ever once mentioned that he was considering a job change. "I think we shouldn't be living together any longer. We've talked about long-range commitment, and neither of us wanted it."

Sandra couldn't speak for a few seconds. She wanted to scream, "Neither of us ever said that. It's a lie." But she controlled herself. "You've been unhappy with me? And you haven't told me? You've never acted discontented."

"I wasn't. It's not you I'm discontented with, Sandra. I don't like working in television here. I want to write a story that's longer than four sentences. You know exactly how I feel about that. You've made that same decision. I don't like Washington anymore." His voice grew louder. "The pressure, the favoritism, the dishonesty in journalism here ... it's taken me many months to realize it—partly because you and I have been a distraction—but my job's nowhere. This will give me new opportunity, a new world."

And after his shocking announcement, he'd taken that opportunity almost immediately. Two weeks later, Charles had left her, his "distraction," and taken an apartment in Paris. Sandra could barely believe it, her trusted Charles talking like that, rejecting her so coldly, without warning. Or was there warning that she hadn't seen?

Today, in faraway Brazil, she shook her head, tossing her braid around.

"Sandra, what's the matter?" Tomás Mello's words shoved her back into the present. "A second ago you acted overjoyed. Now you look like you're somewhere else—somewhere in a sad past."

"Oh, I'm in the present now—here in Rio, making decisions for children whose names I didn't know a few weeks ago. Tomás, what am I doing? What if this isn't the right thing for the kids?"

"Americans! You think you can fix everything just fine, especially other people's lives." He thumped a balled fist on his desk. "I've been wondering what the hell you're doing all along. You know I haven't approved of your interest in these brats. They've been a lot of trouble for you. But now you've found them a place where their lives will be about a hundred percent improved. How can you possibly question that?"

"It's just such a big responsibility, and I wonder if I have the right to make decisions like this for veritable strangers."

Tomás took a ferocious tug at his beard. "Now you wonder? You rushed in where angels fear to tread! Isn't that how you say it? You should have minded your own business. But if you had to do something, it sounds like what you did was reasonable. I've never understood Americans, not to mention women, and I never will." She stared at him, then leaped from her chair.

"Tomás, I'm going to have to miss the afternoon deadline tomorrow. Will you cope?"

"I'm getting used to coping while you play mother to those brats. Far be it from you to do any work." But Tomás sounded more bemused than annoyed.

As she turned away from him, she caught that half-hungry look she was seeing more and more often now. But there was no time to think about it. Perhaps her married boss was just another reason to demand that longed-for transfer.

Because for a nanosecond, she wondered if he actually might be beginning to look attractive to her.

It's just loneliness, of course.
I'll wait until I'm sure the kids are happy and get myself away from this

office.

Tomás Mello, you're not good news.

The following afternoon, Sandra left the office early, soon after the second deadline. Tomás said he would voice her script about the latest flap over accusations of misspent Carnival funds for her daily broadcast. Her legs felt shaky and her head oddly light as she closed the wrought-iron gate of her office building behind her.

Pedro and Zaida sat on the sidewalk in front. Pedro's battered chair, his wooden footrest, and his new backpack lay beside them on the pavement. Sandra caught a glimpse of the blue blanket. Pedro had tried to fold it into the backpack, but some of the tattered material stuck out.

He wore the outfit she'd given him for the futebol game, and he'd put his baby sister into the yellow suit with the rabbit on the front that Heloisa had given her for the match. Zaida looked stuffed in; she'd grown taller and plumper in just the short time since the game. The bonnet was nowhere to be seen.

"Ready, kids? Did you say goodbye to Maria? What did she say?"

"She said she was sad that we were leaving. She said we should come back and see her and the baby." For a moment, Pedro's mouth turned down. But a smile wreathed his sister's pink Valentine mouth.

"Goin' in a car, goin' in a car," she chanted. "Gonna have good things to eat."

"Sure." But her brother didn't sound so certain. After this pronouncement, he looked up at Sandra. Today, his brown eyes seemed dark, blackened. "Will we like it there?"

For what seemed like the hundredth time, Sandra told Pedro what she now knew so well about the shelter. It once was a big gas station, now enclosed and outfitted with a kitchen and bathrooms. She told him it was a place to get out of the rain and the merciless summer sun, a place with cots for the bigger kids, and maybe a smaller bed for Zaida. She wasn't sure exactly what kind of bed it would be. They would eat a meal in the evening.

"And there's somebody there at night to guard you."

"OK."

"You'll be happy to see Father Mulroy again, won't you? You said he used to play futebol with you."

"I don't remember him much now."

Just as Pedro spoke, Mulroy appeared at the intersection, his van looking even older and dustier than Sandra remembered. As she'd seen him do on an earlier occasion, the priest pulled sideways to the curb in a no-parking zone and climbed out. She watched him step down. Again, she thought his walk was odd, quirky. He didn't exactly limp, but he seemed to slightly favor one leg. The mannerism added to the impression of age given by deep facial creases and the iron gray patches that had invaded his dark hair.

He approached the trio, looked directly at Sandra, but not the kids. At last, within touching distance, he boomed in his badly accented Portuguese, "Pedro, it's good to see you again. How you and Zaida have grown."

The kids looked up, way up, at the priest. Pedro took Mulroy's extended hand, but Zaida recoiled. She started to whimper.

"Oh, now I've scared you, have I? Sorry," Mulroy said.

Sandra scooped up Zaida. The little girl stopped sniffling as Sandra put her into the borrowed child seat in the backseat next to her brother.

"Shall we go?" Mulroy hefted Pedro's footrest, shoe-polishing supplies, and the big paper bag into the van. Pedro picked up his backpack slowly, very slowly, and climbed in next to Zaida. "Are you sure nobody will try to separate me and Zaida? And that nobody will try to make me go to school?"

"Yes." But Sandra knew she was lying about school. She would try to see about some education for Pedro. He had to become more literate and learn at least some arithmetic for starters.

It was hard to believe that he knew how to write only a few words of Portuguese, and only enough arithmetic to make sure his shoeshine customers didn't cheat him. But he knew how to survive on the streets and protect a baby sister, and for the last many months, that was all that really counted.

"Kids, the best thing is that you'll be together and safe."

###

Pedro looked around, thinking, observing, processing:

A man much older than Sandra, a man with white hair, is standing in front of the shelter place. The building looks like a big seashell with a cover. The grown-ups make a big fuss over this guy, thanking him over and over. He must be very important. His suit looks that way, though it sure must be hot.

Finally, all the thanking stops and we go inside.

The old man asks how I am today as we go into a big room. But I don't answer because I'm too busy looking around. A few big chairs are against the walls. Funny-looking beds are on the floor, maybe two dozen of them. Some more beds, over in the corner, look like prisons. They're not putting Zaida in one of those, are they? But maybe the bars keep the little kids from falling off.

The people call the old guy Tonio. Sandra whispers that he's the person who got us here and that I must call him Senhor Tonio.

He asks me if I like my new home, but I'm busy looking at his feet. He's wearing some kind of shiny black and white shoes I've never seen before. I wonder if they'd look better with polish on them.

Looks like there's a place to cook in the back, and over there's a room with those upside-down fountains. The priest calls them showers. It would be good to get wet, like jumping in the ocean on a hot day,

Maybe it's okay here. Maybe it will be all right. But will the other kids try to beat me up? What are they like? Some of the big kids on the street were bad, but at least I knew which ones were mean so I could keep out of their way. I don't know about here.

And where are all the kids, anyway?

Senhor Tonio says, "They're maybe working like you do, Pedro. A lot are in schools."

"I'm not going. I'm not a baby. I'm not going to school."

The priest tells me I'm lucky to be here. I guess so, and I guess he's okay, but he's bossy.

Zaida seems happy, though. She's humming that little song she's been trying to sing lately, ever since we went to the doctor.

###

Tonio Campelos showed the kids to the cots that would be theirs. He told Pedro that Zaida will sleep on the cot next to his because she's too big for a baby bed. One of the beds has a blue sheet with a package on it that's wrapped in red paper. The other bed had a pink sheet with a stuffed bear on it.

Pedro grabbed the red package and tugged on the sleeve of Sandra's blue cotton peasant blouse. "Is this mine? What's in it?"

"Open it!"

He pulled off the paper very carefully, thinking he might use it somehow in his shoeshine work. Inside were many small toy soldiers. He looked up.

"What are these for?" Pedro was thinking maybe he could trade them for something useful with the kids under the awning.

"Toys, they're toys," Tonio said.

"We're not babies!" But then Pedro saw Zaida pick up the bear. She rubbed its furry body along her face.

"Urso," she pronounced.

"That's right, Zaida, urso, a bear, a koala bear," Sandra said. "Koalas live in Australia. Pedro, soldiers aren't baby toys. Even grown men line them up and fight battles with them. You can make games with them."

Pedro decided to take her advice. He began arranging the red-coated soldiers across from the blue-coated ones. Soon he was maneuvering the men in his set-up quite professionally.

After a while, though, he heard Sandra and Mulroy talk about leaving. Zaida was busy with her bear and paid no attention to the adults.

"Tia Sandra!" Pedro knocked over one line of soldiers with his knee. "Will you come to see us?"

###

On the return ride from Tonio's shelter, Sandra said not a word. She didn't find her voice for at least fifteen miles.

"Isn't it amazing how hard it was to leave the kids there? Now they aren't going to sleep on the streets, subject to heaven knows-what-all dangers. But I feel guilty and sad for driving away like this."

"That's natural enough. You've been seeing 'em nearly every day recently. You must feel like a mother sendin' the little ones to camp." His brogue sounded especially thick today.

"I'll visit them often, and take them to their old neighborhood sometimes. But, frankly, I need to worry more about work and less about the kids now that they're safe. Right now I'm being noticed; because of Para´, I have new opportunities."

"If you do it right, will you get to the White House or the Capitol Hill?"

Score two points for Mulroy, she thought. "You're perceptive."

"Thanks. Words of affirmation are pretty scarce here."

"You sound more Irish each time I see you. Why is that?"

"Until I met you, I hadn't spoken much English in years—except to myself. And I call the folks back home once in a while. It seems the more I speak English, the more I remember who I am and where I came from."

"And where was that, exactly?"

"My dad was a cobbler before he retired. We lived several places, moving a couple times to where the work was best. I was born in Enniskellen, and we wound up in Portadown. My parents are still there."

"I've been there." Sandra hesitated. She could think of nothing pleasant to say. She'd been in Portadown when it was parboiling with tensions between Catholics and Protestants. For years, Orange Order parades through the relatively small Catholic areas of the city had spurred unrest.

"Don't tell me. Let me guess. You were there on assignment, right?"

"Yes. I happened to be in London on a story, and I was sent there a while back to cover a conference about some recent rough incidents. They really just amounted to pub brawls."

"And did you conclude we were all violent devils?"

"No, I'm sure most people wanted peace and quiet. But…"

"That conjunction always gets in there somewhere." Then, before she could speak, he added hastily, "As it should, of course. After all that has been negotiated and the violence suppressed, there's still an occasional fit of madness in the Six Counties."

"There's madness almost everywhere, isn't there?"

Mulroy stretched his long arms and leaned back from the wheel of the ancient van. "Not so much here, maybe. Here, on my own patch, it's apathy more than rage that's the enemy. Lots of people are too poor and hungry to be angry. I've actually been encouraged by anti-government riots so long as nobody gets hurt. The activism shows that people are gaining energy and will try to make things better."

"Is there anyone with enough money in your parish?"

"Not very many, and there's no hope of money or comfort or betterment for the others. Some folks are even half-starved."

Sandra stretched, too. "Ah, but they'll have their days in paradise, won't they? Pie in the sky by and by?"

"I hear disaffected Christian, don't I?"

"You do. Recovering Catholic, actually."

"And do you expect me to try to win back your soul?"

Now Sandra smiled. "Well, perhaps it would be interesting to hear you try."

"I won't do that. We're partners in helping the children, Pedro and his baby sister. Your soul is your responsibility."

"What? You have no easy answers, no facile sayings to get me back into the fold?"

"You understand you're bein' obnoxious, don't you?"

Sandra thought for a moment. "Yes, I guess I am. I guess I'm bitter. I took a lot of punishment from the nuns at high school, but it was the idea of God as Hell-keeper and the demeaning of women and criminal priests and—"

"Let's don't go down those roads. I don't proselytize. If it's a heretic I am, may the Lord forgive me."

"But proselytizing is part of your job description, isn't it?"

"I have more than enough to do to dissuade my people from their superstitions."

After Mulroy dropped off Sandra at the cafe where she'd parked her car, the drive back to Saint Teresa's seemed longer than usual. The air conditioning in his van had worked well while they delivered the kids to the shelter, but now he was afraid to run it lest the van overheat. It did that often these days. The Lord alone knew how old it was, and the parish couldn't afford even a second-hand replacement.

The image of Pedro and Zaida in the shelter kept leaping before his eyes. Pedro had sat on his short cot next to Zaida, who was curled up in an even shorter cot. She blinked sleepily as the adults made conversation. He'd hoped she wouldn't scream when Sandra left, but the little girl was occupied with the koala bear, and her eyes were drooping toward that instant sleep that's characteristic of small children. Mulroy thought the boy looked puzzled, a little frightened and pleased all at once.

The priest counted the months and realized how long it had been since the children had a bed, or the assurance of a meal provided by someone else. The toys, gifts from Tonio, struck him as especially poignant.

Pedro had been suspicious of the toy soldiers at first, but managed to keep his dignity while arranging them on the floor. And Zaida had immediately snuggled the brown koala. He wondered if a love for stuffed animals was inherited; he was pretty sure she'd not had many toys in her little life.

A memory of Camila de Andrade's home after her death stabbed at him. Food, sleeping bags, ashtrays, or sometimes just cigarette butts littered the floor. All cleanliness, all organization, everything of value that had belonged to Camila disappeared after she died. She'd had toys for Pedro, but what had happened to them?

Mulroy wondered if Camila's son could really be a child any more. Or had the loss of his mother, his responsibility for his young sister, and their life on the streets made him into a small, pinched adult? But at least—miraculously—it had not yet turned him towards crime, which often happened to kids on the street.

Sandra had had a difficult time leaving the children, that was plain. But she'd talked about it freely in the car, and he thought her openness would help. Wasn't confession good for the soul? The thought endowed him with a rueful grin. If that weren't true, he was in even more trouble in his profession than he thought.

Funny about Sandra. She's a journalist, after all; they're usually a shallow and self-seeking lot. And she's an American woman journalist at that.

But she isn't what I'd have expected. For some reason, she accepted the kids as her responsibility.

He couldn't think of a logical reason. So he decided there must be an illogical one, a reason of affinity, of charity, something like that. Certainly it wasn't a religious reason, from what she'd said. But then, maybe she was just repeating cynical journalist cant. He jerked the wheel to the right, realizing that he was too close to the median line.

As for him, he thought children had been his curse. His mental movie screen blackened out Pedro and again showed the dead child on the street in Portadown, lying in the blood of his short, lost life. And for the 10,000th time, the priest thought, maybe I could have stopped that murder. Maybe I could have saved that boy.

I didn't. And ever since I've preached about forgiveness, but it's only forgiveness for other people.

His mind time-travelled to Kieran and Hugh, talking in the shed back of the family's tiny row house.

"It's good, I think." Kieran was twenty at the time. As Peter Mulroy moved closer, he saw what his brother was holding.

"Primitive, nothin' much more than a Molotov cocktail." Hugh was nineteen then.

"What're you talkin' about?"

"Yeah, well, basically it's only a drink can, but I 'spose it will do. When do we go?"

"Soon, soon. Calm yourself. You'll never make it if you don't calm down."

"Who's tellin' who to calm down? And who's tellin' who about getting in?"

That was the first that Peter Mulroy knew that his brothers were trying to win trusted membership in the Irish Republican Army. He heard them talking as though he were playing a radio. If the mind can have an eye, why can't it have an ear?

All these years later, the brothers' talk was just as audible, just as real to him as it had been on that day when he was sixteen years old.

He'd been coming through the back garden when he caught snatches of the conversation. He remembered the soft swishes of the breeze blowing through the leaves of the ash tree near the shed, the birds calling to one another, the grass arising from sleep near the well-trodden footpath. He kept himself hidden as his brothers plotted in the nascent spring.

It was a moment that he might have changed. It was long ago, and it was just a minute ago. And those seconds of overheard conversation had shaped the many years that followed. It was the moment when he could have jumped out from the bushes that hid him and tried to intervene.

Or, he could have run after them as they took off for their act of protest that turned deadly.

He heard them name just the spot where the explosion would take place. It was in front of a market that was closed on Sunday. Everything on the street was closed on Sunday. No people would be around, his brothers said. They'd said it would get attention, and nobody would get hurt.

He thought he might have stopped them. But how? He couldn't have gone to the authorities. He couldn't surrender his own people to the hell that was the Maze Prison.

But, yes, he could have, somehow, without giving up his brothers. Maybe, just maybe, there might have been a way to expose the plot without betraying them. But how?

He didn't find a way.

Eventually, he'd run to the scene of the bombing, but he was only in time to see the carnage, the child's bright red blood that flowed outside the supermarket. Others from the van walked around dazedly, a couple nursing much more minor wounds. The child had been in just the right place in the vehicle to assure that he would die.

Peter Mulroy arrived too late—except to be shot by a constable. The officer assumed that the young man running away from the scene, the only supposed perpetrator he could see, was responsible. Kieran and Hugh had disappeared.

The bullet caught Mulroy in the heel. But somehow he'd gotten away. A doctor friendly to the I.R.A. tended the wound, but the young man didn't dare try to have the surgery he needed. He often still hitched a little from months of favoring the foot as it healed.

Weeks went by before he saw his older brothers again. Mulroy still lived in the family home, and the brothers shared a flat near the printing plant where they had some of the few jobs Catholics could get in those days.

The reunion came in a pub not far from Peter's family home.

Mulroy spied Kieran across the room, strode over and surprised the older brother with a blow to his jaw. The pub was crowded, and Kieran half-decked another man as he reeled from the punch. Mulroy leaned forward, righted his brother on his feet, and grabbed the collar of his work shirt.

"How could you?"

Kieran didn't pretend not to know what he was referring to. He shook off Mulroy's grip, grabbed his arm and dragged him to the street door. Unless surprised, the older brother was stronger.

"I never meant nothin' more than to set off a small bomb, nothin' more than to say we were there and have rights, for God's sake. How could we know that a van with a kid was comin'? I'm sorry the kid had to die."

Peter thought Kieran had expressed his regret in a tone suitable for scratching a car fender or accidentally stomping on someone's foot. If he'd spoken with even a hint of remorse, Mulroy wouldn't have hit him again. This punch sent Kieran to the hard pavement. He shouted in pain.

Mulroy ran. He wasn't sure afterward where he'd run to, but he ran for hours. Finally, his feet came to a stop at the scene of the bombing, now deserted. Only the police tape and a chalk outline of the child's body showed that a crime had been committed here.

It was just a dreary street, lined with the market and small shops like cleaners, jewelers, and the like. Yet Peter thought of how many people's lives the explosion at that place had changed—the dead child, the grieving family, the traumatized witnesses. And there were his brothers, who'd become murderers. The town grew more troubled, and the incident helped fuel retaliatory violence by the Protestant majority.

Mulroy also had arrived at the bomb scene too late for the life he'd planned with the auburn-haired Orla, his girlfriend from down the street, his girl since their mothers pushed the two in their strollers. He'd told Orla about his brothers, about how maybe he could have stopped the bombing and didn't. She was horrified. But she forgave him. She still wanted him, still wanted to spend a lifetime with him.

"What could you have done? You couldn't have stopped them. All you would have done is to turn on your family, your own blood."

He remembered saying goodbye to her. When he'd first told her of his decision to begin preparing for the seminary, for the priesthood, she'd clung to him and begged him to reconsider. But when the time came for them to part, she seemed cold and steely.

"You're makin' a mistake. You're tryin' to get rid of your guilt. But you can't do that. And you'll never make much of a priest, neither," she'd said. "Carryin' guilt don't make a vocation."

But he was not quite eighteen by then, and he'd experienced a forming moment on that Portadown street, a moment that made him what he was.

At this moment, decades and continents later, a bump in the Brazilian road jarred Mulroy into the present. The air conditioning in his van wasn't working at all now, and the temperature must have been close to one hundred. Still, he felt chilled.

Olivia Kattah had the day off, and she was just getting out of her swimming pool when she heard the abrupt squealing of tires in the driveway. She threw back her head to get the hair out of her eyes, dried her face, and stared through the wrought-iron fence. Yes, it was Efrain the Dangerous, as she had begun to call him in her head.

Olivia opened the gate and frowned at the black-haired man with touches of gray around his temples. He seemed more attractive each time she looked at him.

And each time he'd arrived at her home, she'd known she should tell him to run along—to leave her alone. He was a just an extended version of a one-night stand, for God's sake, just that and nothing more, just a distraction acquired at the end of a desperate day.

After all, she knew nothing about him except that he worked in the import-export business. She wondered what he imported and exported. He was a tender lover, but she sensed in him great cynicism and a restrained rage.

He was like a leopard or cheetah, she thought—sleek, fastmoving, and beautiful. But with his elegance, he carried always a sense of threat.

As soon as she opened the gate, Efrain grabbed her around the waist and lifted her off the ground.

"Goodness, you're pretty exuberant, aren't you?" she said. "And I've gotten your clothes all wet."

"That's all right. They won't be on long."

She could feel the anger rising in her body, making its way to her throat. She pulled back from him. "Aren't you being a little bold? Pushy? Presumptuous? Nobody invited you here, and nobody said you're going to take off your clothes."

He grabbed her again, held her more tightly. "Hush, all I meant was that I want a swim. That's all right, isn't it? And you did invite me, you know. You've invited me every time I've come here. Maybe you forgot?"

Olivia considered pushing him off, but his embrace tightened. She could feel him growing against her. She wanted to protest, but she felt herself relaxing, almost as though her body had a mind of its own. Her anger melted into a giggle.

"Yes, let's take another swim."

An hour later, they emerged from the pool. Olivia was still laughing.

"A first for you, my dear?" she asked. She dried her hair with a turquoise towel that was almost impossibly thick and soft. "A first at underwater ..." To her astonishment, Olivia found herself about to say "love." But she quickly amended the word to "games."

Then something unexpected happened. The breath of Rio—the hot wind from just a tad off the Tropic of Capricorn—turned chilly. Quite suddenly, a breeze blew over the swimming pool deck. The palm trees bent a little in homage to the unaccustomed wind. The lovers recoiled against the surge of cool air on their wet bodies.

"Come inside," she said as they ran shivering from the pool deck. "We'll have a drink to warm us up."

Fifteen minutes later, they were lying on the plush rug in front of the fireplace, their naked bodies wrapped in thick quilted comforters Olivia had located in a utility closet. Efrain's head rested next to hers. Every so often, they would sit up enough to sip brandy from her crystal snifters.

Efrain felt like talking. He was telling Olivia how beautiful she was when she interrupted.

"Come on, sweetie, can the line. I'd like some information. What's your Spanish accent about, Efrain?"

"I'm from Buenos Aires."

"Hmm, I was sure it was Argentina. What brought you to Rio?"

"Necessity."

"Oh?"

"Trouble. I got into trouble."

"Is your name really Efrain de Carvalho?"

"Sure, part of it, anyway."

"Carvalho's a Portuguese name. Was your dad Brazilian?"

"Not exactly."

She decided that following up on that question would be futile.

"What kind of trouble did you get into?" She rolled halfway over, propped herself on her side, and leaned on her elbow. Her face was very close to his.

"I thought you were a kids' doctor, not a shrink."

"No shrinking. But I'm curious."

"I take it I'm not your usual bill of fare."

"That's a crude way of putting it, but you're right. You do intrigue me, though—a lot. You know that. It's natural that I'd want to know more about you."

"Fine. I'll tell you the story of my life."

"Will it be true?"

"Some of it."

"So, start."

"Pour me another brandy first."

"Efrain, I think you're spoiled. Do your women always wait on you?"

He smiled. "Certainly...but maybe I'll make an exception. How 'bout if I get us both some more?"

When he returned, Olivia and Efrain settled down again in their quilts.

"Olivia, I'll tell the story of my life in one long sentence. You're not to interrupt with questions. You may make sympathetic noises, though." He cleared his throat, ran a hand over his long scar. "I grew up in Buenos Aires. I didn't know my father, and my mother had nine other kids. There were men around sometimes, but there sure wasn't anybody we called 'Papá.'

"I went to school long enough to read and write and add two and two—that's about all." He stopped, looked hard at her, started to speak again.

"You've heard this kind of story before, I'm sure. How do you call that American guy—Horatio Alger? That's it. I'm Horatio with a Spanish accent. After I left school, I sold newspapers and loose cigarettes in the streets. I had to give Mamá all the money. Eventually, I didn't go home anymore.

"I fell in with a gang. We stole stuff, tires and car parts. We used to operate along Avenida Royal. There was a snooty Catholic girls' school there." Efrain cleared his throat, took another sip of his drink, swished the liquid in the glass.

"One afternoon, a girl came out of the school when it was getting dark, and one of the guys decided to have a little fun with her. It wasn't my idea. I was just there. Okay, not innocently. I was stealing hubcaps. But scaring the kid wasn't my idea.

"Anyway, she left the school, and we ran in front of her. This guy, Paco, grabbed her shoulder and said something to her. She grabbed back at him, trying to fight him off, and he pulled out a knife. I was right behind him. I tried to get the knife out of his hand. But before I could do that, she got the knife away from him, and I got in the way."

Olivia ran her forefinger along the scar. The ugly keloid that ran from his cheek down his neck looked reddish, instead of livid, in the light of Olivia's living room.

"Spoiled your perfection, did she?" Olivia arched her eyebrows. "My God, you deserved it."

Efrain tensed and lifted himself to a sitting position. "I was in the wrong place at the wrong time. I meant no harm to any girl. I tried to protect her."

"So, what happened next?"

"She hurt me bad. I ran. We all ran. But we knew the girl would go to the police, and she got a good look at us, especially me. We were sure she was a foreigner, so of course I'd be hunted down and probably put away for life." To himself, he thought, because of a very white-skinned foreign bitch of a girl in a short plaid skirt and black knee socks. Because of her.

"I had to leave town. I made some money along the way. I landed here. I made a new life. I got some education, and now I've got a good business and lots of money."

"And a wife and six kids?"

"No wife. No kids."

His last words hung in the air.

TWENTY-ONE

It was after midnight, but the shelter was still noisy. A couple of young kids cried and mumbled in their sleep. Pedro rolled around restlessly on the soft cot. It seemed almost to swallow his body. He'd often longed for a softer place to sleep than the pavement, but now a cot seemed kind of flimsy for him.

He dreamed of ice cream with pieces of chocolate cookies in it. He dreamed of his mother, her wide red and blue cotton skirt swishing as she pulled up the threadbare sheet to his waist, patted at the deflated, torn pillow under his head on the mattress. She spoke softly as she leaned over him.

"See, it's your favorite."

He remembered smelling the sweet coldness of it, wanting it badly. He'd wanted to talk to his mother, to ask her about the store, to tell her about playing futebol. He wanted to, but he was so sleepy. And in the morning, she was gone, and the ice cream was mushy.

Pedro woke up in the shelter, momentarily terrified by the unfamiliar surroundings. He jumped out of the new bed. As his feet touched the warm linoleum floor, he remembered where he was. He looked over at Zaida, who was lying on her stomach. She snored a little as she slept. She rolled over onto her back and reached for the stuffed koala and snored some more.

Pedro leaned down, picked up a toy soldier, and put it beneath his pillow.

###

Sandra also dreamed of ice cream that night. The dream, strangely, was a vivid, nearly accurate re-creation of a real scene from a few days before, when she'd bought ice cream cones for the children. She could have sworn that for a second, she'd seen Pedro's chin tremble. Then he wolfed the ice cream. But in her dream, after scarfing it down, he cried and called for his mother.

Next, her dream fast-forwarded to Georgetown, the bedroom in Georgetown she and Charles had shared. This dream was another realistic re-run of a true incident.

It was a summer day, or seemed to be; she and Charles wore shorts and T-shirts. And they were not wearing those clothes for long. In her dream, as in uncounted times in their life together, they'd undressed quickly, pulled back the cotton window-pane-checked comforter, and dived onto the sheets. Strands of Charles' black hair lay over her arm. She remembered how dark the hair looked against the whiteness of her skin.

On those mauve sheets—and underneath the comforter in the winter— she was certain there were no other lovers in the world like her and Charles.

Their lovemaking always made her think of the tropical island where their relationship had begun. Oh, they'd nodded to each other before at State Department briefings or at the Defense Department, but their life together had started in Grenada. Their editors had sent them there to mark an anniversary of the American invasion of the island in the 1980s. They were to observe and chronicle the island's economic progress, or lack of it over time, and also write some features.

At the time of their assignments, they worked separately, then together. And after three days, they'd found themselves making love in the big rope hammock by the empty hotel swimming pool at four in the morning.

And over the years, their lovemaking continued to remind her of a tropical night, even in the middle of dreary Washington winters. She often felt she could sense the moist breeze on the frangipani bushes, the sweetness of the hibiscus.

"So, what do you want to do tonight?" she'd said after they made love.

"More of this."

Sandra awoke, probably because of the tears on her face. She thought, improbably, of a *Star Trek* episode in which one character from a far flung planet had an unusual ability. He could banish others' memories with a special touch. She wished she were a character on the sci-fi program. She wished this assassin of memories would carve away parts of her past. She wished she were someone else, someplace else.

Finally, she succeeded in waking herself up. Just the other day, she was happy to tear up Charles' phone number. But on this night, thoughts of their former happiness left her bereaved.

Isobel Kwenten sat in her living room in Misericordia. She'd just poured herself a Guarana instead of her usual cocktail. Efrain was out somewhere on his new business. But never mind. She was especially delighted that he'd said she could help him with his new business. Never before had he trusted her with the details of his work. Though she'd picked up some suspicious conversations over time, she preferred to vaguely hope that Efrain's work was mainly honest.

She knew the Misericordia organization dealt with marijuana—harmless, of course—and sometimes prostitutes, as she had been. Most had been very poor girls, like herself, who'd learned that they couldn't make a living in the city any other way. But others wanted to use their youth and looks to make as much money as possible. Some had repeated abortions.

Not me, though. Never me. My sister and brothers never even answered my letters after I came to Rio. I was alone in the world except for my Ana, at least until Efrain came along.

For a moment in the chilly, air-conditioned living room, Isobel saw herself at fourteen, helping on the farm. With all the kids in the family, there was almost never enough to eat. One day, a tourist lost on a nearby road passed by. He spotted Isobel planting corn in the scalding heat, hailed her to ask directions. He'd remarked on her beauty and asked why such a lovely girl was working in the fields instead of becoming the darling of Rio.

"Don't be a peasant," the man had said. "Find a place where you can have a better life!" In return for driving directions, he'd sewn the idea of going to Rio in Isobel's brain. She waited two years before hopping onto a truck for her new life, which was to be in the most glamorous and beautiful place on earth, the place where the Carnival never stopped.

Then came reality—and Efrain. He was her man, and she longed to please him. He was her salvation.

###

Next evening, Efrain and Olivia Kattah again were drinking Cuban mojitos at The Breezes, where they'd met. The place suited her well. She was sure she'd never see anyone she knew there. The nightclub was like Efrain himself. His murky world held a strong attraction, but she would not have recommended the club to people in the world she normally inhabited.

She stirred her cocktail, trying futilely to extricate a leaf of mint from beneath several ice cubes. Other customers looked at them with admiration. She wore a white linen dress and Efrain wore a white sharkskin suit. Olivia thought they looked like a handsome couple who'd planned their outfits that way while dressing at home.

"So, my love, you're a kids' doctor," Efrain said. "Do you know any kids without homes? Gotta be very little—like two or three and under. Preferably under."

Olivia lifted one dark arched eyebrow and half-smiled. "Let me guess where that came from. You long for fatherhood. You are so paternal that you want to adopt a baby."

He snorted.

"Right. Actually, I've met an American couple who are desperate for a kid. They're customers of mine. They're already in their late forties. He has diabetes and something the matter with his heart. He's Buddhist, and she's Catholic. Or, was it the other way around? Anyway, they didn't fit the picture of ideal adoptive parents back home. No agency there would give them a baby. And the Chinese also said no."

"How do you know about these people?"

"Met them in my import-export business."

"Efrain, is that what you really do?"

She felt, rather than saw, a shock go through him. Was it possible he didn't know she suspected he was lying?

"I told you, import and export. You know, textiles: Everything from tapestries to silk for fancy T-shirts." In the half-light of the room, his scar looked green, outlined by the greenish light from the bar. She recalled how it got there and winced.

"Hey, do I scare you? I'm just tryin' to do a favor for some customers."

"Look, you can't just buy them a baby. There's the bureaucracy to go through. It can take months, maybe even longer. And, you know, if these people are unacceptable as adoptive parents in the United States, they're probably just as unacceptable here."

"But foreigners get kids down here, even older people. I know they do. Where do they get them if they can't go through normal channels?"

"Dunno." Olivia's voice came from behind a mint leaf.

"Come on, Olivia. You must know some kids who don't have homes."

She yawned. "I never work in the charity clinic or anyplace else where I'd see orphans."

"Why not?"

"They're not my problem."

Efrain shook his head. "Somebody ought to take an interest in poor kids."

Her voice hardened. "Efrain, are you telling me that I ought to be a do-gooder? Why, you're probably on the very edge of the law. You're probably still wanted in Buenos Aires. You've got your nerve."

Efrain's face darkened, making the scar more distinct. For an instant, he looked as though he might yell at her. Instead, he gulped his mojito and said, "Cool down, honey."

Olivia realized that her head was beginning to feel as though it had been placed crookedly on her neck. The mojitos, of course. The usually icy air conditioning of the bar seemed to have warmed up, too.

"Actually, I did run into some orphans the other day. It's an odd business. An American reporter brought them in to my boss, Dr. Gomes, for exams and shots. A very scruffy boy, almost eleven, and a cute girl getting on toward three."

Now Efrain was taking a turn at fumbling in his mostly empty glass in search of the green mint leaf. "What did she do that for? She's trying to adopt them?"

"No, she's not adopting them. I think she's just assigned here in Rio for a while. I helped her get them into a shelter the other day, Antonio Campelos' shelter. You know, the man who made his fortune in the mines. Those kids don't have much of a future. But there's less of a chance of their being assaulted or used as sex slaves." She realized that her words were starting to slur.

"The boy's hopeless," she said. "He's too old to learn anything, I'd imagine. The little girl could clean up nicely and be educated if she had a chance. I thought she seemed very bright. Actually, she might be adoptable if someone didn't care that she's a toddler, not a tiny baby, and that she hasn't had normal care. But hell, Efrain, why are we talking about street kids?"

He smiled. "Because, my dear, I think it bothers you that the little girl's life is going to be wasted. Why, she'll be taking tricks by the time she's ten."

"You might be right. But it's not my business."

"You could make it your business. You could help her get a good home."

"I got the kids into a shelter. I don't want any more involvement."

"You wouldn't have to be involved." His grin broadened. "The kid could just find her way to that couple who want a baby so bad."

"Forget it, Efrain. Let's talk about something more interesting."

###

Two hours later, Olivia and Efrain were again lying on quilts in her living room. She looked up at the high ceiling with its rococo drawings. One of them depicted Leda being raped by a swan. Though Olivia had seen it perhaps 1,000 times, she giggled.

She felt muzzy, befogged by the mojitos. She couldn't remember inviting Efrain back home with her. Now, after their lovemaking, she wanted desperately to go to bed—alone. "Efrain, please go home. I've got to be at the hospital early in the morning." She withdrew her left arm, which was asleep, from under his neck and looked for her watch. But she'd taken it off.

"You were going to tell me more about those kids, Olivia."

"What?"

"The kids the American reporter was dragging around. The ones you got into the shelter. What shelter?"

She sat up, looked down at the face of Efrain de Carvalho. "Efrain, that little girl is cute enough, but she's a street kid. She has a family of sorts, that brother of hers. He's too old to be placed with a family. Nobody sensible would want him. He's too far gone. And it would be cruel to break them up."

Olivia paused, looked again at the high ceiling with its mahogany beams. "Surely your friends wouldn't want to deal with children with a background like the kids I helped. Anyway, I think foreigners would have to wait at least a year for a child. They have to be affiliated with an international adoption organization before they can even apply. That group needs to be certified and licensed. The paper shifting must be awesome. Forget it. Your friends will just have to look elsewhere."

Efrain fixed his gaze on her.

"My love, you have clout. You must have great clout to get those kids into that rich guy's shelter. You could get that little girl for me quickly—for my friends."

Efrain, you're becoming tiresome. "Get going, will you? I have to get up at five o'clock and be alert. Hello, I'm a responsible kids' doctor, remember?"

"Stop pestering me about those kids," Olivia said as she and Efrain emerged from the swimming pool the following night. "I'm beginning to wonder if it's me you want, or information about some grungy children so you can sell them."

Efrain toweled his face carefully, as though it were sore. After all these years, his scar sometimes still felt tender when his skin was wet. "I don't love you at all, mi querida amor. I'd sell you for ten reais." He snapped the towel smartly at her rump, which was barely covered by the smallest polka dot bikini bottom. She wore no top. "For goodness sakes, if you're so anxious to find out about that little girl, go talk to Tonio Campelos' people who run the shelter."

Efrain stopped drying himself. "Which shelter? Where is it?"

She told him. "End of subject, OK?"

"Ah, yes." He pulled her close, feeling her bare breasts harden against his chest. "End of subject."

TWENTY-TWO

Tomás Mello answered the landline telephone in the Worldwide office to hear the voice of the network's managing editor in New York.

"Listen, you've got to get that girl to write more features. She's a find."

Usually Tomás thought the boss in New York was a pain. But he'd got it right about Sandra Shelton. "That girl" was indeed a find, both as a writer and also as a…well, what? Tomás had a black book filled with women's names. But he had no real feeling for them.

This woman, this uppity American reporter, was different.

I made a mistake dismissing her interest in those street urchins. But I'm going to change that.

He took a puff on his expensive Cuban cigar and inhaled deeply, savoring the smoke.

###

Midnight in the shelter. Silence. Only an occasional snore or sigh emanated from the two dozen or so cots in the big dormitory room.

But something awakened Zaida.

Quiet…bed so soft…not hard like the street. Pedro there next to me.

Where's Urso? So sleepy. But I'm moving, being lifted up. Tia Sandra? No. No. Big man with scratchy whiskers. Pedro! Where are you? Where are we going? Pedro, wake up!

NO NO NO NO NO!

She screamed and kicked the man, but he ran very fast through the room. Clutching her in his arms, he ran right past someone at the door.

"Pedro, help me!"

Her brother roused quickly and ran after the man holding her so tight, hurting her. It was no use. Zaida and the man were out of the building in a dreadful minute. A few seconds more and Zaida de Andrade was in a car, screaming in terror as it sped into the night.

TWENTY-THREE

Olivia Kattah was drinking her customary strong coffee with a spare teaspoon of cane sugar in the doctors' lounge. Her boss, Dr. Gomes, entered with stooped shoulders. Instead of his usual cheerful wave, he shook his head.

"Something wrong?"

"It's the damned weirdest thing, Olivia. That little homeless girl we both saw in the office, you know, the one you got into the shelter. She's been kidnapped."

Olivia placed her coffee cup on the table before her. Her hand moved very slowly and deliberately. The top of her head burned, as though lightning had struck her hair. Her throat thickened. A few seconds passed before she found her voice.

"What? What happened? How do you know?"

"That reporter who was looking after the kids called me. Tonio Campelos notified her. The boy, the brother, is hysterical. Campelos was pretty upset, too. The guy he hired to watch the place during the night hadn't locked up the front door. So Campelos is blaming himself. Now, who the hell would steal a street kid?"

Olivia hesitated. The sensation in her forehead resembled a physical blow. She willed herself to sound casual. "Well, at least there's no terrified, grieving parents. I mean, the kid has no family." Gomes looked at her curiously.

"But you saw those children. There's the brother. He managed to take care of that baby, alone, on the streets of Rio. He has no one else in the world. And I just told you, he's hysterical."
"Of course." But this time, Olivia's voice sounded uncharacteristically soft in her ears. "I'm not registering information very well this morning because I'm getting a migraine." She hesitated. "Would you mind terribly if I went home?"

Olivia turned her ankle as she hurried over the steaming hospital parking lot pavement to her car. She cursed aloud but continued running on her stiletto heels. She needed to talk to Efrain.

Had he betrayed her trust?

No, she thought, she'd gone off on a silly, illogical tangent. Been reading too many whodunits. The kidnapper was some pervert who'd seen the pretty toddler on the street and followed as she was taken to Campelos' shelter. Or he was a nutter who just happened to invade the shelter and grab a kid at random, a disturbed person showing the world what he thought of it, like those shooters in the United States.

That was it. That was horrible, but it had to be like that. Why was she jumping to conclusions? Wasn't she supposed to be analytical?

As she started the car engine, Olivia asked herself exactly where she would look for Efrain. He'd always been close-mouthed about where he worked and lived. He'd given only his cellphone number, and never a street address. And he hadn't called her in several days.

Olivia made a right turn into the street from the hospital parking lot, narrowly missing a woman pushing a stroller. The woman waved a fist.

"I have to get control of myself!" Olivia said aloud. She pulled over from the boulevard into the nearest side street and punched in Efrain's cellphone number. The phone rang several times. Then his voice came through, insinuating and inviting.

"This is Efrain de Carvalho. Leave me a message." No please, no name of his business, nothing but a terse, "Leave me a message."

She deliberately honeyed her voice. "Darling, I can get the morning off. Any chance you'd like an early swim?"

Efrain hurried from the copying machine in the drugstore, hands full of duplicated documents. The papers looked impressive. For the first time in months, he couldn't wait to get home to Isobel.

So far, luck was with him.

The American couple who wanted to adopt a child had swallowed his story about the kid Efrain was going to present them with. He had all the proper papers forged, including a document showing surrender of parental rights by a fictitious biological mother.

Efrain thought either they were terribly naïve, or they understood the situation and didn't care. But that wasn't his business. He also wondered how they'd get the child out of Brazil with the phony papers. That wasn't his business, either. But he felt a little nervous, needed to reassure himself. He was used to peddling cocaine, not children.

This deal will go down all right, and by tomorrow I'll have satisfied Rodrigo Suares with that lovely huge pile of American dollars I'll get for the kid. Unlike what he'd heard about most people wanting to adopt tiny infants, these people were especially excited about getting a two-yearold.

"Gee, maybe she won't wake up in the middle of the night to eat, and we probably won't have to do potty training," the prospective mother had exclaimed.

Tonio's telephone call about the kidnapping had awakened Sandra before first light the morning after Zaida disappeared. Somehow, she showered, dressed, threw some food at Marmalade's bowl, found her car keys, and drove to the shelter. But as she pulled in, she couldn't remember doing any of that.

"Let me in! I brought Zaida here!" she exclaimed to the policeman on the sidewalk in front of the entrance. She tried to control the fear in her voice. "I was responsible for her coming here." But the cop blocked her way.

"Senhorita, you've just crashed through the crime-scene tape. You're violating police regulations. And there's a priest in there now. He says he brought the girl and her brother here. He's trying to calm the brother and help us get answers from him."

Sandra attempted to move around the officer. But he held up his hand, arm outstretched with the palm straight up like a traffic cop at a busy intersection.

Her own hands shaking, Sandra tried the priest's cellphone. It took her three tries to get the right number, but she heard only a message that she should leave her name and Father Mulroy would return her call as soon as possible. Her throat tightened; she felt she might choke.

One child, a child with no parents, had disappeared into the Brazilian night, disappeared with no trace of her captors. Would the police try hard to find Zaida? Maybe they would, but how could they even begin a search? Something like fourteen million people lived in Rio.

Who might have broken into a shelter for homeless kids and taken the little girl? Tonio was offering a healthy reward for information. Yet the cop at the shelter door told Sandra that the mining millionaire hadn't received any sort of note or call. He said the police didn't think the motive for the snatch was financial.

The thought of another possible motive, a pervert grabbing a little girl for sex, made Sandra sick.

After what seemed like many minutes, Mulroy and a tall, very dark-skinned man in plain clothes emerged from the building.

"How's Pedro?"

"Terrible." Mulroy rubbed his forehead as if to remove the image of the child as he'd found him. "First he was hysterical, and then he went quiet. He refused to answer any questions. Truth is, I don't think he saw anything much. The kidnapper was quick."

"Oh, God, how could this have happened? What can you do to find Zaida?" She grasped at the arm of the policeman, who introduced himself as Delegado Ademir.

"We've put out a bulletin, of course, alerted the city, and the posters with her photo will be online and all over within a few hours.

And the PF, the Policia Federal, have entered the case."

Ademir took out a handkerchief and rubbed his sweating forehead. "But the security guard didn't see the car in the dark, so we don't have a description or license plate. And he didn't even get a fleeting impression of the guy who snatched her. All we know is that it's a man." He freed the arm Sandra was holding captive and waved it in an arc to indicate the neighborhood. "We'll ask around, of course, but there's not much possibility of witnesses. There wouldn't be very many people up and about at that time of night."

He spoke slowly, not really looking at her or Peter Mulroy. In his words, Sandra heard no hope.

"But, don't you see, you have to find her!"

"We can only try." The cop turned away.

"Mulroy, we need to talk to Pedro."

The priest put a hand on Sandra's shoulder.

"Tonio called a doctor and Pedro's had a sedative. He's sleeping now. The truth is, you may be the person who can do the most to find her. Why don't you get back to your office and write about what happened? Put the kids' picture on your website. I heard your broadcasts about Para´. You can move people."

TWENTY-FOUR

It was morning by the time she arrived at the office, but Tomás wasn't in, and Nilda wasn't around, either. Sandra fell, rather than sat, on her chair and stared at the screensaver on her desktop. The image showed an ocean scene in which waves lapped on a tropical shore. The beach was surpassingly beautiful; perhaps it was nearby—at Copacabana, maybe. The image was not identified. The lush scene spoke of pleasure and contentment, and here she was, half-wild with fear. How could anyone possibly trace one tiny child among multitudes?

Sandra felt nausea coming, then scolded herself. Wasn't she an adult, supposedly a smart one? Hadn't she spent years as a reporter? Couldn't she ask questions, badger the officers on the case? Get public support? Stir people up? Somebody among the Cariocas, somebody besides the criminal who snatched her, must know what happened to Zaida.

Sandra banged out a short broadcast about the missing child and posted both kids' photos on Worldwide's website. Taking action made her feel better. Other media were picking up the story. Tonio Campelos made a televised appeal for help from the public.

Then she heard a key in the door.

"Olá," said Tomás. "What's up?" He gave a long look to her loosely hanging hair and flushed face. "Why do you look so flustered?"

Damn, she thought.

To her horror, Sandra could feel the moisture forming in her eyes.

"Zaida's been kidnapped," she said. "Snatched from the shelter."

Tomás stared as he processed the information. She could see total disbelief on his face. Then he walked purposefully toward her desk.

"Taken from the shelter?" He tweaked his mustache. "Ridiculous! She just got up and left."

"Right! She's not even three years old and she wandered out for a stroll in the night. Tomás, the watchman hadn't locked up when the kidnapper pushed him and ran out the exit door. The guy saw the man throw her into a car and drive off."

"You're not making sense." Tomás barked. "It could be a pervert who saw her on the street and wanted her for…." Seeing Sandra's face, he hesitated, decided not to finish the sentence. "You said she was a pretty little thing. And light skinned. For all I know, there's a black market for babies here."

"But who would know there was a cute young child there in the shelter?"

"Maybe somebody who saw the kids on the street and figured the little girl was marketable."

"How will I ever find her?"

"You won't find her. Millions of people live in Rio. Why are you so obsessed with these children?"

He was shouting. Sandra sobbed. She felt she could almost watch herself, the supposedly competent professional woman, making a scene in front of her boss. He could never understand, just as it seemed he could never quit trying to get her to bed. Somehow she willed herself to stop crying.

Tomás leaned way down, his face close to hers. He reached for her hand. "I think you need a drink."

Like a child, Sandra stood quietly while Tomás called Nilda and asked her to come in and take over the next broadcasts. Like a child, Sandra let herself be led from the office. Maybe Tomás was right. She needed a drink.

###

As Mulroy entered the dormitory room at the shelter, he found Pedro sitting near his cot, staring straight ahead. Next to the bed lay Pedro's footstool and clean clothes, all in a heap topped by Zaida's koala bear. The stuffed animal stared forlornly at the ceiling.

A dark-skinned woman wearing jeans and a blue oilcloth coverall stopped the priest as he approached. Her lapel pin read "Volunteer."

"You won't get him to talk, Father. He's acting mute ever since somebody snatched his sister. Strangest thing we ever saw here. Senhor Tonio created this place because nobody wanted these homeless kids. But somebody wanted Pedro's little sister." She wiped her perspiring forehead; the shelter's air conditioning wasn't working well that day.

"We're keeping an eye on him so he doesn't run away to try to find her. But we think he knows his best bet is to stay here while the police look for her."

Mulroy nodded. He didn't think the cops were going to get anywhere. They didn't have much to start with, after all. No witnesses. And, searching in the children's immediate background, they'd had no luck in the homeless encampment under the awning. Almost nobody there acted as if they knew the kids.

When interviewed, it seemed that only a teenage girl called Maria would even admit knowing them. She was terribly worried and blamed Sandra, whom she called "that gringa," for taking Pedro and Zaida away from the awning.

Mulroy moved around the volunteer, whose stout body had blocked his way.

"Pedro."

The child continued staring, not replying.

Then: "You! You brought me here. You and Sandra. You said everything would be better here. And now Zaida's gone. Get away from me!"

"Pedro, I'm trying to help."

"You've ruined everything. You've let them take my sister." He began to flail his thin arms at the priest.

Mulroy switched to English. "I'm sorry. I've never done right by you or your family." He switched back to Portuguese: "But I'm going to find your sister."

Pedro howled even louder.

Mulroy suddenly understood that if he didn't find Zaida, he'd die trying.

TWENTY-FIVE

Sandra woke up in her bed when Tomás left. She heard the creaking of the front door over the whistling of her apartment's inadequate air conditioner. Her watch said it was midafternoon, and her head hurt badly. She stretched tentatively in her Brazilian bed, which still felt foreign. It took her a few seconds to remember what had happened. She'd left the office with Tomás for his club. He'd tried to get her to eat something. But instead, she'd drunk some strong Brazilian liquor without taking a bite of food. As he signed the check, he said he'd take her to her apartment.

"No! My car is back at the office."

"Don't you realize you're high? You're slurring your words. Your car will be fine there. I'll take you home."

Now, hours later, she looked out the window of her apartment at the street below.

People were walking up and down carrying groceries, carrying briefcases. Right in front of her building, children were playing hopscotch. A little boy grabbed a small dog, a terrier that was chasing a ball dangerously near traffic. The boy carried the dog to safety on the curb.

Life was continuing. But Zaida de Andrade, not quite three years old, might be dead. "What have I done?" Sandra said aloud.

Marmalade padded into the bedroom, looked at her curiously. Sandra returned the stare and talked to the cat.

"Good for you, Sandra! Your blundering meddling's helped ruin two little lives—maybe end one of them. And you've committed the ultimate cliché. You got drunk and took comfort with somebody you don't care for. A somebody who's your boss, yet. Your married boss."

The trouble is Charles. It's having to work in this country. It's being so homesick. It's having to work for Tomás. It's everything. And I've managed to hurt kids who were already victims.

Marmalade continued watching her, unblinking yellow eyes wide with accusation.

"You wanted to see me?"

Dr. Olivia Kattah stood in the door of the first-floor conference room at Wilson Azevedo Hospital. She scanned her visitor curiously. He was a tall, weary-looking man of middle years wearing the black suit of a clergyman. His white clerical collar looked dingy and gray.

"Is one of your parishioners a patient of mine?" But from his appearance, she didn't think so.

Mulroy accepted the wave of her well-manicured hand as an invitation to sit in a mahogany chair. "I came about a homeless child you treated recently. Little girl. Zaida de Andrade by name. I understand you helped place her and her brother in Tonio Campelos' shelter."

"And...?" Olivia pulled a pencil from the pocket of her white coat.

"Well, the child has disappeared—kidnapped, it seems. Her brother is..."

"Catatonic. Dr. Gomes told me about it." Her hand shook around the pencil. "We'll see him here if you want to bring him."

"No. I don't want to consult you as a doctor. I'd like to know if there might have been anyone else besides us and a few volunteers who knew that we took the children to the shelter."

Olivia feigned a gasp. "Surely, you don't imagine that the kid was selected on purpose? That a homeless kid was the deliberate target of a kidnapper? I mean, she's been on the street a long time. Anyone, any pervert, might have spotted her and wanted to…"

The priest said nothing but watched her carefully. There was a long silence before she spoke again.

"I heard the caretaker wasn't alert and didn't even see the intruder enter, didn't know he was there until the guy grabbed the girl and was leaving. Maybe the old guy accepted money to let someone take her."

"No. That man's an old employee of Tonio Campelos' mining company. Senhor Campelos hired him as a guard to boost his retirement. The guy was asleep on the job. But he's not a criminal."

"Then you've talked to the guard, or to Tonio." Her eyes narrowed. "May I ask what your interest is?"

"The children were in my parish out beyond Flores. They ran away to Rio. Just a few people knew they'd been moved into the shelter. Just you, Tonio, the reporter Sandra Shelton, me, and a couple of shelter volunteers, very good people. I'm trying to find out if any of us might have mentioned it within earshot of someone who might conceivably be untrustworthy."

"As for me, certainly not!" Olivia raged inwardly. How could this shabby-looking man possibly think she mixed with people who'd know a kidnapper? But she instantly recognized the bitter irony in that thought. How had she reacted to the news of the child's disappearance? With immediate suspicion of Efrain, that's how.

Days and nights passed in front of Olivia's eyes, days and nights with Efrain. Was that even his real name? For in the past hours, he hadn't responded to her many messages. He'd removed her suddenly and surgically from his life.

She'd known he was shady. That was half the fun of their affair. But she'd thought he truly cared for her, at least a little. They had great sex. But now it seemed she'd become only a conduit to what he wanted even more than her—a child to sell for an illegal adoption. Efrain was not just an excitingly mysterious lover. Efrain was a criminal.

The man who now sat in front of her was twice her age, a representative of religion, something she cared nothing about. There was no reason to answer his questions. She could get rid of him in a tick. But her rage at Efrain surfaced in the priest's presence.

"I did talk about those kids to someone…a man." She stopped, fingered the nameplate on her white coat.

She could see Efrain's face before her, with its scar that ran down to his collarbone. Maybe he was laughing at her—a rich-bitch who'd gone slumming and fallen for his romantic presence. He'd been attracted to her, all right, but the attraction gave way when he thought he could use her to gain what he undoubtedly wanted.

Olivia watched her relationship with him again flicker on fastforward across her mental screen. She understood that she'd become an object, a step toward a goal. She no longer meant anything to Efrain.

Mulroy waited.

Olivia cleared her throat, trying to control her visions and her rage.

"I did speak about those children to a new friend. After all, it was hardly a secret. He could have said something in front of a dishonest employee, or someone working on his cars or…"

Hearing herself sound ridiculous and fumbling in the large and mostly empty conference room, Olivia coughed and cleared her throat again. She hesitated for almost a minute. Mulroy let the silence work on her.

"I guess… I guess…" She stumbled, then resumed. "I could tell you what little I know about that man."

TWENTY-SIX

Sandra put many ice cubes on her eyelids before returning to the office by taxi. She wanted to see Pedro. But she thought the priest was right. The important thing was to keep writing broadcasts about his missing sister. She could gain attention that way. Once again she was at her computer.

"A child has been taken from the only family she has known in her not-yet-three years of life. Zaida de Andrade was sleeping in a shelter, clutching the only toy she has, a stuffed koala bear, when…"

She spun out the children's story, relating how she'd met them and grown to care for them. She realized she'd rarely written with so much emotion.

As she typed, local television channels called and invited her to record a plea for the little girl's return. Minutes later, CNN International and France 24, in need of human-interest material, set up live interviews. Twitter and other social media exploded with tips, good wishes, prayers.

I've become part of the story. It's because I went to Pará and wrote about it that there's so much interest in finding Zaida. Who knew that one little girl with no family and no home could arouse so much caring?

Sandra didn't look away from her screen when Tomás entered the Worldwide bureau. He said "Oi" and sat down and banged away on his keyboard while she pounded, harder than usual, on hers.

Neither looked each other's way. Nilda appeared, assessed the atmosphere in the room, and began to chatter about her personal botanic garden.

"I just think these amaryllis are doing beautifully. But they need some soil-food." She bustled from plant to plant with a package of fertilizer and a small watering can, humming as she quenched her charges' thirst.

Hurrah for her, Sandra thought. Nilda the office tropical gardener was playing Nilda the welcome distraction.

Sandra was starting another feature about homeless children in general and the missing little girl in particular when Mulroy strode into the office. He charged up to her desk without looking at Nilda or Tomás.

Peter Mulroy wore khaki slacks, a green sport shirt, and his venerable loafers. Without his cassock and priestly collar, he looked like a middle-aged, slightly down-at-the-heels businessman. His face expressed determination.

He spoke uncharacteristically fast. "Dr. Kattah says she told some guy about helping the kids get into the shelter and told him where it was."

"But what does that have to do with anything? I doubt the doctor hobnobs with kidnappers who snatch little girls in the night."

"There, you could be wrong. The doctor worded her information very carefully, very defensively. But it sounds like she confided in a sleazy guy. She had a fling with this man. She said he's been nagging her to find him a kid for friends who want to adopt and can't do it legally." He took a breath and resumed. "She met this man in a crummy nightclub when she was slumming, lookin' for a little excitement on the shady side, it sounds like. She doesn't know where the guy lives or works. He told her he was in the import-export business. She has only a cellphone number, and he's not answerin' now." Mulroy's words ran together.

"I've been doin' some research. She said her friend calls himself Efrain de Carvalho, the name of a drug trafficker in Misericordia. He's kind of a middle-level crook in the operation of a man named Rodrigo Suares. I think our man may be using his real name."

"That doesn't make sense, Mulroy. Why would he give his real name?"

"Don't know, but maybe it's out of sheer ego. Maybe givin' his name to an unsuspectin' woman so far from his world was a kind of private joke. He's got no address, no licenses for his vehicles, no nothin.' The police know about his criminal activities. But he's smallfry compared to his boss, Suares. That's the man the cops'd like to send to prison. They've never been able to pull together a case that would stand up in court."

Sandra whistled. "You'd make a good reporter." Then the tsunami of her deep gloom rolled over her again. "But how in the world could we follow up on Olivia's suspicions?"

The tall priest loomed over her desk. "I've got one idea." His speech sounded more Irish with every word. "Dr. Kattah said they met in The Breezes, an American nightclub near Rocinha. She said people there seemed to know him, that he'd been frequentin' the place. Maybe we can find out where he lives."

"Whoa! How did you get all that information out of the woman? I mean, why would she admit knowing some low-life crook like that?"

"Give me credit for a few skills, will you? I hear confessions all the time." He grinned ruefully, then sobered. "She was embarrassed at first, for sure, but she's very angry with this man. That was plain. After she thought it over, it seemed like she was happy to give me information that might harm him. It's obvious she wouldn't mind seein' him interrogated by the police."

Sandra stood up. "I can't imagine what we could learn at that bar, but it's better than doing nothing. Let's try."

She swept out of the office without a word to Tomás. He didn't look up as she and the priest passed his desk.

###

An hour later, Sandra and Mulroy stood at the bar at The Breezes nightclub. It was still very early, and the place was quiet. Sandra sipped her mojito slowly, her head still aching from her night of whatever that fatal liquor was, her night with Tomás Mello. She watched as Mulroy quickly downed a Skol beer from a chopp.

Sweat poured into the frayed neck of the priest's open-collar shirt, although the air conditioning was frigid. Except for his very Celtic complexion, she thought he looked like the few other customers in the bar—a little shabby, but not destitute, either. She wondered again what they were doing there, why they'd jumped at this chance for information when their plan seemed dubious at best, hopeless at worst.

What's the saying? Desperation is the mother of invention—something like that.

Could they possibly find some trace of a man Dr. Kattah had met here during an evening of excitement-seeking slumming? Sandra doubted it. Instead, she thought they were acting like something out of a cheap detective thriller or a television soap opera—but without any training or skills in detection.

She kept looking around. She found it strange to think of the elegant Olivia Kattah in this place. Sandra's impression of the young Brazilian had changed greatly in the last few hours. The woman who got the children into the shelter—an instrument of mercy, almost—might also have been their inadvertent betrayer. In search of adventure, she might have triggered a tragedy.

"Aren't you surprised by Olivia Kattah?" Sandra asked the priest.

"She's complicated, that one."

Sandra caught the attention of the bartender. She began to ask if he knew a man with a scar just here. She gesticulated at her eyebrow and her collarbone, following the description Olivia had given the priest. But Mulroy stopped her in mid-phrase.

"My turn," he said. He opened a tight fist just wide enough for Sandra to spy the corners of Brazilian notes.

"Do you know a man named Efrain de Carvalho?" he asked.

"Nah."

Mulroy pulled another two or three notes from his pocket.

"I'll bet you know Efrain, don't you? Handsome guy, but with a scar on his face and neck. They tell me he's in here sometimes with a beautiful black-haired young woman."

"Don't know those people." The barkeep swiped his dingy rag over the counter vigorously. But he was watching the priest's fist.

"Maybe your memory could improve?" Mulroy pulled more bills from his pocket.

The bartender never straightened, never looked directly at the priest or Sandra. But he began to mumble. She couldn't hear him very well above the blaring samba music. Mulroy leaned in close, surrendered half the bills.

The barkeep spoke slowly. "One of Rodrigo Suares' men, right? I've heard people say…on the bottom of the hill, just inside the favela where Rua Amazonas ends, a pink house, walled, with an electric line hanging over the fence. Iron fence. There might be dogs. Lots of Rodrigo Suares' guys have guard dogs. Looks like a dump from the outside, but they say it's very posh inside."

"Obrigado." The priest steered Sandra steadily by the elbow for the exit door. As she had many times before, she wondered at how quickly the big man with the strange gait could move.

Safely in his dusty van, Sandra and Mulroy looked at each other. The priest ran his hand through his hair in the wrong direction, causing some strands to stand straight up. He looked pale. She could see that the likes of Efrain de Carvalho kidnapping a little girl sickened him.

"At least now we've got a location for Efrain to give the police," said Sandra.

"But we haven't learned anything else."

Would the cops question Efrain? And even if they did, how could they possibly get him to admit that he had even the slightest connection with Zaida's disappearance? They had only Olivia's suspicions. Still, those suspicions might be true, or somehow lead them to the truth. Efrain de Carvalho ran his district in seeming safety. If he could be shown to have links to a kidnapping, it might be easier to get him on his drug crimes.

Sandra pushed back her bangs.

"Now what?" he said.

"What choice have we got? The police are our only hope. There's a police posting in Misericordia."

"Sure, it's flimsy, but they might be interested in Olivia's story. Efrain may be small potatoes compared to his boss, but he might give up information helping them nail Suares if he's caught for kidnapping."

Mulroy nodded and backed up the ancient dusty van, the tires screeching as they pulled out of the parking lot onto the steaming streets.

Sandra remained quiet while the priest, the more experienced Portuguese-speaker, talked to the officer at the main desk at the delegacia. Its walls and floors were dirty and scarred, and the place teemed with people, most looking extremely unhappy. After a long wait, a thin middle-aged man with a shovel chin emerged from a back office.

"Delegado Carneira?" Sandra greeted the man with an exclamation of recognition.

"Yeah, miss. You're doing a good job of circulating the story about the snatched kid with your stories and television appearances. The police are doing all we can. But what do you want of me now?"

Mulroy spoke before she could, spinning the possible connection between the kidnapping and the Misericordia drug criminal. But Sandra thought this was no time to demand gender equality. The more fluent language speaker, an authority figure in a Catholic country, might make their case better.

Mulroy told the story of the young pediatrician, her shady boyfriend and her suspicions, speaking as fast as he could. But when he stopped for breath, Sandra blurted, "We found out where Efrain lives! You could get a search warrant."

Carneira shook his head, emphasizing both his many deep facial lines and his sharp chin. "Are you kidding? Do you think the police don't know where Suares' men hang out? Or that, even if Efrain had the little girl, he'd be dumb enough to keep her at his home? Are you seriously asking me to get a search warrant for Efrain's house?" His tone indicated amusement as well as annoyance at their naiveté.

He nodded his shovel chin up and down in a strange motion. "You want me to act on intuition, on a mere notion, maybe even a delusion?"

The cop rubbed the balding spot on his head and chortled without humor. "What the hell would Efrain want with a street kid, anyway? He's a drug salesman and a go-fer, a foreigner from Buenos Aires. The story is that he was in a street gang there as a kid, wanted for assault of an American high school girl—not important enough for Argentina to want him back." The policeman scratched the bald spot again, pushed back a lock of his thinning gray hair to hide it, and addressed the priest.

"I know this woman here is goofy; she tried to get into Misericordia right after a double murder, with the perp still at large. But you, Father, ought to have a better sense of what the police can do."

Sandra twisted her braid as he spoke. She pulled so hard that her scalp hurt. "You have to help us. A crime has been committed and you're saying you won't even question the only person who might know what happened to Zaida?"

Her voice grew louder. "What kind of police are you, anyway?"

The lieutenant's eyelids seemed to squeeze together. She saw his hands clench just as she felt Mulroy's restraining hand on her shoulder.

"Lady, you do yourself no favor," Carneira's voice sounded sharp and icy. "I've been very patient. Now, go. You're wasting police time."

But as they turned to leave, he called to them. "Try a private investigator. Maybe that person can find out something about what happened to this kid in unofficial ways."

###

After Mulroy had made a series of frantic phone calls, the man behind the large, gleaming metallic desk came highly recommended. It seemed that Drengo Vargas, private investigator, was a friend of a friend of a man who had once made a gift to Mulroy's parish.

Vargas had a round face that looked like it had been squeezed from crown to chin to make it wider. His nose was flattened, but it took an unexpected turn-up at its end. Sticking out from this remarkable head were ears similar to the handles of a flower vase. When he spoke, his voice was so soft that Sandra had to strain to hear him.

The combination of the subdued voice and very rapid Portuguese made him all but impossible to understand. Nettled, Sandra realized she would again have to depend on Mulroy. She, supposedly proficient in Portuguese, had to rely again on the in-flesh representative of religion, a concept she thought she'd outgrown.

After Drengo Vargas spoke a few sentences, Mulroy turned to Sandra, started to explain. But she was understanding better now and waved off the translation. Halfway through the priest's story, however, Vargas arose. His face expressed both distant sympathy and a faint mockery. He swiveled his head toward Sandra and frankly inspected her.

"I don't often go inside Misericordia, Ms. Shelton. I don't usually work in favelas at all. Besides, I'm sure surveillance to determine if this gangster is connected with the kid's disappearance would be too expensive for you."

He's afraid, Sandra thought. Unless law enforcers were occupying the area, not so many outsiders ventured cheerfully into the lairs of criminals.

She heard herself say, "Try me." But as she expected, he mentioned a per diem that nearly exceeded her weekly salary.

He shook his head dismissively. "Even if the man you seek is the real Efrain de Carvalho—and I really doubt that—and if connecting him with this kidnapping were possible, your cause doesn't look very hopeful."

After leaving the detective's office, they drove toward the ocean. It lapped a peaceful obbligato on the sand.

The priest looked at Sandra. "So what's next?"

"How 'bout if we try to talk to Pedro? Maybe take him out for a meal or ice cream, divert him in some way?"

"I doubt we'll divert him. But we can try to make him understand how lots of people are workin' to help."

TWENTY-SEVEN

Isobel Kwenten sat in her living room, holding a squirming, shrieking little girl in her arms. The child's adoptive parents would be coming in a couple of hours, and if things kept up as they were, the first meeting between the little girl and her new mother and father could be a disaster. The child hadn't stopped crying since Efrain had dropped her off many hours before.

Isobel had tried reading Ana's books to the toddler. She'd sung to her. She'd offered her food and the best of Ana's toys. The kid just kept sobbing. At times, she'd fall asleep from the exhaustion of crying. But the respites lasted only for minutes.

At wit's end, Isobel turned on the television to drown out the noise. She picked up the remote and was about to choose a soap opera when the image of a pretty blonde woman caught her attention.

"If anyone knows of information that might help us find Zaida," the woman said, "please call the police at…" The talking head hadn't gotten through the number when the little girl in Isobel's lap stopped crying. She murmured something Isobel couldn't understand. A name, perhaps?

Isobel turned the volume up, but the image faded. The little girl started sobbing and whimpering again. But by this time, Isobel thought she understood that the child was saying a name—'San-dra, San-dra."

The chilly room grew warmer. Sweat moistened Isobel's face. *It couldn't be.*

She changed the television to her local channel, calming a little as the announcer talked about the rowing competition in the coming Olympics. But up popped the blonde woman again. The woman explained that Zaida de Andrade had been snatched from a shelter at Number Eleven Avenida Georges Noves in Rio's South Zone. Her brother Pedro, who had cared for her alone for many months, was beside himself with grief.

Isobel opened the channel's webpage and read a longer plea for her return, a story of the children's lives. It was accompanied by a large, very clear picture of the girl Isobel held in her lap.

Efrain appeared in the living room. She thought he seemed out of breath.

"Why is the kid screaming like that? I have to pick up the parents at their hotel in Barra now, bring them here." His face reddened. "That's why I set the kid's handover for here—a nice domestic atmosphere with a gentle caretaker."

He started to say more. Then he spied the television screen.

Isobel stood, still awkwardly holding the little girl.

"Efrain, you liar! Her mother didn't give her up. What have you done?"

The woman on television continued with her recital: "Zaida's brother has been catatonic with grief."

Efrain grabbed Isobel's shoulders, causing the howling Zaida to slip down to the rug. "Listen, this couple trying to adopt won't be watching television or reading the papers. They don't know a word of Portuguese. I can still get the money, and they can still get their kid."

"How could you lie to me like this?"

"Isobel, for God's sake, don't you see? This is our chance. I won't tell Rodrigo about my new business. I'll keep all the money for us. I'll take you to Paris, like I always promised."

"You're a criminal. You've tried to make me a party to a kidnapping."

"Is it possible that you actually believed what I told you about the kid?"

"This is a crime! I'm not going to help you."

"Don't you see that this kid will be better off with parents than in a homeless shelter?"

"Criminal!"

"Worthless bitch! Weren't you a criminal when you tried to steal dresses? When I saved you from prison? I keep you and your brat all this time and you show me this kind of gratitude? You whine because I ask you to babysit for a few hours?"

"I'd die first rather than help you!"

"Fine. In return for everything—everything!—you can't keep this kid for a few hours without playing drama queen. You have moral qualms. You guttersnipe, I'm sick of you. I'll be back in two hours with the couple. You get that kid to stop crying and make nice for them. If you don't help me, I'm going to kill you!"

Efrain's voice broke and he turned away. But she saw the tears on his face, anyway.

Isobel remained motionless in the same place she'd occupied during her lover's tirade. She stood like a model posing for an art class in figure drawing. A few minutes passed.

Holding the squirming, screaming toddler tightly, Isobel carried her into the bathroom and washed her face. She tried to run a brush through her wild curls. She slipped one of Ana's prettiest dresses over the plain gray pajamas Efrain had brought her in.

"Stop crying, sweetheart. Your name is Zaida, right? I'm going to take you to your brother and that woman on TV. I promise you." The little girl quieted.

Isobel dashed into the playroom, where Ana had retreated to flee from the interloping toddler's screams. Her mother lifted Ana from where she was playing with her dollhouse and hugged her. Isobel thought that Ana would have been a little waif like this one, had it not been for Efrain. But that was over now. And she would end it, not Efrain.

"Will you play with me?" Ana waved around a doll with long red hair and a mermaid tail. "We could pretend that Ariel is just meeting the prince in the ballroom." But Isobel was trying to think, and dolls were not on her mind. The answer struck her so hard she yelled, startling her little girl.

Isobel ran back to the living room. Yes, an extra set of keys to the blue van were in the big desk where she'd once tucked them. Efrain had said the desk was a present for her, purchased at an antique sale.

She had at least a dim idea of where to go, of what to do.

Maybe somehow, deep inside, she'd known that this day would come, that her life might drastically change. She'd make a life for herself and her child somehow, away from Efrain. She believed he hated her now. And now, at last, she hated him.

Tears still clouded Efrain's vision as he gunned the BMW toward the prospective parents' hotel. He turned on the radio. The station was airing the same interview he had seen on his television at home. The woman urged listeners to turn to the streaming video on their computers to see the kidnapped girl.

A sudden sharp pain ran down his scar; the memory of Isobel's voice sliced through his mind like a burning knife.

She betrayed me. She said hateful things. Maybe I'm being a fool to trust her. But she wouldn't dare disobey me now.

Would she?

He slowed the car, thought hard.

OK. New plan. Forget the kid. When I get to the hotel, I'll force that couple to give me the money. I'll take it and run. It'll be plenty for me to start out someplace new. But there's something I need to do first.

He doubled back toward home. As he'd feared, the blue van was gone. A baby blanket lay in the driveway. The Rhodesian dogs were tearing it apart.

Efrain de Carvalho reached in his glove box and withdrew a nine-millimeter Glock. The gun felt cold and comforting in his hand. *Isobel, I'm not through with you yet.*

TWENTY-EIGHT

It was almost dark by the time Mulroy and Sandra parked near the shelter. They couldn't get very close because of long streamers of crime-scene tape that blocked off parking places. They walked slowly toward the entrance. Their steps were heavy, and Mulroy's hitching gait was more pronounced than ever. They were still a few yards from the shelter when Sandra spied a man standing inside the center door.

"Now they've got a younger guard. Too late for Zaida."

"T'wasn't the old guard's fault. What happened to Zaida happened in a few seconds. And, think of it this way. It's doubtful he could have…"

"Look!" Sandra's voice soared.

The new guard grew larger in their vision as they neared the door, illuminated by a very strong halogen light. But a steamy haze still hung over the scene.

A blue van punctured the tape and swept up within yards of the door. A woman leaped out, the light catching and playing on her amber hair. She held a child in her arms.

Seconds later, another vehicle pulled up close to the door, a BMW. The driver also leaped out. He took a few long steps until he was nearly touching the woman. She turned, looked at him. He pointed a gun at her chest. She dropped the child on the pavement.

Zaida! That's Zaida!

The reporter and the priest moved at the same instant. Sandra threw herself on the little girl and shoved her back toward the shelter door. Mulroy ran to the shooter and the woman, who were so close to each other they could have been dancing. But Mulroy shoved his large body between them.

"Isobel, you traitor!" the attacker shouted. "I'll send you to hell." He fired. Mulroy took the bullet meant for the woman and collapsed to the cement.

The shooter fired again. The bullet exploded to the side of the woman, missing her.

Sandra pulled herself halfway up, took a few steps and hurled her body onto the shooter, catching him off balance. He fell. They wrestled on the pavement, the man still screaming epithets—this time at Sandra. The security guard rushed back to the struggling attacker and Sandra. He tried for a second to disentangle them. Defeated, he fired at almost point-blank range into the back of the man's head.

Sandra felt warm blood on her face and arms and wondered for a second if she'd been hit, so close was the retort and the yellow flash. She waited for the pain, but none came.

She turned the attacker's head. In death, he stared fixedly. Blood spurted from his ruined skull.

She studied his face: regular features, electric blue eyes and dark hair gracefully running to gray at the sideburns. She realized she knew that face. She'd seen it uncounted times in her nightmares. She looked at his scar. It was raised but thin, evidence of a knife wound.

She heard the voice of Carneira a few hours before: "Buenos Aires, gang kid, wanted for assault on a girl."

Time fell away. Twenty years rolled back.

Sandra and Efrain were once again sixteen years old, two strangers meeting as the sun set and the dusk settled on a quiet street in Argentina, a long time ago.

###

Sandra thought she and Mulroy looked like they might have been waiting in an emergency room instead of on picnic benches outside Tonio Campelos' shelter. Sandra had cuts on her face and arms, and one leg had a long gash. Her wrestling match with the attacking Efrain had cost her many stitches. Mulroy, just released from the hospital, had a shoulder sling, and he wore a neck brace. The doctor had told him that had the bullet been located a few centimeters to the right, he might not have survived.

Sandra looked at the priest and shook her head. She felt the need to fill the silence, but didn't know what say.

"Did you get your tetanus shot?"

"I did. I can't imagine why. The scratches were from the pavement. Nothin' rusty involved that I could see. They're surely cautious, those medical people."

"Right, I've never heard of rusty cement," Her laugh sounded hollow. "But maybe you get tetanus shots if a bullet hits you."

Peter Mulroy seemed to look through her. She wondered if he was reliving the moment when he'd shoved himself between the woman Isobel Kwenten and her enraged lover Efrain.

"Mulroy, you saved that woman's life. I don't know what to say."

"Don't say anything."

"You very nearly sacrificed your own life."

"It was owed, y'know."

"What?"

She started to ask him to repeat. But just then, Pedro and Zaida came running to join them. Pedro piled a couple of blankets on the bench so Zaida could be raised to table level. Her face and arms were covered with scratches. Like Sandra, she had a big bandage on her leg. Zaida hadn't said a word about being taken away from her brother by a stranger, about being in a strange home, about the melee at the shelter. But Pedro said she wouldn't let him out of her sight.

Get with it, Sandra. Find a good children's therapist for her—and for Pedro, too.

Sandra handed the little girl a small dish of peaches and a spoon. Zaida, long accustomed to eating with her hands, took the proffered spoon, rolled it in her chubby hand, studied it. Then she aimed the spoon carefully at her mouth. Having found the target, she chewed and swallowed.

"Want more, more, more." She smiled angelically. "Very, very dee lush us."

"She's learning a lot of words." Pedro sounded proud.

As he spoke, Tonio Campelos joined the group. Tonio sat down next to Pedro, the impact of his girth on the bench making the boy bounce a little.

He switched to English so the kids wouldn't understand.

"Soon this little girl will be learning the kinds of words that street kids always learn. The kidnapper had one thing right." Tonio shifted on the hard wooden bench. "That man may have been hired by people who might have given her a good home, an education, the advantages of money."

The other adults had frozen expressions. Then, seeing their faces, Tonio switched back to Portuguese. "But, of course, Zaida will have a good home, anyway."

"No home without me!" Pedro's voice suddenly sounded deeper and louder than usual.

Tonio put a restraining arm on Pedro's shoulder. "No, you'll be together, as you need to be." Tonio tipped his head and looked at the priest, then at Sandra.

"I can endow a small children's home on this property. I'll rebuild this shelter, make it bigger. The orphanage would take in all the kids here now as well as others. They could get instruction in the house, so to speak."

"No school for me," Pedro said. "I'm not a baby!"

"Hush!" Sandra said.

"The kids' friend from the awning camp, Maria, could also live in the children's home if she wants," Tonio continued. "She could have a job or take some classes while keeping her baby close. This place will be pretty full service—beds, daycare for the little ones, three meals a day, medical care. Speaking of medical care, Olivia Kattah has offered to provide it."

Sandra and Mulroy stared at him.

"And that's what I can do, folks. I'm rich, but that's the best I can do." He smiled. "After all, I'm a selfish capitalist businessman."

"You can't take my sister away," Pedro said.

Sandra reached across the table and grabbed his arm. "Pedro, you're not listening, Tonio is saying he is going to build a place—a nice home—where the two of you will live together."

"We wouldn't be separated? Nobody would steal Zaida?" The boy's tone was softer, but still suspicious.

"Kid," said Tonio, "a lot of my idea for a children's center came from the need to keep you two as a family. This way, you'd grow up together."

Mulroy rubbed a hand over his graying hair. "But…it would take years to get permission to do this. The paperwork, the applications…"

Tonio frowned. "Don't you think I've already spoken with the authorities? It can be done in a hurry. This property is hardly the Copacabana beachfront, for God's sake. Nobody's competing with me for the land."

He didn't mention the obvious, that money was no object.

Mulroy nodded slowly.

Sandra said nothing. The events of the last few weeks had stunned the reporter. In that time, she'd accepted responsibility for two homeless children—with nearly disastrous results. She'd been in physical danger in Pará. She'd slept with her married boss. She'd stopped dreaming about Georgetown and Charles. And she'd fought with the man who'd blighted her dreams for twenty years, the man whose life of crime she might have set in motion.

"I talked at length with the cops about Efrain de Carvalho," Tonio said. "His real name was Efrain de Caballero, and he came from Argentina. The cops there fingered him for an assault on some teenage Catholic schoolgirl in Buenos Aires."

"What'll happen to his mistress and her child?" Mulroy asked.

"Ana will stay here for a little while, while her mother's in custody. But I think the mother'll get off because she tried to return Zaida. And it sounds like she really didn't know of the kidnapping plot and meant to turn in Efrain."

Sandra's face felt numb, wooden, almost paralyzed. She smiled at Pedro, surprised that her facial muscles responded to the impulse. "So, it sounds like you and Zaida will have a new home, much more of a real home. And before you ask me, yes, you can polish shoes if you want to. In the meantime, Pedro, is there anything we can do for you right now?"

The peach-pit skin of the child's face seemed to light up.

Mulroy spoke before Pedro could say anything.

"Sandra, I'll tell you one thing you can do for the kids right away. You can stay in Rio a while."

"Yes." She gulped from a water bottle as though dying of thirst.

If Tomás Mello would behave professionally, maybe I'd stay with Worldwide a little longer. It might be fun to try to help build up our struggling bureau. And after all, it was Tomás who ordered me to Pará. That assignment made me a reputation in reporting that helped return Zaida.

No, but first I'd better consider those job offers from France 24 and CBS.

Pedro interrupted her thoughts. "These peaches they give us here are all right. But couldn't we have some ice cream?"

"Ice cream, ice cream, wanna ice cream."

Pedro patted his sister's strawberry blonde curls and stared into the distance. "Could we have some plain vanilla ice cream with chocolate cookie chips in it?"

Mulroy looked at Pedro. "You're going to have lots of ice cream and other good stuff from now on. No more sleeping on the street. No more worrying if you have enough food or if some other kid will try to take your money."

His words seemed to release Sandra from her trance.

"And we don't need to live in the past anymore," she said. Her face relaxed into a broad smile, and she raised her water bottle in a toast. "For all of us, here's to fine days ahead."

ACKNOWLEDGEMENTS

I'm grateful to Miles Watson, James Whalen and Tom Phillips for early readings and to Kelly J. Kelly for letting me share a delightful anecdote of her toddler niece. I'm especially appreciative of the help and support of my extraordinary editor, Michael Dell, and many gracious Brazilians.

ABOUT THE AUTHOR

Jerilyn Watson is a Chicagoan by birth. She reported for a daily newspaper in the city after graduating from Northwestern University, where she later served as an adjunct lecturer in journalism. Moving East, she wrote news stories and features for an international news operation. She is the author of *Welcome to Bedlam*, a nonfiction book of reflections, memories and tales from life, and feature stories for newspapers across the country.